TANGLED TRUTH

A gripping private detective murder mystery

DIANE M DICKSON

Published by The Book Folks

London, 2025

First edition published 2017

© Diane Dickson

Mass market paperback

ISBN 978-1-80462-307-7

www.thebookfolks.com

Many thanks to Mandy and Bill for their help with my
research.

Chapter 1

It was after finishing time at the industrial estate, so Simon was surprised to see a figure standing by the shop door. Now and again reporters had tried to get him to talk to them, offered him money, and he had given them short shrift. He prepared himself for another confrontation.

"Can I help you?" When the figure turned, it was obvious that this was no reporter, he was much too old.

"Are you Fulton, Simon Fulton?"

"I am. And who are you?"

"I'm Charles Clegg. I've been waiting to speak to you. I want you to help me, Mr Fulton. I need you to help me."

"How? I don't understand. How do you think I can help you, I don't think we've met?"

"No, no we haven't but I've read all about you. All about what you did and how you found those buggers that killed your Sandie. I want you to help me, Mr Fulton. I can pay. I can pay you for your time whatever you want, but just say you'll help me."

He was going to turn the man away but something desperate in his eyes stirred up the emotion that hovered constantly just below the surface. The anger and hurt that eased but never quite went away.

"Why don't you come inside Mr Clegg? Come on in and I'll put the kettle on."

Chapter 2

Simon led the older man into the dim interior of his messy shop. Charles Clegg peered around. "What's going on with this?"

"Sorry?" Simon opened the door at the bottom of the stairs and waited for him to catch up.

"Well this, it's neither shop nor office or nowt else. Some nice wood though." He stepped up to the counter and ran a hand along the dusty wooden top. "A nice piece of mahogany, worth a bit. Folks like all this old stuff now. You could sell it."

"It's not mine. I don't own this place. I rent it." Simon glanced at the counter and the shelves. His mind filled the empty spaces with paper samples, books of designs and patterns, all the stuff that lay around when this was the display space for the small printing business operating here. The place of his apprenticeship, before desperate events left his family decimated and himself in jail for murder.

Why he was here still puzzled him, but it was just the way it was. He'd come back to Ramstone, paid a year's rent and allowed himself to settle, even begun to turn it into a home. Sometime, and probably quite soon, he would need to make more decisions about the use of the shop and where his life was heading. His granddad's legacy wouldn't last forever and he needed to create an income.

In an attempt to move things along, Simon turned and stepped into the stairwell hoping that the stranger would follow him.

He didn't really want to do this now. He'd had a long day with his father, and now he planned an evening with a glass of whisky and his book. He glanced at his watch. "What was it you wanted to talk to me about Mr Clegg? I don't really understand why you're here to be honest."

"Aye, right." With a sigh the other man crossed the floor and followed Simon into his flat.

"Do you want a cup of tea?" Old courtesy, dyed in the wool. As he spoke, Simon waved a hand in the direction of the kitchen but again Charles Clegg was turning his head back and forth, taking in the newly decorated room and the mix of furniture, some newly bought and other stuff picked up from car boot sales and junk shops.

"This is nice. Wouldn't have thought it from the look of downstairs. You want to have a word with the landlord. He could sub-let the shop. Cut your rent perhaps." Simon struggled with his patience.

"I haven't decided what I want to do about downstairs yet, but really Mr Clegg I don't think we need to discuss it. What was it you wanted to talk to me about?"

Clegg pursed his dry lips and let out another heavy sigh. He lowered his head and shook it a little, dragged out a huge white handkerchief and blew his nose loudly. "Oh, I don't know lad. I'm probably being downright daft but I just bethought myself that maybe you could do for me what you did for yourself."

"Tell you what, why don't we have a drink? I've got some decent whisky or a Guinness. You tell me what's on your mind."

"Aye, that sounds grand." As Clegg lowered himself onto the couch, Simon dragged a bottle of Scottish malt whisky and glasses from the cupboard built into an alcove beside the chimney breast.

He handed the generous measure over and took his own place in the armchair by the window. Clegg began to speak again, his voice low but firm. "Of course I know who you are lad. I know your history and I know what they did to you. I don't know your family, though I did see your dad round town now and again. Folks were always happy to point him out as he passed, shaking their heads and tut tuttin' but not one of them reaching out a hand in friendship." Simon stirred uncomfortably and the old man coughed and took a sip of whisky. "Aye, well that's done isn't it, all done and justice served at last. Well it will be by the time the police round all them buggers up and the courts work their way through it. I suppose it'll go on for years, hanging over your head as well I expect."

"Yes, but at least I cleared my name, eh?"

"Aye lad, you did that. That's why I came to see you. It's a cheek, I know it is but well, once the idea took hold I couldn't shake it." He leaned forward now and stared straight into Simon's eyes. "Would you be willing to do for me what you did for yourself?"

"What, you mean clear your name? What is it that you're accused of?"

"No, it's not me, it's our Colin. My brother-in-law. He's been locked up, two years now. Manslaughter. They reckon he was going too fast and he was drunk. He'd been at a do, but he said he'd only had one drink, his so-called colleagues were a lily-livered bunch, not one of them would say aye or nay. By the time they came for him it was too late for blood tests and what have you."

"Oh no, no. I'm sorry Mr Clegg, you need a private detective, something like that. Not me. Or maybe a solicitor who can go to the police for you. No. I'm sorry."

"Oh, I've been to solicitors and I've looked into private investigators but they're a cold bunch, talk about fees before owt else. It struck me, you see, that you'd know, you'd know what it's like to be beatin' your head against the wall. He wouldn't do it, he really wouldn't."

"Yes, I understand but really, I don't think it's me you want." Clegg leaned forward and fixed his eyes on Simon's.

"She's dying you see. Our Colin told us to leave it, said he'd serve his time – another three years to go and then he'd put it behind him. I tried to talk him out of it but it was no good. He said it was all too much stress for them, as a family, and that he wanted something left at the end of it, something of what it used to be like. That was before she got sick though. Doctors reckon she has maybe a year. We haven't told him about it, says she doesn't want to, but it's not right. I'm driven mad with it all. Please, won't you just see what you can find out? Please. He wouldn't have done it, driven, if he didn't think it was safe."

An idea had tickled at the back of Simon's mind for months now, just a nub of a plan and now here it was.

In jail, he'd taken some courses in law. He had not kept it up after he sat the exams that had won him a diploma, and it was years ago. He had been planning an appeal that never happened. It had kept his mind alive and his spirit lifted from the hopelessness that had threatened every day. The feeling of relief and vindication when he cleared his own name had made him wish he had gone further. If he had, maybe now he would be in a stronger position to help people like this distressed old man. He could never be a lawyer, it was too late for all that, but surely some of the knowledge would have stuck, and he could make use of it.

Not surprisingly, most of the people he had been incarcerated with had protested innocence. But he knew that some of them were telling the truth and that the only thing they had done wrong was to be victims of fate. Fate, and the system, and human fallibility.

He sipped his drink and spoke slowly to the old man in front of him. "I can't make any promises Mr Clegg but I'll tell you what, I'll have a think about it and if I can help you I will." His stomach clenched as he spoke, his own case had taken him into danger, disaster and the loss of a developing relationship with Gloria – what on earth was he doing?

Chapter 3

There was no point going to bed, his mind was buzzing. Simon sat in his chair looking out at the empty road and the dark hulk of the moors above sleeping houses. He hadn't a clue where to start. With the flat to himself and time to think second thoughts, he realised it was silly to have told old Clegg he would help him. This just wasn't the same as his own story. Even though the man was right and he understood the frustration and the pain of being wrongly convicted, there were so many differences. First of all, he had known for certain that he hadn't done what he had been convicted of. He had been driven by the need to clear his name and he had all the facts seared into his brain.

What proof did he have of the very basics of this case, of the innocence of 'Our Colin'? He had no right of access to any legal information. He had made a rash promise that brought the light of hope to flare in old eyes. But there was this other thing. Even though he knew from personal experience that, although it might be unexpected, inconvenient and the repercussions shattering, in the end, it was the truth that mattered.

It would probably go nowhere, but really the old man would be no worse off. He had made him promise not to say anything to his sister, not for the time being at least, so really, what harm could it do? They had agreed that if and when Simon made any progress they would talk about some sort of payment. In the meantime, if there were costs, Charles Clegg would pay. *'I don't want charity young man; I can pay my way don't you worry.''*

* * *

The sky was smudged with grey – a couple of early morning trucks had rumbled past. He stood up and stretched his cold muscles. He took the glasses into the kitchen, checked the locks on the front door and in the quiet bedroom, he slid under the duvet. He would ring Charles Clegg tomorrow and ask for a meeting, find out as much as he could and feel his way forward.

The talk of payment made him wonder if there was a way to formalize things. He could look at whether it would ever be possible, given his history, for him to apply for some sort of licence. Then he knew just what he would do with the space downstairs, it would be his office. He grinned – Simon Fulton Enquiries. It sounded good. He'd have a website; he'd need a car. He tried to imagine doing this, properly, on a permanent basis. He wished that Gloria was with him, longed for her support, just longed for her anyway. Seeds of doubt niggling in the back of his brain taunted him but he ignored them. He was heading for forty in just a few years and he had never achieved anything. His developing career, such as it was, had been cut short and although he had studied in jail he hadn't actually taken all that knowledge and used it. It was brute force, violence and luck that had been his salvation and he wouldn't be able to rely on those things forever. Rolling with the tide, blown with the wind – he could hear his mother's voice telling him that this was just more of the same.

She'd been right. He had never applied himself, maybe now was the time.

* * *

They met in the pub, a table in the corner away from the bar and the draught whenever the door opened. "Thanks lad, thanks so much. I was so pleased when you called."

"I'm not making any promises Mr Clegg."

"Call me Charlie, I've been Charlie all my life, to friends and family anyway."

"Look, all I can say is that I will find out what I can, it might be nothing or it could be something you don't want to hear, but if I think I can help Colin, I will. I need your help though."

"Of course you do lad. What do you want?"

"Well, first of all I can't stress how important it is to me that you don't mention this to your family. I don't need the added pressure of your sister's hopes. Secondly, I need you to jot down all the important stuff. The dates, the places Colin had been, the names of the police officers who dealt with it – anything really that you can remember. I need to know what happened to the car..." Clegg opened his mouth to speak but Simon held up his hand. "Don't start telling me about any of it right now, it'll just get confusing and it's better if you write it down, carefully. Except for the dates, I need the dates so that I can start to do some research."

"Aye right, what sort of stuff are you going to look up?"

"First of all, I'm going to have a look at the papers, what they said about it all at the time. I'll be honest with you, I'm just feeling my way here but I know that with my own case the reporting in the papers crucified me."

"That's it, that's it exactly. They decided he was guilty and wouldn't let it go. I don't know how he was ever supposed to have a fair hearing."

"Okay then, the date?"

"It was February, two years ago. February fourteenth, easy to remember." The old man nodded his head. "February fourteenth, two thousand and twelve. It'd been sunny all day but the weather turned, in the late afternoon, it rained."

"Okay, let's stop. Write down for me the time it happened, how it was reported and of course the name of the woman who died."

"She was nowt but a girl, barely a woman at all. Poor thing, she was only eighteen." He coughed and pushed the ends of his fingers against his closed eyelids. Simon picked up the empty glasses and walked to the bar to give the man time to collect himself. A young woman dead, a man wrongly imprisoned and a wife dying with Simon as her last hope. The magnitude of this task he had taken on was starting to become frighteningly clear.

Chapter 4

They parted with a handshake outside the pub and Charles Clegg promised to deliver his notes in the next day or two. Simon watched the other man drive away and then rubbed his hands over his face. This was messing with other people's lives and he had to admit that it scared him.

After the court cleared him of his sister's murder he had been ecstatic. For several days, he had been unable to concentrate on anything for long. He had walked miles on the moors alone, relishing his freedom. Then had come a period of anti-climax which almost dragged him into depression, until he understood that now he had his life back, he had to find a way to live it.

Proving his innocence had truly set him free in a way that his release from jail had never done.

* * *

Once he was home he surfed the web, reading online copy.

The papers carried the story for a few days after Melanie Walker had been killed and left beside the road, her blood flowing with the rain and muck into the roadside ditch. They stirred again when the net had closed around *a local man*, then came the naming, shaming and the harassment, followed ultimately by coverage of the court case which found Colin Bliss guilty of manslaughter.

Simon printed pages. He needed to organise his thoughts, it was possible to do it on the screen of course but he wanted paper, a pen, some hard copy, something to make it all seem real.

He learned about a young woman studying at a hairdressing college, *a beloved daughter* who met a violent and premature end. There had been a time when this would have been too close to home but he was learning to compartmentalise. Everything couldn't be about his own murdered sister. Other girls had died, other families had fallen apart and turned against each other, and other truths had been lost in the mire of accusation and false belief.

Melanie had been out with friends but left early saying she would walk home. According to her friend, it wasn't uncommon for her to do just that.

He read press releases and watched videos of statements outside the police station, and later on the court room, where a small crowd of camera men battled for space with local television crews.

"Was there CCTV on the moorland road?" The answer had been no.

"How then had they found the blue Mondeo and the *local* driver?" It had been seen at the end of the bypass and then later, on the road to Ramstone.

"Were there no other vehicles there as well?" There had been none at the same time until the one driven by the man who found the body.

It had been damning and all of it reported in the local papers and for a while in the inside pages of a few nationals.

The minor road was unlit and winding. There was damage on the front wing of the car and when the police tried to follow up the story of a near miss with a double-decker bus in the town centre in Leeds, they could find no evidence. None of the bus drivers had reported anything.

When the case came to court Colin had argued that it wasn't until the next morning he realised the extent of the damage. He was asked to explain the fact that the car had been washed thoroughly and repeatedly. There was no blood and the defence had made much of this, but it had rained heavily and the assertion that there would always be some blood was dismissed. "She was thrown aside before she began to bleed," said the prosecution, "and the road was wet, no blood would have a chance to creep into the crevices." Bliss had insisted that he washed his car regularly, he was a pharmaceutical rep, he had to present himself well, it was routine at least twice a week in the winter, more so if the weather was bad. The cleanliness of his car was meaningless.

There was heartbreakingly little reported about the girl's background. She had been ordinary right up until the gory details of her death. She had lain in the road for several hours while her parents phoned friends and paced from room to room in their home, trying to believe that all would be well. Her poor broken body was soaked, her torn clothes filthy. The only comfort for those who had loved her was that the injuries were to her head and it seemed that she would have been dead before the car sped away. It had been a hit and run by a drunken driver in poor visibility. What more was there to be said?

Her sobbing parents told those gathered on the steps of the court, after the verdict, that they couldn't understand why she was up there in the dark on her own. They had begged her not to walk alone at night. Her father had always been willing to collect her from college, and now they would never know. They were glad that they had seen justice done, but now wanted to be left alone to live with their loss and to try and rebuild their lives. Sound bites and headlines, a brief posthumous notoriety, and then nothing more.

Simon dragged his paper and pen nearer. He would start by finding out about Colin, try to ascertain why Clegg was so convinced that he was innocent, for surely there was nothing in the information online to cast much doubt on the verdict. The facts had been gone through by solicitors and the police and examined over and over, why should he believe that anything was other than it seemed? Except he knew from his own experience that it could be.

* * *

The sun was beginning to dip and the light through his window was fading. It was a favourite part of the day and he pulled on his jacket, laced up his walking boots and left to have a hike across the hills before it became too dark.

As he walked for an hour in the quiet and gathering dusk, he tried to empty his mind and leave room for thoughts to find their own way. Birds spiralled overhead, sailing through the turquoise sky and sheep ran from him onto the short moorland grass, the rhythmic thud of his boots and the peace soothed him as he had known it would.

Perhaps if he could start to understand Colin it would help. The man himself had said he wanted it leaving alone. It was odd but hadn't Simon himself done something similar? When he had been beaten, slashed and stabbed in the showers in jail he had let go of any ideas of appealing his conviction, kept his head down and waited out his time. It was easier and he was tired of the struggle, and nothing could bring Sandie back anyway.

He knew he should try and talk to Colin. He would speak to Charles Clegg and try to persuade him to tell his brother-in-law just what was going on, and then arrange a visit. Even if he succeeded, it would probably take a couple of weeks to arrange. He had no legal standing and so could only go as an ordinary visitor. For the moment, he put the idea aside and a tiny knot of tension unwound. The thought of visiting a prison, any prison, appalled him. It seemed inevitable that it would have to be faced in the end, but the longer he could avoid it, the better.

He kicked out at a loose rock beside the footpath. Maybe it was the thought of going to a prison, maybe it was just good sense prevailing but he was again beset with doubt. This was stupid, the whole idea was ridiculous. He couldn't do this. He climbed the stile and turned back to his home. He'd ring Charles Clegg tomorrow, tell him he'd changed his mind; then he'd stop putting off the inevitable and start looking for a proper job.

The route took him past the end of Mill Street. As always, he glanced towards Mill Lodge, one small window glowed with light. It was the kitchen of Gloria's little flat inside the bed and breakfast — that was something he should be dealing with, something real. He had to go and see Gloria, they had to sort things out.

Chapter 5

Sun filtering through the curtains dragged Simon from a deep sleep. The insomnia that he'd suffered for years now was improving and this had been a really good night. The walk had cleared space in his mind. He should just live an ordinary life, find a regular job. It was sensible, it would be easier, he couldn't handle anything as heavy as Colin Bliss and his dying wife.

Today though he would face up to a difficult thing. He would go to Mill Lodge, knock on the door again and hope that this time Gloria would at least come and speak to him. Not all that long ago, they had been close, and her support and belief in him had been the only thing that had kept him going when it all seemed hopeless. He missed the occasional, uncomplicated sex, her positivity, but most of all he missed her friendship.

By the time he'd had his tea and toast the weather had deteriorated. It was drizzling and miserable grey clouds turned the town monochrome and obliterated the hills. He put on an anorak and tugged up the hood. Shoulders hunched against the cold, wet wind, he walked towards the town centre. Half way down the hill he turned right into Mill Street and past the old people's home, the Clearview Hotel and then into the double gates of Mill Lodge. The garden looked sad and overgrown, dirty water dripped from blocked gutters. Obviously Gloria had told the gardener not to come. Possibly at the same time as she had dismissed Rebecca, the young girl who helped with cleaning and breakfast service. The teenager had snivelled and sniffed and told him that Gloria had hidden away in her room after the horrible events in the betting shop, leaving Rebecca to cope on her own. Then, when the last two guests had gone, Gloria phoned and said that she didn't need her anymore, the hotel was closing.

A few days later she received a cheque for a month's wages in an envelope holding a small card with just one word printed across it – *Sorry*. She knew no more than that. Several visits over the following weeks had been abortive – no-one had responded to her knocking on the door. The phone was never answered and she couldn't even reassure him that Gloria was still there. "I've given up now, Mr Fulton. I've got another job. It's okay – they let me go in and do the bar in the evening as well as cleaning. It's more money. I'm sorry about Mrs Bartlett, she was always good to me but I need a job." He had patted her on the shoulder, told her she had to look after herself after all, and that had been the last time he had seen her.

Over the weeks, when he had walked down the back snicket between the garden wall and the moor, there had been a light in her bedroom window. Sometimes on his way back from the pub he had noticed a glow from the kitchen on the side of the building. But by day the place looked empty, neglected and unloved. He could just let it all go. He didn't have to do this now. This new life had been hard-earned and there was no need to complicate things. But he owed her, she had believed in him when nobody else did, stopped him overdosing on pills and booze and bullied him into carrying on. Without her, he would most likely be lying in the churchyard now with Sandie and his mum. He wouldn't have this life if it hadn't been for Gloria.

He tried the bell first of all and heard the jangle of it deep inside the hotel but there were no footsteps across the hall, no rattle of keys. He glanced at the bay window but that was the guests' lounge so it was no surprise when there was no flit of shadow across the window or twitch of the drapes. He raised his hand and hammered on the wood and then bent and stood with his mouth close to the letter box, lifting the flap and shouting through. "Gloria, it's Simon. I really need to talk to you. I know you're in there. I'm not going away this time so you might as well open the door." He straightened up and glanced around. Perhaps he was being too confrontational, it could work against him, drive her deeper into the darkness which was all he could see through the narrow gap. "Come on love, please. I'm worried about you. I really want to see you. I miss you, Gloria. Can't we try and sort this out? I don't blame you. I've never blamed you for any of it. Shit, I could never have got through it without you. Gloria, please, these aren't the sort of things I want to yell through the door. Let me in!" Still there was nothing.

He turned and walked across the front of the building, stopping to press his face against the grimy glass of the second bay. The tables inside were bare, no cloths, no shining cutlery. It looked more like a furniture warehouse than a dining room.

He went down the side alley, past the kitchen window, stopping again to peer inside. He could make out a plastic box full of empty bottles and the big waste bin next to it was lidless and overflowing. As he took in this evidence of neglect and despair his spirits sank.

When they had first met, he had been the one lost to black moods and anger. Even now when the darkness threatened, which it still did when he grieved for Sandie and the stolen years, he thought about Gloria and it helped.

He stopped in the back garden and looked out at the stretch of sky and moorland beyond the low wall. The clouds were blowing away on the rising wind and he could see the pewter glint of the river in the distance. He wanted to go out there, to walk and breathe the freedom but first had to sort this out, if he could.

He turned back to the kitchen door and banged with his clenched fist against the wood. "Gloria, for God's sake please just let me in. Just talk to me please!"

He was tempted to break one of the panes and reach inside but he didn't want to scare her. He gave the door one last massive thump and turned away. It was no good, he couldn't do any more. The blind over the window next to the kitchen moved, he held his breath. She pulled it up in one corner and bent, peered out. Her voice was faint but she was shaking her head and the visual clue made her words clearer. "Go away, leave me alone. I don't want to see you. I'm not seeing anyone." Before he had a chance to answer she dropped the blind and the light was turned off in the room.

Before he left he went back to the front door, the letter box. "I'm not giving up. I will speak to you. I'm going to keep coming." He let the thin metal cover fall back into place with a quiet clank and then went to The Oak where he ordered a pint and a pie and took himself into the corner by the window. He felt depressed and stuck. He needed to move on, wanted to, but he just didn't seem able to get going. The past had hold of him still. He would break loose and it had to start soon. *Bugger it,* he thought, it had to start now. He'd been treading water and it was time to stop procrastinating. He muttered to himself, "Get yourself sorted, come on, get your arse in gear."

Chapter 6

On the way home Simon called into the little stationer's shop at the top of Bradford Road; he bought a couple of notepads and a pack of blank postcards. He felt a bit stupid, as though he was play-acting, he was copying this from books he had read in prison, making notes on little cards. He had to somehow make this real, it was not a novel, not a film – there were people involved, real people and none so real as *Our Colin's* dying wife.

Once back in the flat he made a pot of tea. He sat at the desk by the window and opened his new book. He copied down the names, the dates and the very few facts that he had and then stared at the almost empty page. He printed out another copy of the newspaper report and cut out the image of Melanie. He stuck it to the wall with a piece of Blu-tack. That made it real, looking at her shining eyes and wide, young smile – oh yes, that made it real. He wouldn't take that down again until he knew as near as possible that he had done all he could to find out what really happened. If it was true that Colin Bliss had killed her, so be it.

The personalities were important, weren't they? Colin, the dead girl, they were the crux. He had to know much more about them and for that he needed Charles Clegg.

Okay. It was happening, he was going to do this. If he made a pig's ear of it at least he would have tried.

* * *

"Come in, Charlie, take your coat off. More rain, eh?"

"Aye lad but it wouldn't be Yorkshire without it. Are you well?"

"I am, thank you. How are things with you?"

"Well, about as you'd expect. Our Maureen's up at the hospital, some God-awful treatment. My Beryl goes with her, drives her home after. It touches us all, sommat like this." Simon nodded and pursed his lips, tried to look sympathetic. He had to believe in these people. He had to care about them as much as he had cared about his own family. How did you do that? He would have to find a way.

"Tell me about Colin?"

Charles leaned back in the chair and crossed his legs. For a moment he didn't speak. "Well he's younger than me. 'bout ten years I reckon, same age as Maureen, my kid sister." He stopped for a moment and turned to look at Simon who acknowledged the unspoken recognition of a link between them. "He was born down round Manchester, came here when he was a kiddie. Met our Maureen when they were teenagers and they tied the knot when they were 'bout twenty. They've no nippers of their own. Don't know why, they never said and – well sommat like that you don't ask. He works for Stamforths, do you know them?" Simon shook his head. "They're based down near Leeds, they distribute drugs. Take in orders, buy them and then supply chemists, vets, that sort of thing."

"Vets?"

"Aye, not that much difference is there, vets, doctors, all the bloody same, you ask me, though if I were sick I'd rather trust a vet. Well, our Colin, he has to go round and try to get orders and then sometimes, with the animal stuff and that, there's deliveries an' all. If it's needed quick like and it's a regular customer. At the end of the day it's just reppin' really."

"So that's what he'd been doing on the day of the accident?"

"Aye. Well no, not really. he'd been to some sort of meeting. I don't really know that much about it. That's not my world but it was some sort of gatherin' I understand. Manchester way I think, anyway he said as he had a pint but just one and it had been with sommat to eat and he was nowhere near drunk."

"Colin and Maureen, were they – I mean, are they happy?"

"What, happy? Oh yes, why wouldn't they be, eh, not sommat you talk about is it? But yes, they're happy. Why do you want to know?"

"I'm just trying to get a picture of him in my mind. An idea about his life really. I know you think he must be innocent. I understand that, but I'm trying to get an idea about him for myself."

"I see. Well, now then what can I tell you? He liked his job well enough, used to talk about it plenty anyway. Bragged a bit now and again, truth be told. How he was their top salesman and all that. It was nowt but a little bit of an outfit, not as if it were Boots or whatever but anyroad he liked it well enough and he seemed to make a fair living. He was just ordinary, but I'll tell you this." The old man sat upright and jabbed a finger towards Simon. "He wouldn't drive drunk. I know that, I know that for a fact. I've written it down why but I'll tell you anyway. He wouldn't drive drunk because his own mother was killed by a drunk driver."

"Oh."

"Aye, a lorry it was, out on the bypass. Mowed her down and killed her when he was so drunk that he couldn't hardly stand up. So, you see…" Now he simply shook his head.

"Yes, yes I see. I understand."

"I'll leave you this." Clegg held out an A4 sized envelope. "I've written down all that I thought might help and I put my phone number on there. Not the house, don't want you speaking to Beryl and her pesterin' me with questions, but you ring me any time you like."

"Are you retired, Charlie?"

"Nay lad, not me. I reckon I'll work till they nail me in my box."

"And what is it you do?"

"I've me own business. Transport. Clegg's International Haulage."

"Oh right, I've seen your trucks."

"Aye, I reckon you probably have. We've done well. I'll let you get on and I'll be off, I'm sure we both have plenty to do. Keep in touch, won't you?"

"I will, I'm still not sure how much I'm going to be able to help you but I'll do what I can, and if your brother-in-law is innocent I'll do my best to have him cleared. I don't know what it might lead to, whether we'll have to involve solicitors or what have you, we'll just have to see."

"It's up to you lad. You've taken it on, you sort it and I thank you." With that he stood, offered his hand and then clattered down the stairs and was out in the road with no further word.

After he'd gone, Simon logged on and typed in *Clegg's International Haulage*. It was huge and Charles Clegg lived in a grand house in the countryside between Ramstone and Leeds, a place with acres of land and imposing buildings. Surely he would have had the best solicitors at his disposal, probably a whole legal team and they hadn't been able to save Colin from jail. How then was he, no more than feeling his way in the dark with no experience, going to be able to? Simon puffed out his cheeks and spoke to the empty rooms. "Bloody hell, what have I let myself in for?"

Chapter 7

He read through the notes. They were mostly the things they had just discussed but there were details about the evidence, the damaged car, the CCTV film. Simon had already found most of it for himself online. At the end of the second page there were a few notes about the dead girl.

She had been out with her friend after a day at college, they hadn't been drinking and it hadn't been particularly late when she said she was going to walk home. She had done it before and always the same quiet road.

Although Simon had spent years locked away, he'd watched television in jail, he'd listened to the conversations when someone went missing, the speculation and brutal opinion. He knew that over and over they were cautioned about putting themselves at risk but Melanie's closest friend had been clear. She often walked home alone. She had repeatedly asked her not to do it but Melanie was confident that there was no danger and brushed aside any concerns. It was unusual but young people thought they were immortal, didn't they? They believed that bad things only happened to other people.

In the end the danger hadn't come from thugs or rapists but from a cowardly driver who sped away leaving a young girl in the rain, dying alone.

* * *

He went through to the kitchen and took a beer out of the fridge. He carried it back to his table. Charles Clegg had noted the friend's name. He'd obviously had access to this information through the solicitors working on his brother-in-law's behalf and he had been thorough.

They had attended the sixth form college together. Melanie a trainee hairdresser, with her friend studying to be a veterinary nurse. They had been friends since school.

It had happened over two years ago, they would have finished with college by now, gone on to jobs or no jobs or marriage. He would need to find this friend. It seemed logical that he should do that. He must speak to her.

It was quiet in his flat, sitting beside the window as darkness grew and the yellow glow of lamps appeared along the roadsides and in windows. He stood and gazed out at it. From here he could see down Bradford Road, almost to where it became the High Street. Half-way down was the turn into Mill Street, and Mill Lodge and Gloria. He would give anything now to be able to talk to her about this. She had been so bright, so sharp and it would be wonderful just to have someone to toss the ideas back and forth with.

He slapped his empty bottle onto the table and snatched up the papers. Dragging on his jacket he thundered down the stairs and out into the chilly evening. He strode down the hill, his hiker's legs carrying him quickly into town, around the corner and through the gates of the B&B. He lifted the letter box flap and yelled through.

"Hey, Gloria. Gloria, if you can hear me just come and let me in. I need you to help me. I need you to stop wallowing in self-pity and tell me what to do. I know you're in there, it's time to get on with stuff. There's a girl dead and a bloke accused who might not have done it — does it sound familiar? And if you want to have a chance to make up for what your brother did why don't you make yourself useful and help me with this?" He thumped again on the wood. "Come on, you're better than this. Help me, Gloria." He didn't hold out much hope but was driven to try. He stood before the door now, his heart thumping, his rapid breathing clouding the chill air.

A light came on inside, the leaded windows glowed red and blue and behind it he saw the wavering shadow of someone coming nearer. "Go away, Simon. I don't know what you're trying to do here. We fixed it all, you cleared your name. You found the truth. Let it be enough and leave me be. I don't want to see you – go away and if you come back I'll call the police. How can you come yelling this stuff through the door – don't you think I've suffered enough? Go away. Sandie is at peace, my brother is in jail, where he belongs."

"It's not Sandie, I'm not here about me – it's someone else, Gloria. I need you to help me. Please. I need to see you. At least let me talk to you. I've said I'll help someone and I don't have a clue how to go about it. I know it'll help to talk to someone and, Gloria, you're all I have."

"You don't have me, Simon."

"Open the door please? Let me in and we can talk."

He held his breath as the shadow leaned forward, deepening against the coloured glow and he heard the click of the latches and the slide of the chain into the runner. The door opened a crack. He could see only a thin slice through the gap, her hair messy and unwashed trailing to her shoulders, her eyes were bloodshot and sore-looking in a pale face. Her voice was just above a whisper, desperate and full of tears. "Why won't you just let me be? Have you any idea what it's been like?"

"Yes, I think I have an idea but this can't go on and now I really do need you to help me. There's a bloke in jail and his wife is dying and I said I'd help. God knows why, but I did. Please help me, Gloria. I know you can."

She shook her head and the door closed with a sudden slam but then he heard the chain rattle against the wood and she opened up again. "Come in, come on in and just have a look at me and then tell me again that you think I can help you, Simon." With that she pulled the door wide and he stepped into the dusty, untidy hallway. The air was stale and thick with the smell of tobacco smoke and Gloria stood before him, dressed in a baggy, stained track suit, a lit cigarette gripped in her fingers. She had lost weight and deep wrinkles ran from her nose to her mouth. "Shit, Gloria, what have you done to yourself?" As he reached a hand towards her tears sprang to her eyes and she brushed them away impatiently.

"I'm having a drink. You can join me, just for one, say your piece and then leave me." She turned and stalked away from him down the hallway and into her own flat at the back of the house. He followed her into the dim and grubby rooms.

Chapter 8

The once bright, tidy room was gloomy. There was one small side-light turned on, an ashtray on the coffee table was overfull and there were glasses on sticky coasters. A soft pink blanket was heaped in the corner of the couch and Gloria's slippers were pushed together underneath. Her feet were bare and as Simon glanced down she shuffled in front of him to retrieve her footwear. As she passed he smelled body odour and tobacco with an undertone of the perfume that she wore. He reached a hand towards her but she pulled away and walked over to the drinks cabinet. "I'm ploughing through the spirits pretty well now, Simon. Do you want one while there's some left?"

His first instinct was to shake his head but he nodded just once. "Yeah, why not?" She poured a large whisky and held it out to him.

"Say your piece and then go away and really, Simon, don't come back. It's over."

"What is, what's over?" She shook her head and looked at him sadly.

"Everything really. But, us, that's gone and the hotel… finished… and, well, me – there's nothing left."

"Don't be stupid." She drew in a hiss of breath but she didn't speak. "You can't let this go on." He swept his hand around, taking in the untidy, sad room. "It stinks in here, you look a wreck and the hotel is a mess inside, outside. What are you thinking? Why have you let this happen? What is this going to solve?"

"I told you to say your piece and go. I don't want to hear your opinion of me, I don't need it. You said there was a dead girl, do I know her? What has it to do with me?"

"No, you don't know her. But a bloke is in jail and I'm pretty much convinced, from what I've heard, that it could be wrongful – like me. Apart from that his wife is dying and if nobody does anything she'll be gone before he gets out."

"But what the hell has all of that to do with me? Why would you bring more trouble to my door? Don't you think I've got enough?" Her voice cracked and Simon took a step towards her but she raised a hand and glared at him. He paused for a moment and then lowered to the settee where he sat with his head bowed, sipping on his drink.

"What I don't understand is why you have gone down this route. Why this, locking yourself up, letting it all go – why?"

"Shame." The word was whispered and as Gloria sat in her chair before the dead fire she repeated it. "Shame and disgust and grief."

"But, Gloria, you have nothing to be ashamed of." She gave a harsh cough of a laugh. "You didn't do anything wrong. You helped me to find justice, not only for Sandie but for that thug Jason Parr as well and maybe he didn't deserve what happened to him, but it was right in the end."

"Yes, and how many others? I don't know, do I? We might never know. Peter's locked up and I hope they never let him out but we don't know if he killed anyone else. Shit, Simon, he raped your sister, a young girl. What sort of monster is my brother? What sort of people was he caught up with and what sort of family are we that raised a creature like that?"

"But it wasn't you."

"He was my younger brother, we were close, we cared for each other and yet I didn't know. I knew he was becoming a thug, he was a bad lot but I could never, never have believed that of him if I hadn't heard him confess with my own ears. And then there's me isn't there?"

"You, but love, you didn't do anything."

Her voice rose now, became shrill, "Didn't do anything, bloody hell, Simon, I threw boiling water at him, I blinded him in one eye."

"But you saved me, doing that saved my life."

She shook her head again and thrust her fingers through the tangle of her hair.

"Well, maybe."

"Never mind maybe. I'm sure of it, you saved me. So you should stop all this wallowing in guilt. You didn't turn him bad and what you did with that kettle, it was brave and it saved us both."

"And what about my husband, what about Dave?" There was silence for a moment and she stood and picked up the framed photograph from the top of the sideboard. "I thought we were close, happy, and I thought I knew him."

"Yes, well – I see that must hurt."

"I didn't even know he was in debt, he killed himself and I didn't even know he was in trouble. What sort of a bloody wife was I?"

He couldn't bear to watch her any longer, tears slid down her cheeks and she wiped them roughly away with the back of her hand and sniffed loudly. Simon stood and took her in his arms as she gave way to the crying that caused her body to tremble and her breathing to change to gulping sobs. He rocked her gently back and forth and held her close until the worst of it had passed and then he pulled her down beside him onto the settee and held her hand and looked into her drowned eyes.

"Gloria, love. You can't blame yourself, and you can't let yourself go like this. The horror is over, you have to move on. Please."

After many minutes, she raised her head. She looked at him with eyes that were red and puffy but she managed to dredge up a smile. "That felt good. Oh, don't worry, I've had many a good roar but it felt good to have someone to hold me." She sniffed again and pulled away from him. "God, Simon, I'm rank." Now she created even more distance by moving back to her chair, but he slid along the settee so that there was just a foot or so between them. "It's no good though. If crying could make it better, then it would all have gone away by now."

"This can't help." He raised his glass tipping it to make the amber liquid inside swill back and forth.

"Ah, but it does. It smooths the edges, it takes some of the sting and if I drink enough it takes me away completely."

"But you know that's not wise."

"Simon, wisdom and sense have gone long ago."

"Hey, come on now. Please, Gloria, don't say things like that." At her huff of impatience, he slid from the seat onto his knees in front of the chair. "Do you remember when I tried to take all those pills and you wouldn't let me? You said that you weren't going to let me make you regret not doing enough. Well, here we are. I'm not letting you do this to yourself. I had no idea. I thought you just didn't want to see me and didn't want to run the B&B, if I had known that it had got this bad I would have been down here far sooner."

She dragged a creased and shredded tissue from the end of her sleeve and used it to wipe her nose. "I just don't see how to get through it though, I can't see a life beyond this horrible guilt. When I close my eyes, I can hear Peter screaming and then I wonder how many other people there were screaming and I can't shut it out."

"Gloria, love. You poor, poor thing. You don't deserve this."

"Well, it's what has happened, isn't it?"

"Let me help you."

"I don't think you can. I don't think anyone can and I don't know what I'm going to do." She took the last big gulp of her drink, lowered her head into her hands and hid herself from it all and Simon leaned close and wrapped her in an embrace and knew that he had to save her from herself and the misery that her life had become.

Chapter 9

"I don't suppose you've been eating properly, have you?" Gloria didn't answer. Her self-neglect was obvious. "Tell you what, I'll go and get us some fish and chips. Let's just have a meal and – well you know, let's just be together." She stared at him for a couple of moments and then gave a nod.

"Go on then. But, just this, just now. Fish and chips aren't going to fix me but by God I could eat some. Can you get scraps on top?"

"Of course I can. Do you want a pickled onion?"

"Bloody hell no, don't you think I stink enough as it is?" He didn't answer as the blush spread over her face and neck. "Go on, you go and I'll try and sort myself a bit before you come back."

"Good enough."

Simon took his time walking down to the local chip shop. She had been so lovely, bright, bubbly and mentally strong, it was incredible that she had deteriorated to this extent. He felt guilty. What sort of a friend had he been? She had saved him more than once and when she needed help, he had let her down.

By the time he arrived back at the B&B she had taken a shower. Her hair was loose around her face and shoulders, still damp, and he smelled steam and shampoo as he walked in. She had emptied the ash trays and tidied the living room.

"Shall I put the kettle on?" She was bustling about, avoiding eye contact.

"Great."

She ate slowly and there was little in the way of conversation until the plates were empty and they pushed back from the table. "So, was that okay?"

"Yeah, I have to say it was pretty good."

"What have you been doing, Gloria? What's been going on with you?"

She sighed. "Nothing. Really, just nothing. I know you saw me at the court, for your thing and then Peter's. Of course, I had no choice, did I? I was part of it. But apart from that, now and again I have gone down to the shops and so on, that's about all, just the essentials to keep things running. There were reporters outside a bit and I just couldn't deal with it. Then I started online shopping, for my groceries I mean, and since then I've just stayed in."

"On your own?"

"Yeah. Just me. Who would want to be with me for God's sake?"

"Me."

"Yes, well. I heard you knocking but I just couldn't face it. Couldn't face anyone."

"Are you going to let me help you?"

She didn't answer.

"Well, thing is, I came down for a reason, I need you to help me."

"The dead girl?"

"That's it."

"If I don't know her, how can I help you?"

"To be honest I don't know why I've taken this on, except that I felt sorry for the old bloke. Mind you I didn't need to as it turned out, he's not some poor old codger, he's rolling in it and running a huge business. But his sister – she's got cancer and – it's his sister."

"Hmm."

"Anyway, I just said that I'd see what I can do to find out what happened but it's no good on my own. I need someone – well you really, to talk it through with."

"Just to talk?"

"Well, any help at all you can give me."

"So, what did he do, this bloke that's in jail?"

They sat in the scruffy room while he outlined the problems. As he spoke he saw the lines of tension soften a little and interest spark in her eyes. She asked him questions, made more tea and he saw a glimpse of Gloria begin to reappear.

Simon glanced at his watch. "God, look at the time. I'll get off, but I'm coming back, you know that, don't you?"

"Okay."

"And will you help me?"

"I don't see how, but if you want to just talk about it I can do that. I've got plenty of time after all."

"Great. Thanks, Gloria."

"No, no. Let's just see how it goes. I might well get up in the morning and decide I want to be on my own after all."

"No, that's over."

"Well, we'll see. It's been good and if I can do anything that might help this other bloke, well really this woman, the one that's dying, that'd be good, yeah I'd like that."

"I'll see you tomorrow. Maybe we can go for a walk? Just a short one, up to the riverside maybe."

"Oh, I don't know about that." She was shaking her head again.

"Well I'll come down and we'll see how you feel."

He kissed her on the cheek and then listened as she locked and bolted the door behind him. As he strode back up the hill to his flat his feelings were scrambled. It had been an intense and unsettling evening and he understood that he had taken on yet another responsibility. It was a bit overwhelming after all the years of keeping his head down and letting no-one come close. It felt like he was beginning to care again and he wasn't sure it was a good idea. He could step back, there was still time and life was simpler without other people. But it was lonely and he had had his fill of loneliness.

Chapter 10

If the streetlamp hadn't been vandalised, he would have seen it much sooner. The damage wasn't evident until Simon had already crossed the road towards his shop. At first he just registered that something was odd in the way that the light reflected from the big plate glass window. Once across the road, he was cursing under his breath as he took in the evidence of catastrophe. The old glass was shattered, there was a huge hole in the centre and jagged shards hung perilously from the wooden frame.

Simon glanced around expecting a damaged car pulled up to the kerb. But there was nothing. So, whoever had hit the frontage had sped away and left him to sort it all out. "Bloody marvellous. Just bloody brilliant." He kicked at the door.

He pushed into the dark shop, glass screeched and scraped across the floor. The door jammed against the boards, glass grinding under the wood.

He kicked away some large splinters so that he could force the door closed. He had insurance so it should all be okay, but it was shocking and annoying. There didn't seem to be any other damage, just the ruined window. He stepped across the space and turned on the light. A clatter from the storeroom at the rear had him striding across the room until he smelled the unmistakable odour of petrol.

While he was still struggling to take in everything that was happening, he heard the rumble of a car in the side road. He dashed towards the back of the building, to the big storage space and pushed open the door. A low wall of flame was spreading rapidly across the room, licking along the dusty floor, burning on the surface of a pool of fluid. Flames were dancing along rivulets of liquid slithering down the cracks and faults in the concrete.

He was panicked and frightened, he wanted to run but the urge to fight was strong, the rooms upstairs were his first home. They had become precious over recent months. He had to save his flat. It was his and he couldn't just leave it to burn.

The heat intensified rapidly and he felt his throat scorched with each breath as fire licked at the skirting boards and ran over the boxes and packing materials he had stored, ready for recycling. It was beginning to roar.

The chance to act was getting away from him. He pulled his jacket up over his mouth and made a frantic dash for the rear door where a pile of old blankets was folded neatly in the corner. The hair on top of his head sizzled and he felt the flush of heat on his exposed skin. But once on the other side of the pool of flaming liquid he was able to grab some cloths and throw them down all across the floor, stamping and pounding on them over and over, denying the fire the oxygen it needed. He smothered the final vestiges of flames and when he was as sure as he could be that there were no lingering hot spots he leaned against the wall and gave himself over to the shock and surging adrenaline. His shoes and jeans were blackened and when he ran a hand through his hair a cascade of singed and stinking bits fell onto his shoulders.

Should he call the fire brigade, the police? He no longer thought he needed the first and didn't want the second. His thoughts tumbled and spiralled. What the hell was all this about? Any explanation that he came up with harked back to last year, to the gang of thugs whom he had crossed and bested and to the men he had hurt on the way. Was it coming back to haunt him now? He had truly believed all of that was over.

His phone vibrated and he let it go to voice mail. Time enough for that later when he'd made sure everything was safe and he'd calmed down.

He filled a big bucket with water and then pushed open the double doors into the yard. By the time he had finished sluicing and swilling, gallons of water had soaked the floor and skirtings and he threw yet more up against the doors. He was scared stiff of the fire rekindling while he was asleep. Eventually he climbed up to the flat, took a long shower and then pulled on a pair of soft trousers and T-shirt.

There were planks in the yard outside and he nailed them over the broken window. Tomorrow he would make the calls and get someone to come and sort the mess out properly. It was only as he gathered up his tools and began to sweep the broken glass into a pile that he saw three bricks laying against the base of the counter. He lifted them, turning them back and forth. So, no car colliding with the frontage, this was as deliberate as the attempt to start a fire. If he hadn't come back when he had, the whole place could have gone up. The realisation turned his stomach and bile rose into his throat. He had to lean against the old wooden shelves to steady himself.

Though he tried to settle in the flat he was drawn back over and over to the rooms downstairs, to check and double check that everything was alright.

After a couple of hours sitting in the chair by the window he went to his desk to log on to the insurance company site. He might as well use the sleepless hours to organise his claim. His phone battery was flat and as he plugged it into the charger it beeped. He clicked through to listen to the recording. It was short – a low, breathless, staccato of words, difficult to tell whether it was male or female. "Keep your nose out of things that don't concern you."

Chapter 11

The next morning he phoned Gloria. At first she was adamant that she wasn't leaving the hotel, that she wouldn't meet him, she'd changed her mind. Didn't want to go out and about. "But there's something I need to tell you, something happened, last night."

"Tell me now on the phone or come here." He kept at it, wearing her down until she agreed to meet him for breakfast in the little café by the bus station.

* * *

"So, there was nobody around?"

Simon thought for a moment before responding, "No, no-one. I heard a car but I didn't see anyone."

"It's odd though."

"Yes, it bloody is, and scary. What if I'd been in bed?"

"Exactly, that's my point, that's what I mean by odd. How come the fire only started when you arrived? Did you hear the window breaking as you walked up the hill? It must have made a hell of a crash."

"No, not that I can remember."

"So, the window was broken before you got there but the fire started after you were inside. That's odd?"

"I still don't understand what you're getting at."

Gloria put down her cup and raised her eyes to look straight at him. "I don't think it was ever meant to burn the place down or for you to be hurt." He stared at her without speaking.

"So, what was it all about then?"

"I reckon it was just to scare you."

"But..."

"Yeah?" She nodded.

He felt the need to verbalise what they were both thinking. "But in that case, it doesn't make sense for it to be anything to do with last year. All that stuff is finished as far as I'm concerned. It's not going to involve either of us. Your brother will be part of it but not us. So..."

"So! Got to be something else. Do you think it's to do with the hit and run girl?"

"No, it can't be. Nobody knows about it. Only me and Charlie and now you. I made him promise me that he wouldn't tell anyone else."

"Well, Simon, unless you have even more enemies than you thought, I can't see why anyone would do this. Then there's the message. It doesn't make sense unless it's to do with Charlie and his brother-in-law."

"Shit. Thing is, if that's the case then..."

She screwed up her eyes and nodded.

"Yeah. It means that there really is something off about it and somebody wants you out of the picture." She waited for what she knew was coming.

"Well, in that case..." Simon stopped when he saw the look on her face.

She leaned across the table and laid her hand over his. "Don't, Simon. Don't get into it. Not after all that stuff last year. You were nearly killed. I was nearly killed. We're lucky to still be here. You could have walked away then, walk away now. Learn from what happened, please."

Before she had finished speaking, he was shaking his head. He had put down the coffee cup to take hold of her hand. "You know that's not happening, don't you? After this, there is no other way. You're right, I could have walked away last time, it would have been easier. I can't do easy, Gloria, not anymore."

She pulled back and lowered her head into her hands, her elbows on the table amongst the crockery and crumbs. "Oh hell, Simon. When you came yesterday, after you'd been to see me – I thought maybe I could pull myself together. I thought that if you'd really forgiven me I could drag myself back and now – this."

"I'm sorry. I'm so sorry but there's no choice. I remember what it was like, when I knew the truth and nobody believed me. I can't ever forget how it made me feel. Look, if you like I'll just keep it all to myself. You forget I asked for your help. I understand, truly I do, and at the end of the day it was me who took this on. You don't need to be involved."

"Yeah. Right. So, that'll work. Oh bloody hell, Simon, I should have thrown you out right at the start. That first day you came to the hotel with the stink of prison still on you and that lost look in your eyes." He watched quietly and he saw her strengthen.

"Well, I suppose as I'm not running the hotel anymore, and you've got no car and to be honest you're not fit to be let out on your own..." She raised both hands, palms upwards and shrugged. "Let's go up to my shop" – she grinned as she reminded him gently that she was in fact the leaseholder for the time being – "and see what you've done to it."

He helped her on with her jacket and as they left the stuffy warmth of the café, he took her hand in his and squeezed it gently. She glanced at him and shook her head.

Chapter 12

The shop looked forlorn with the old planks nailed across the front and they sighed and shrugged when they saw that 'Gazo' had already tagged it. It didn't matter. The insurance company had arranged for a glazier who was coming by the end of the day.

Gloria scanned the inside of the empty shop. "There's no real damage is there, apart from the window? Did they break in by the back door?"

"No, I reckon they must have come in through the broken glass. Bloody dangerous, those big shards have been dropping out all the time, whenever a car goes past. They could have been sliced in half. Whoever they are they're very stupid."

"Oh, don't!"

"No, you're right. It was messy but now it's all drying again, there's nothing much to see."

"It makes me even more sure that this wasn't meant to do real damage, not meant to hurt you. You haven't said but I'm guessing you haven't called the police?" Simon shook his head.

"I don't see what they could do and I can't face it. Plus, I don't want to risk the papers finding out. You know what it's like."

"Yes, but they would have access to any cameras and might be able to see the car. At that time of night there wouldn't be much traffic would there?"

"I think for now at least I'd rather not."

Gloria wasn't ready to let the idea go. "The insurance people might insist. What about that bloke, Prentiss, from before? He was one of the good guys, wasn't he?"

"He was but you know at the end of the day, me and the police" – he shrugged – "there's always going to be some of them who don't believe they got it so very wrong. I don't reckon they'll ever think of me other than being the bloke who got away with it."

"You didn't get away with it, you served time."

"I know, I know but, then there's the other thing. I don't particularly want them up here, nosing around."

"Nobody knows about all that. Well, nobody but us." She knew that his actions when he was first released from prison tormented him. He had been bent on revenge and on a road to self-destruction. He had chained up one of the people who he thought had been responsible for his wrongful arrest, locked him in the warehouse and beaten him badly. He had planned even more violence. This new Simon, whom she liked to think of as the real Simon, was a different person to the tormented man she had first met. "That's all gone, there nothing left of that is there."

Simon shrugged, "No, but I don't want them poking around, looking for stuff."

"You can't go on feeling guilty, looking over your shoulder all the time. You have to move on. Just call him, see if he will help you, sort of off the record."

"I can't, Gloria, I just don't want them in my life. I just don't want them here. It's my home as well as everything else."

"So, what are you going to do? Are you going to call Mr Clegg?"

"I need to speak to him but for now I'm not planning on mentioning this. I don't want to worry him; he's got enough on his plate."

"Okay, I've been thinking about it all though, since last night. It's not like it was with you, is it?"

"In what way?"

"Well, in nearly every way. You fought it right from the start, you denied everything even after they locked you up. Yes, you knuckled down later but at the beginning you told them it wasn't you over and over, you said. But this bloke hasn't. Isn't that a bit weird? I can't help thinking that for the time being at least you have to keep in mind that he might actually have done it and it's Mr Clegg who is just clutching at straws. With his sister so ill and everything."

"Yes, I have to admit that was starting to be my thinking but what's happened here sort of puts a different light on it, doesn't it?"

"I guess it does, so what now?"

Simon shrugged and for the first time in months Gloria laughed aloud, it surprised her as much as him. "You haven't got a clue, have you?"

He raised his eyebrows, "Well, that's not strictly true. I have found out about her friend, the one she was with that night. I thought if I could find her and have a word, that might help to understand her a bit and what she was like. I also want to go and have a look where it happened. Charlie gave me a plan, it's out on the moors."

"What do you know about her mate?"

"They were at school together and then college. She was a hairdresser and the other one was training to be a veterinary nurse."

"Well, that shouldn't be too difficult."

"How so?"

"I would have thought a veterinary nurse would be registered somewhere."

"Brilliant. See, I knew I needed you." He leaned and hugged her. She smelled like Gloria, shampoo and perfume.

"I'll go online and see what I can find out about it. Hopefully I can at least find out whether or not she qualified and then, if it comes to it, I'll just start ringing round the veterinary surgeries."

"When the bloke's been to fix the window, I'll drive you to the accident place. I'll go back home now and make a flask and some sandwiches. Let's have a picnic."

"A picnic, it's bloody cold and it'll be even colder up on the tops."

"I know but I feel like a picnic. I'll make soup. Don't be a wuss." She paused for a moment and then raised her eyes to his. "Thanks, Simon, I feel so much better already. I can't believe the difference a couple of days has made. God, I have been a stupid cow."

"Yeah, well."

She thumped his arm and then turned to leave. "Give me a call when the glazier's finished." And she was gone. Simon went up to the flat with his spirits in a much better place.

He was surprised that a female voice answered when he called what he understood to be Charles Clegg's private mobile number. "Hello. I'm trying to reach Mr Clegg. My name's Fulton."

"Hello, Mr Fulton, this is Beryl. I'm sorry you can't talk to Charlie just now." Simon caught the break in her voice.

"Is he okay, is everything okay?"

"No, not really. We're at the hospital. Charlie's having an operation, he broke his leg."

"I am so sorry, did he fall, is there anything I can do?"

"No, he didn't – he didn't fall, Mr Fulton. He was in a car crash; his car went into a ditch. We're lucky he's still alive. If it hadn't been for a young woman passing on the road, I dread to think what would have happened."

"I am so sorry. Will it be okay if I call again, in a little while? Just to see how he is?"

"Yes, alright. I'll tell him you rang. Thank you."

Simon turned off his phone and stared out of the window. Poor Charlie, his money wasn't saving him from trouble heaped on trouble.

Chapter 13

"Poor old thing. Did you get any details?" They were driving away from Ramstone. They passed the bungalows on the outskirts of the village and then it was all dry stone walls and fields dotted with shaggy sheep and low, wind-formed trees. As soon as he had closed the car door, Simon had blurted out the news about his 'client'.

"No, not really. I'm going to try to go and see him but his wife was really upset so I didn't want to seem like a ghoul."

"Do you know where it happened?"

"Yes, I looked at the local news online. It's not all that far from where Melanie was killed, it's a bit odd that isn't it, you know, quite a coincidence. It's not the most direct route but it is the nicer one, going over the tops as it does but…"

"Did you make a note of whereabouts?"

"Yes, can we go and look, can we do that first?"

She nodded.

Simon turned to look at her. "I know these roads can be dangerous but what are the chances? Although I'm probably overthinking it, looking for stuff that isn't there."

What had promised to be very little more than an excuse for a winter picnic had become something else and the atmosphere in the little car was tense with anticipation.

It was easy to see where the accident had happened. The grass beside the road was torn and muddied. Great clods of soil had been thrown up the bank and huge gouges scarred the slope where the big four-wheeled drive had plunged down the embankment. Yellow paint on the road, marking the start of the skid and swerve, evidenced the police investigation. Simon and Gloria walked back and forth. A wet wind began to blow and grey clouds streaked low across the sky.

Gloria pulled her collar closer. "Not much to see really is there? He's lucky someone came along, it's not that busy."

"It was a young woman, who'd been taking her daughter to school apparently and just coming back a different route from normal."

"I wonder if we can find out who that was?"

"Perhaps. I'll go to the hospital as soon as they say he's well enough to have visitors and maybe Charlie will be able to tell us more."

"Well, I wouldn't bank on it. If he was knocked out, he might well not remember anything."

"No, but – well, I can ask." She nodded as she climbed back into the warmth of the car.

"So, the other accident, the first one. Can we work out from the plan exactly where that was? As we're here we might just as well carry on."

Simon studied his map for a minute before replying. "Down here, there should be a narrow turn off and it was just before that."

"It's an odd place for a young girl to be walking about on her own, isn't it?"

"I've puzzled about that myself but according to the reports, her friend said that she often walked this way. Did it because she enjoyed being on the hills alone. I can sort of understand that because I love it myself but it's not that usual for women, girls, is it, even these days? Plus, it was winter, latish in the day; all just a little bit of an odd choice to make."

"Well, I guess she must have been pretty self-confident. Didn't do her any favours though in the end. Here we are. Is this the turn?" Gloria slowed the car as she spoke.

"Looks like it. It's very isolated."

"Yes, but once you get over the dip there are houses, not quite as lonely as you would think. I wonder where that turn off leads to?"

"High Hill Farm according to the OS map."

Clouds had gathered in grey heaps on the tops of the moors and they lowered now over the peaks and flowed into the valleys. Sheep huddled at the foot of low walls and in minutes they could see only a couple of hundred yards in any direction.

"God, the weather's turned now. Did you bring something hot to drink?"

"I did but I don't think this is going to clear, do you?"

"Let's give it a little while, it might blow over. Anyway, I like it when it's like this. As long as you're not out in it without your foul weather gear it can be fun and it certainly makes you appreciate a hot shower after."

She poured soup into mugs and gave him a packet of cheese and ham sandwiches and they ate quietly, watching through the streaming windows as the moors, the road and the walls vanished in swirls of mist.

The roads ran with water and fine rain whispered against the windows. But every now and again a glimpse of blue peeked through and as suddenly as it had begun, the drear weather cleared. Beams of light speared through the remaining clouds and the pools and puddles shone in wintery sunshine. Grass and leaves twinkled with moisture and as a hawk spiralled up into the rapidly clearing sky, Simon sighed and leaned forward to wipe with a cloth at the condensation on the inside of the windscreen. "This is what it's about for me you know. This is the closest thing to magic that I can imagine. I know it's lovely in the summer but this, this wildness is what I love."

"Yeah, it's pretty special, I used to enjoy it back in the day, with Dave you know." She sighed. "Anyway, we need to get back, if you've seen all you want to."

"I think so, to be honest I'm not sure I've learned anything much but it's been good to come here, it all helps to make it real."

Gloria pulled out onto the narrow highway and gave a little squeal as a horn blared loud into the quiet. She wrenched the wheel over as a Land Rover, its headlights flashing, streaked past them down the gleaming tarmac.

"Bloody hell. That's a bit quick for the conditions, isn't it? I'm beginning to think this road is jinxed." She puffed out a sharp breath and then slipped the stalled car into neutral. She turned the key, indicated and turned to look back through the window, no longer trusting what she saw in the mirror, she pulled slowly onto the road.

Simon reached over and touched her leg. "Are you okay, you've gone pale?"

"Yeah, yeah, I'm fine, it just made me jump that's all. It came out of nowhere."

Chapter 14

Charles Clegg looked old. The life force that was so much a part of him had been subdued by drugs and confusion. He lay in a quiet room in the local private hospital. Once out of danger he had been transferred from the infirmary and was now well enough to have visitors. Simon dragged a chair up to the side of the bed, he was shocked at how ill the man looked.

There were large floral displays and cards on the window ledges and tables, and the hospital smell was drowned by the heavy scent of lilies. It was overheated and in spite of the attempts at luxury, the old man was still lying in a hospital bed with wires and tubes attached to his bruised body. Muffled noise leaked into the room and it was all pretty depressing. Simon couldn't see any point in staying. They had said Clegg was conscious but there was no indication that he was going to be able to talk, so, with a brief squeeze of the age-spotted hand, Simon stood and prepared to leave.

"Don't go lad. I'll be with you in a minute. Just give me a bit of a chance." The voice was just above a whisper but the words were clear.

"I thought you were asleep." Simon lowered back onto the seat.

"No, it's the dizziness. I can't see straight, it's bloody awful." His eyelids flicked open for a moment and Charles Clegg moved his head a little towards Simon.

"Don't worry, I can come back. When you're feeling a bit stronger. It's fine." He was surprised at the strength in the hand that reached out and gripped his wrist.

"Wait. Just wait." The old man forced his eyes open again and pointed at the glass of water on the bed table. Simon helped him to take a drink and then settle back against the pillows.

"Bloody drugs have me confused. I'd rather feel the ache in my leg to be honest but they've got me in their clutches and they'll do what they will. Bloody doctors."

He lay with his eyes closed but the slackness in his face had lessened. "Good of you to come lad. Appreciate it."

"I wondered if you remembered what happened?"

Clegg groaned as he shook his head, his concussed brain paying him back with pain and nausea. He breathed deeply and raised a finger to indicate that Simon must wait.

"I'd had a busy day, out and about and what not. I remember leaving the yard. I decided to drive over the top. I do quite often, usually mid-week, even though there are memories up there. It's no good letting stuff like that dictate what you do. I don't know much more than that. I remember that young lass, the one that helped. She clambered down to me, somehow opened the car door, called the police. Saved my life I expect. I'll tell you sommat but you must promise not to say a word – right?"

"Erm, yes okay."

"I didn't have my belt on. Bloody belts, I hate them, always have and every now and again I just leave it off. If I'd not been such a stupid, stubborn old bugger I could have walked away from this. Well, serves me right. I was probably goin' a bit quick, truth be told. No point having a powerful motor if you don't let it off its leash now and then." He gave a throaty chuckle but it caused him to cough and Simon helped him to take another drink. "Bit of slide on corners you know, bit of a twitch in the rear, just for the hell of it. Bit of sharp braking, testing her metal, you know? They're saying they think I fell asleep but that doesn't feel right, not right at all."

"No, not from what you've just been saying."

"Aye, well I don't want them pryin' too much, crash investigating and what have you, so I'll let them have their way and take the hit on the insurance. Serves me right and I'm paying for it now. But truth is I don't remember anything properly, just flashes. I can see that girl, but it's odd because sometimes it seems that maybe there was another one, happen a woman, happen not, but anyroad it's all a fog. It's just the drugs and my poor scrambled brain but… let's be honest, I reckon they know, about the seat belt I mean, they can tell these things from bruises, stuff like that, but sometimes, well if you show folks an easy way out, they'll likely take it." He flapped a hand weakly against the bed covers. "It's no good, I'm befuddled. They reckon it might come clearer in time but right now I just don't know what happened. Been drivin' for more than fifty year and only ever had one other accident – years ago when I was a daft kid." Simon saw exhaustion and medicine take Charles Clegg away again. He left the little get-well card on the table and walked quietly out of the room.

It would be useful to speak to the woman who had helped him. Maybe her name would be in the paper by now. He pulled out his phone and made a note to check.

So, it would be back to the computer. He hadn't been able to do anything about tracing the veterinary nurse though, he had spent hours well into the night bent over his desk.

When he phoned Gloria they decided the only route left open to them was to call all the local veterinary practices. They had taken half of the listings each to work their way through, just calling and asking if Fiona Carpenter worked there.

"You know they might start with the stupid privacy stuff, don't you?"

"Yes, I know, but at least we'll have tried."

He called at the little convenience store and picked up a lasagne ready meal for lunch and a six pack of lager. He was seeing Gloria for dinner but for now he liked the idea of getting on with what he was thinking more and more of as his job.

The shop front looked smarter with the new pane and he decided to have it painted. Now they were talking again he would speak to Gloria about making an offer to buy it. It would be much simpler having cleared his name and he would love to own his own place. He was settling and becoming attached to his home. It was a good feeling. He knew it would please his dad as well, so that was another plus.

Chapter 15

When the phone rang, Simon was puzzled to see Charles Clegg's name on the screen. "Charlie, this is a surprise. I thought you'd still be out for the count."

"No, Mr Fulton, this is Beryl, Mrs Clegg."

"Oh, is everything okay? He's not worse, is he?"

"He's alright. They say he's not in any danger now and it's just a question of time. He's tough so he's going to be champing at the bit to get out of there as soon as he can stand up."

"Well, that's a relief. What can I do for you Mrs Clegg?"

"I want you to stop what you're doing."

"I'm sorry?" The woman took in a shuddering breath, when she spoke again her voice wavered.

"I know what Charlie has asked you to do and I want you to stop. Don't stir things up."

"Mrs Clegg, I don't understand." He had thought that Charles Clegg had been as keen as he was to keep his wife away from the enquiry. "I'm not sure what you're talking about."

"Yes, you know. I haven't been married to Charlie for all these years without knowing how his mind works. I've put two and two together and I understand what's happening here. He means well, I know he does – God bless the man. But I want you to make an excuse. Tell him there's nothing you can do. Our Colin will be out of jail in a few years and we'll look after him. It won't be like with you, we'll make sure he has work, his dignity, a place to live."

"But your sister-in-law, Charlie's sister? He said that they don't think she'll last."

"Aye well sometimes things are best left as they are. Listen to me, the least said soonest mended. An old saying but in this case it couldn't be more true. Leave it all be. Will you do that, for me and Colin and Maureen?"

"Mrs Clegg, I've taken the job on. I told him I'd do what I could."

He heard her sigh, "I know. But you're not listening. Leave it be, that's all. If it's money you're worried about I'll pay you. What did he promise you?"

"Nothing, we didn't talk about it. Except for expenses and there haven't been any. No, it's not about money. I haven't got very far but… well, things have happened that lead me to think there's something off about all of this and…"

She didn't let him finish.

"I'll give you a cheque for five thousand pounds tomorrow if you tell Charlie you can't find anything."

"No, I'm sorry but no, I can't. I promised."

"What do you mean you can't? Of course you can – just do it." Her tone became stronger now, hectoring and bullying. She was making him angry, he tamped it down – the woman was under stress. "I realise you've had a nasty shock, but really I think if you have a problem with me trying to find out about Colin and the accident you should talk to your husband. I gave him my word. I can't let him down. Apart from that I need to do it because I think he might be right about some of this. I can't turn my back on that. I just can't."

The quiet click told him that she'd cut the connection. He replaced the handset on his desk and stared at it for a minute. He pulled one of the little cards from the pile and wrote out a rough precis of the conversation.

* * *

It was wonderful to be back in Gloria's living room. She had cleaned and tidied in the last couple of days and it was almost like it was when he had first seen it, downstairs in her private rooms at least. She had cooked roast lamb for them and now there was her favourite jazz music, heavy with saxophones, playing quietly in the background, and she'd turned on the fire. The atmosphere was cosy and relaxing. Simon sighed. "I thought I'd lost this forever. It made me sad."

Gloria nodded. "I've had trouble remembering what life had been like. The world turned nasty so quickly and I hated it. Now, here tonight that side of it is unreachable. Life is odd. I hope I'm better, but sometimes it sweeps over me, the whole bloody thing. Ah well." She deliberately pushed the maudlin conversation aside. "Anyway, back to what you were telling me."

"Yes, so at first she was really upset I think but then towards the end she sounded more… angry."

"God, this gets more and more complicated every day. Will you tell Charlie?"

"I don't think so, not right now anyway. I can't see how it will help and it will probably cause trouble between them, and I wouldn't want to do that."

"She must know something though, mustn't she?"

Simon nodded. "Yes, I reckon. But obviously she's hiding what she knows from her husband." They sat in silence for a while until Gloria moved forward in her chair and leaned towards the coffee table.

"Do you want another drink?"

"No, I'm fine thanks." She raised the whisky bottle, uncorked it and then looked across the space between them.

"I'm just having another little one. I know, I know – I'm drinking too much, but this is nothing compared to a week ago. I'll cut back, I will, but not just now." He shrugged, though he wanted to speak, to tell her that he had smelled the alcohol already on her breath when he arrived. He held his tongue. It was all too delicate, building this new bridge.

"For now I'm going to just carry on, trying to find that girl first of all. Oh yes, and I'm going to go and see that woman who found Charlie. I've got her name from the paper – Michelle she is and an unusual surname, it sounds Italian or Spanish maybe, so it was easy to find her address in the phone book. She lives in Keighley. I just thought I'd ask her what she saw when she found him, although like with everything else, I'm just working on instinct."

"So, for now we'll just keep on, shall we?"

"Yup, that's it. Cheers, Gloria. Thanks for the meal. It was lovely but I think I'll get back now. I'll come down early tomorrow and we'll go and find this Michelle – will that work for you?"

"Yep." Tension crackled between them but she moved and picked up his coat from the back of a chair, holding it out to him.

"See you tomorrow, Simon. Maybe some of this will start to make sense in a while."

"Well, I bloody hope so." As he turned at the end of the drive, he heard her lock the door and imagined her moving through the rooms, sliding under her duvet and laying there in the dark, alone. If he had pressed it, she may have let him stay. He would have liked to stay. He picked up the pace until he was pounding up the hill, his heart racing and his breath quickening.

Chapter 16

The address took them to a small, neat, terraced house and as Simon walked up the narrow path the blind at the front window lifted in one corner. He rang the bell and smiled as a dog inside set up a racket and a distant voice sent it to a basket.

A tall, slender woman with shoulder-length dark hair opened the door. A little girl of about five years old, dressed in a cute school uniform peeped out from behind her. "Yes?"

"Hello, sorry to bother you. Are you Michelle? Sorry I'm not sure how you pronounce your name."

The woman grinned and nodded. "It's okay a lot of people have trouble. "Yes, that's me. Who are you?"

"Sorry. My name is Simon Fulton. I'm really sorry to bother you but I wondered if I could talk to you about the accident you saw on the moors the other day?"

"Are you the police?"

He was aware of her fight to drag her eyes away from the scar that snaked down his cheek and under his chin. He never thought about the wound from his time in jail until he met someone new and saw them struggle between curiosity and good manners. His solicitor had once tentatively suggested that he could have the state pay for plastic surgery on that and the slashes across his belly. He didn't care about the way they made him look, and they made him remember. Every time he looked in the mirror, he remembered it had happened because he let his sister down. If he hadn't become bored waiting for her, then she would still be alive today. No matter what happened, he knew it was a guilt that would be with him forever, so why not wear the scars it had caused.

He carried on as if he hadn't noticed, "No, no I'm not. I suppose you've already spoken to them?"

"I did. I gave them a statement. You're not a reporter, are you? Because if you are you can get lost right now. Anyway, I'm in a hurry, I have to get my little girl to school. We can't be late."

"No, I promise you I'm not a reporter. I'm… well, I'm sort of working for Mr Clegg. The man in the car."

"Oh right. How is he?"

"He's doing alright now thank you. He reckons you saved his life, he's very grateful."

"I'm glad he's okay but anyone would have done what I did."

"Well, maybe, maybe not. It must have been pretty shocking for you."

"Yes, it was. I was just glad Keira wasn't with me." As she spoke, she wrapped an arm around the child's shoulders, drawing her close.

"You had to drag the door open?"

"Yes, I did, had to clamber up on that car, the air bags were in the way and I had to shift them. It was horrible but once I saw he was breathing and not bleeding too badly, just a couple of little cuts as far as I could see, I just left him as he was, I didn't want to make things worse by moving him. I called the ambulance and just talked to him while we waited. I didn't think he could hear me but you know, just in case."

"Well you did a good job."

"Look, I really do have to get going. Thanks for coming by, tell him – Mr Clegg, is it? Tell him I'm glad he's okay."

"I will. I did wonder if you could just give me a few more details though?"

"How do you mean?"

"Well, did you see the accident for example?"

"No, I didn't but it must have happened just before I got there because the engine was still hot, I burned my hand on the exhaust." She held out her arm and Simon saw the nasty reddened skin on the back of her hand. "Bit of a nuisance to be honest, I'm a beauty therapist, I can do without something like that on my hand."

"It looks sore." She nodded and frowned as she studied the damaged skin.

"Well it's nothing compared to what happened to that poor old bloke, is it?"

"No, I guess not. So, you didn't see any other cars, nothing like that?"

"No, nothing. Oh, well – hmm."

"Yes?"

"Well for one thing he didn't have his seat belt on. I didn't tell the police, these older men, I know what they're like. My uncle's always doing it, stubbornness that's all it is. They possibly thought I'd taken it off, but I hadn't." She smiled and shrugged. "There was something else and again I haven't mentioned this to anyone. I wondered if I should have told the police. To be honest when they came I was still a bit upset about it all and it was only afterwards I remembered. I thought about it and decided it didn't really matter anyway because they had pretty much assumed that he'd fallen asleep at the wheel or something. You know, him being an old bloke and that."

"Yes, I think that's their explanation. But you saw something else?"

"Well, I don't know. While I was sitting waiting for the ambulance. I saw a woman, or maybe a girl. Just on the top of the hill. Off towards where that narrow road goes. I think there's a farm down there. She was standing on the rise and then she disappeared. I did wave to her, I thought she might be able to bring a blanket or something but she didn't wave back, just vanished. I thought she'd probably gone to get help but I was already talking to the ambulance by then anyway, so it didn't matter. Look I really do have to get going."

"Sorry yes of course. If I need to, could I come back and talk to you again? Could I take a number so I can ring, in case you're busy or whatever?"

"No, I don't think I want to give you my number but I'm here most days after five, you can come in the evening if you like."

"Great, that's great – thanks."

"Tell Mr Clegg I hope he gets better soon."

"I will, yes I will, thank you."

Simon slid into Gloria's car and they pulled away as Michelle buckled her daughter into her own vehicle. When they reached the junction at the end of the road the two cars were alongside each other. He turned and waved at the child in the rear seat, grinning at him through the window.

"Did she say anything that might help?" Gloria didn't look at him as she pulled into the line of traffic.

"I'm not sure. She didn't see another car or anything like that but she did say she saw a woman, watching from up by the farm."

"Oh, well maybe that should be somewhere else we could go, see if they saw anything?"

"Can we go there now?"

"Might as well, as we're out anyway."

Chapter 17

Half an hour later they were bumping and sliding down a rutted narrow road across the top of the moor. They could see a collection of buildings in the distance and sheep scattered across stony grassland as they passed.

There was no gate. A dry-stone wall with a small gap flanked by two pillars showed the entrance to the farm lane. As the car drew to a halt, a couple of black and white dogs came around the corner of the house. They didn't bark or leap about but they were alert in every muscle and sinew, watchful and on guard, heads lowered.

"Do you think they're okay? I mean they won't attack us or anything?" As she spoke, Gloria was grasping the handle tightly as if attempting to pull the door closer to the frame.

"I'm sure they're fine. They are just doing their job, aren't they? Guarding the place. Anyway, you stay here, I'll go and see if there's anyone around."

As Simon climbed from the car, the smaller of the two dogs took a couple of paces forward, barked just once and then took a position foursquare in front of the door. "Hello there. It's okay." He moved towards the house his hand held low in front of him as he called out. "Hello, is anyone there?" The dog moved aside to let him pass but they both stayed close, waiting.

He banged on the dried-out paint of the front door but there was no response from inside.

He walked to the corner and peered along the side wall. Behind the house was a small flower garden and a wooden seat positioned to look out over the rolling hills. He called again. "Hello. Anybody home?" Then he glanced over his shoulder to where Gloria was peering through the windscreen, shrugged and raised his hands. She shook her head in response. The dogs had followed, still watchful but the tail of the smaller one wagged once as he spoke softly to them. "Alright boys. Good dogs."

Across the yard, on one side of the rectangle formed by the wall and buildings were a couple of sheds. Set further back on the third side was a large barn with doors open to reveal rolls of hay stacked in the corner and farm equipment parked in the middle, some of it rusted and dilapidated. There was an old green Land Rover parked alongside. Beside it, against the wall was a large tool cabinet with drawers and doors. There was a pair of ramps propped against the fence. The whole place felt deserted but it was obvious people had been around at some time not that long ago. The dog bowls on the ground beside the kennel had clean water and some bits of dried food sticking to the sides. There was a pair of muddy boots on the step beside the front door and a wind chime swung gently in the breeze.

Simon leaned into the car. "I think we're wasting our time, Gloria. I suppose they must be out working somewhere or… well, whatever it is famers do in the day. It was probably nothing anyway. We might as well head back. We haven't got very far today, have we?"

A sudden crack, followed by a shutter of small impacts against the side of the car caused him to yell in shock. The second one, coming shortly after kicked up a fountain of dirt from the ground beside him and sent the dogs running for cover.

"Bloody Hell. Shit, was that a gun?" He tore open the door and threw himself into the car.

"I don't know. My God was it, was it a gun?" As she shouted back at him, Gloria turned the key, put the gears into reverse and began a skidding three-point turn in the wide yard. "God's truth. Is it? Is someone shooting at us?"

"I don't know, let's just get out of here." They bounced back along the track much faster than when they had approached and skidded between the two entrance posts and, as they sped away, Simon twisted in his seat and peered back towards the collection of buildings. A slight figure appeared from behind the barn and moved across the yard, the gun hanging from her hand. The dogs trotted back from their kennel to join her.

They reached the road and turned towards Ramstone, both shocked into silence. It wasn't until they had joined the main thoroughfare that either of them spoke. "Are you okay, Gloria?"

"Yeah, I am but I'm shaking." As she spoke, she lifted one hand from the wheel and flexed her fingers. "What the hell was that?"

"I don't know. I suppose technically we were trespassing but… Talk about overreaction."

"Did you see anyone?"

"Yes, did you not see the woman?"

"No, I was too busy trying to stay on the road."

"I'm sure it was a woman, came out from behind the barn. She had a rifle thing, don't know what, maybe an air rifle. I don't think it can have been anything more than that though, can it?"

"She hit the car, didn't she?"

"Yes, we'll have to have a look when we get back. I'm really sorry about that, Gloria. If there's any damage, I'll pay of course."

"Oh, I'm not bothered about that so much, but I don't really want to drive around with holes in the side of my car." She gave a nervous laugh. "Then again, perhaps it would make me seem interesting, eh?"

Simon leaned across and laid a hand on her shoulder. "Are you sure you're okay?"

"Yeah, I'm fine now but I could do with a drink." He didn't answer and after a moment she filled the silence. "Well, it's not every day a girl is in an ambush, I should think a little drink is allowed."

"Of course it is. Tell you what, how about we stop at that little pub just before the bypass. We haven't had any lunch yet and they serve food all day and I'll buy you a glass of wine and then I'll drive the rest of the way."

"Done."

Chapter 18

Gloria's little blue car had a rash of small, round dents in the side panel, the paint was scratched and bare metal showed in places. "I'll take it to that repair place up on the industrial estate, they must be okay. They do the police cars!"

"Hmm, is that a good idea then?"

"How do you mean?"

"Well, I haven't much experience but to me this looks a bit dodgy and if the police are up there?"

"Oh, I see. It'll only be the bodywork bloke and I'll tell them it was kids with stones. You can't really tell the difference and at the end of the day who's going to be interested? Only we know what we were doing. It's not as if there's people taking pot-shots every day, is it? And we weren't doing anything wrong, we were victims really."

"It was scary."

"You did well, Gloria; you got us away pretty sharp. Most people would have panicked."

"Yeah, well I did, that's exactly how I got us away pretty sharp." They headed back to Mill Lodge. "Are you coming in for a cup of tea?"

"Please. That'd be lovely. We could have a rethink, see where we are up to."

"What the hell can that have been about? Do you think she shoots at everybody who goes up there?"

Simon took a minute before answering, "Well, I can't see it, can you? I mean if she did, surely somebody would do something; it'd be talked about. You know what it's like round here. Do you remember that old bloke who used to throw rocks at anyone on his land? Everybody knew about him. Oh, maybe that was before you came here."

"Oh yeah, I knew about him, Old Tom the Bomb. But High Hill Farm is right out of the way isn't it. I bet they don't have many visitors, just the postman I suppose, maybe farming officials and stuff." She shook her head. "Or, I don't know, just people to do with the sheep and stuff, perhaps the vet."

"Yes." Simon sipped at the hot drink. "Gloria, you know when we were trying to find out about Sandie?"

"Hmm."

"Well, do you remember how the betting shop kept coming up, over and over, and it didn't mean anything to us because it was just so… every day?"

"Oh come on, just because I said the vet."

"Yes, I know but Colin Bliss dealt with veterinary surgeries, the dead girl's best friend was a trainee veterinary nurse…"

"Yeah and I just said vet! Spooky. Come on, Simon, don't be silly."

"Okay, not the vet, I agree that's daft, but that farm, it's near where the accident happened and it's near where Charlie's car went off the road. Michelle said she saw a woman standing over that way while she was waiting for the ambulance. It's a common factor in everything. I think we should go back and see if we can talk to them."

"Are you mental? Go back! We were shot at!"

"I know, but we did arrive unannounced and as you say it is pretty isolated. If that woman was there on her own, well, put yourself in her place. Perhaps she's nervous…"

"So she shoots people."

"I think I will go back. You don't need to come with me."

"So, how will you get there?"

"It's time I bought a car, isn't it? I can probably pick something up second hand and I do need to be more mobile. I've been putting it off a bit. To be honest I've been sort of hedging my bets about settling down but it's happening in spite of me, so I might as well admit it. I'm back and it looks as though I'm here to stay, at least for now." He had walked to the back window and looked out across the garden to the wide moor beyond. "There's worse places to be after all and this is where I started."

She moved to join him and threaded her arm through his. "You seem settled, I have to say. I thought you might leave, after the court case and all of that, I imagined that you would want to be anywhere but here."

"Well, my dad's here, and Sandie and Mum up in the graveyard." He turned and pulled her closer. "And you're here, Gloria, and so really I don't think there's anywhere else I should be."

As he bent to kiss her, she sighed deeply and leaned against him.

Out in the dark garden a black grouse was startled by a movement beyond the low wall and rose into the air with a crackle of wings.

Chapter 19

He found a car, it didn't take long, there were only a couple of dealers locally. He didn't want anything flashy, and had no real experience, so the first ever vehicle of his own was a VW Tiguan in burgundy red.

As he parked it in the yard at the rear of his shop and plipped the key he felt a moment of claustrophobia. He loved Ramstone but fleetingly he felt trapped, confined. When he'd been discharged on licence there had been no intention of staying here. It was to have been a short, sharp thing, violent and decisive and then it would be time to join Sandie and his mum, forever up there beside the church. Now though, everything had changed.

So, he had a home, a car and for the moment at least, something important to do. He strode up the stairs to his flat. His mum had often said that he let himself blow with the wind, didn't take charge. Well, now it seemed that, belatedly, he was doing it.

With a cup of instant coffee on the desk beside him he logged back into the site to read again about the licencing he could apply for. He downloaded copies of the forms he needed to complete. They needed to know where he had lived for the last five years. He directed them to the copies attached. They were of his university diploma; and probably more importantly, he had written proof that he had been cleared of all wrongdoing. There was no getting away from it though, his addresses were unmistakably prisons. It could be a sticking point. If it was, then he would take that as a sign, yes he would let fate decide about his future career. He muttered a quiet *sorry Mum, I'm doing it again aren't I,* into the quiet of his home. He stuffed the application forms in an envelope with the other paperwork and the cheque for a couple of hundred pounds. He ran downstairs, out into the road and down the hill to the post office. It was only when he was halfway there that he remembered he had a car.

He was putting down roots. After all, what he had said to Gloria was true, there were worse places to be than here, on the edge of the wildness and beauty of the Yorkshire moors.

While he waited for the response to his licence application, he had to carry on with trying to help old Charles Clegg. The unpleasant truth was that in spite of being shot at, he didn't really have any information, except for the fact that Mrs Clegg had told him to leave things alone, and that was odd, very odd indeed.

Obviously, any agency would need to have a decent reputation and if he failed now, in what could be considered, at a stretch, to be his first case, he would be dead in the water. This had to work out.

Tomorrow he would go back to the farm on his own and try to speak to them.

Later, he drove up Hope Street and parked in the little gravelled area. He walked through the quiet churchyard to the big old tree and perched on the tiny wall around his family's grave. "So, now look at what I'm doing eh, Sandie. Who'd have thought it, a Private Eye. Oh, I know it's all a bit daft, isn't it, but what else can I do? The only thing I know about is printing, which is past and gone these days, and crime. Crime and mistakes and assumptions and that sometimes you just have to try and put it right. This might not be the wisest decision I ever made but then, what have I got to lose anyway?" He sat for a while, remembering and wishing, then he stood up and went to surprise his dad with a run and dinner in the pub up on the moors. It was a lovely early spring evening and he told himself he'd done the right thing, taken control.

Chapter 20

The next morning was wet. Simon pulled back the bedroom curtains to look out at the grey striations of cloud scudding just above the rooftops. It would be easiest to stay in, carry on with some decorating and painting in his flat and then maybe persuade Gloria to go with him for lunch in The Oak. He shook his head, that wasn't the way it was going to be. Just because there was no office to go to didn't mean that he could please himself. He stood before the window with his mug of tea and wondered if he truly had the self-discipline that this venture was going to need. There had been no real reward as yet, maybe there would never be if it didn't work out. There was no boss to drive him on, and no routine. It all came down to his own conscience and the need he felt to do the right thing for a dying woman and her husband. The insecurity and sense of play-acting was only a breath away and he had to work through it and find solid ground. All the years in jail he had followed routines laid down by other people and now it was up to him.

He walked through the flat, leaving his mug on the countertop in the kitchen and grabbing his rain jacket, he ran down the stairs out into the yard. He backed his new car into the road and then took a couple of minutes locking up and double checking that the warehouse and shop were as secure as they could be.

The gutters ran with water and the wipers swished away at the windscreens struggling to clear the view but he carried on. Perhaps this would be a good thing, maybe the rain would have kept the farmer at home.

The cars that he passed on the way out of town had their headlights on and he drove slowly. His driving experience was minimal at best. He had borrowed his dad's car a few times after he passed his test but then it had ended along with everything else normal and ordinary. This was not the ideal day to be out on his own for the first time in years, apart from the short drive from the showroom. His knuckles were white as he grasped the wheel and he rolled his shoulders trying to ease the tension in his neck and upper back. It hadn't been too bad driving Gloria's car with her there as back up. He would need to go out for some solitary driving practice, get some real confidence. The idea didn't fill him with enthusiasm, he preferred the pound of his feet on the paths in the moors to this swish of water under his wheels and the flick-flack of the wipers on the screen. He shook his head, this was work, this was necessary.

"Just bloody well get on with it." He spoke aloud into the quiet car. He would need to programme the radio, work out the heater settings and so on, learn this new vehicle's little idiosyncrasies.

Once he was beyond the town limits the roads were quieter and his nerves settled. The rain eased and the sky lifted and brightened. By the time he reached the turn off for the farm he was enjoying the experience of driving alone much more.

He jerked and bounced down the narrow farm track, dirty water flying up around his wheels from the potholes and ruts.

There were lights on in the downstairs windows of the farmhouse as he pulled into the yard. As he reached for the door handle, he stopped and peered around. They had been shot at on the previous visit and still didn't know by whom or why. He twisted back and forth in the seat but there was no sign of anyone around. He banged with his fist on the centre of the wheel, the horn sounded into the quiet. Nothing happened. He blew the horn again. Surely someone would be in on a cold rainy day. There was no sign of life in the little house. He pushed at the door and then swung his leg out, his heart was thumping now and he wished he hadn't spent so long waiting, allowing the tension to build. He peered around again.

From the back of the barn was a flash of colour. The rain had come back, squally now, blowing into his face and he dragged his leg back inside the car and squinted through the splattered windscreen to where the blur of blue had flickered in the edge of his vision. There was nothing to see.

He puffed out a breath. Well, he was going to have to either get out and run through the rain to hammer on the door or just turn around and drive away. He couldn't carry on like some ridiculous jack in the box half in and half out of the car. He pulled the key from the ignition and zipped up the front of his jacket. The flash of blue appeared at the other side of the house now and as he watched, a bent figure ran down the side of the building across the scruffy yard, feet splashing and slipping in the puddles. A face appeared at the window, and a fist hammered against the glass.

"Let me in mate, come on it's proper parky out here. Open the soddin' door."

He leaned, clicked the automatic locking device and a skinny boy dragged open the door and half fell into the car, showering Simon and the dashboard and seats with cold rain.

"Shit, it's a proper bugger out there. Nobody in, you might as well go. They've gone to town."

"There are lights on."

"Yeah, but they always leave them on. It's for when they get back. No point staying. Come on then. You goin' back to Leeds you can drop me up at the junction."

"No, I'm going to Ramstone."

"Oh yeah. Result. Take us to the High Street then?"

"Erm, who are you exactly?"

"Oh right, I'm Fuzz." The youth leaned forward and turned on the radio, twisted the knob back and forth until he found a station blaring out heavy metal music. "Ace. Come on then. If we go now, I can be back in time to meet Jazzer and Kens."

No response suggested itself and so with a small shrug of his shoulders Simon started the car and made a complete hash of a three-point turn, slithering across the farmyard the wheels spinning in the mud until he eventually drew away. He glanced at the boy next to him. He pulled down the hood of the short blue jacket and rubbed his hands against dark, spikey hair. He dragged a handkerchief from his pocket and wiped it across his face, blew his nose and then took out a packet of cigarettes. "Erm. I don't think…"

"Oh, sodding hell you're a bloody health freak, alright I won't light the bloody thing. Sodding no smoking shit." He leaned back against the seat now and with a grunt stuffed the cigarette back into the pack.

"So, do you live there? At the farm?"

"Wot?"

"Do you live at the farm?"

"Who wants to know?" The boy's rudeness was astounding but Simon found himself amused rather than irritated.

"Well, I'm giving you a lift, I should think the least you could do is tell me who you are, what you were doing there."

"I already did, didn't I? Fuzz, I said."

"Well, yes but…"

"No, I'm not no farmer, am I? Shit."

"So what were you doing there?"

"Lookin', I were just lookin'."

"What were you looking at?"

"Stuff."

"What stuff?"

"Ayyup." The conversation, such as it was, had been cut short by Simon taking his eyes from the road and a ewe with her lamb choosing just that moment to leap from the ditch in the dim light.

"Sod it." Simon spun the wheel as the car skewed across the slippery carriageway and then spun it back again as the wheels found some grip and they zig-zagged and slid across the narrow road for a few yards, until he was back in control.

"Shit man, where'd you learn to drive? My gran's better than you and she's half ga ga."

"Sorry. Sorry – I'm a bit out of practice and it's a new car."

"Not new."

"Well no, new to me I mean."

"Well you won't have it long at this rate." And with a shout of laughter, Fuzz leaned forward and began drumming on the dashboard, keeping time to the blare of music from the radio.

Simon gave all his attention to the road and the driving and looked forward to dropping this loud, rude boy in the centre of town and going back to Mill Lodge to see if Gloria could be persuaded to go out for lunch.

Fuzz rummaged in his pocket and pulled out some shotgun shell casings. He rolled them back and forth in his hands, lifted them to his nose and sniffed at them.

"What have you got there?"

"Bullets, or erm, a shotgun shell."

"What? bloody hell."

"It's okay, they're old – whatchamacallit, spent. Yeah spent – look it's empty. She already shot them."

"Who did?"

"The nutter, at the farm, she a friend of yours? What, your sister or sommat?"

"No, no she's not. How do you know it was her, with the gun I mean?"

"I seen her. Seen her loads a times, shoots at everything. I tell you she's a total nutter, a thingy, psycho, yeah a psycho. She's got loads of guns, puts them in the car on a rack. Just like in those American films. Well two or three at least."

"Tell you what, Fuzz, why don't you come back with me. Up to my flat. I've got some beer, some coke."

"Yeah?"

"Oh, the drink, not… you know, not drugs."

"Oh, right." The boy peered out of the window at the constant rain. "You're not one of them paedos are ya? You're not going to want a bum job or sommat?"

"No, no I promise you. I just thought it'd be nice to have a natter. You can tell me about the psycho – if you like. I could get us some fish and chips or a curry or whatever?"

"Yeah. Go on then. Chicken Korma and some naan bread. Sweet." With that he lay his head back and closed his eyes, his fingers drummed on the dirty jeans that were loose around skinny thighs and now and again he would splurt out a few of the words of the songs.

Chapter 21

Simon drove into his yard and splashed across to close the big timber doors. As he walked back to the car Fuzz clambered out and looked around in bemusement. "What's this then?"

"How do you mean? It's my yard."

"Well, it's a yard, I can see it's a yard, but what's it for? There's nothin' in it."

Simon rubbed a hand through his wet hair. "Well, I don't really need it, so I – well, it goes with the shop."

"Oh right, what d'ya sell?"

"No, I don't, erm... Look I just live here that's all. I live in the flat upstairs. Come on, the curry's getting cold."

The young lad shrugged and followed behind into the warehouse. Before he had a chance to say anything, Simon pre-empted yet another question-and-answer session. "This just goes with the flat and I'm not using it at the minute." And he pounded up the stairs with Fuzz behind him.

They ate the curry sitting at the table in the window, the rain streamed across the glass but it was cosy inside. "Have you got any beer?"

"Are you old enough to drink?"

"Don't be daft, how can you have curry without beer?" Simon shrugged, it wasn't his job to look after this kid after all. "Lager, okay?"

"Yeah, great."

"So, come on then, tell me what you know about the woman at the farm?"

Fuzz pushed back from the table, slid his hand into the pocket of his jeans and brought out the shell casings. He handed one across to Simon.

"Well, like I said she's a nutter. I 'spect she's married to the bloke and she just spends all day walkin' about on the hills with them dogs. She shoots at stuff, rabbits and that, well a lot of folk shoot at rabbits but she shoots birds and stuff as well. One day me and Jazzer were out there and it come on to rain and we thought we'd just sit it out in that old barn. Well, bugger me if she didn't come on out yelling and screaming at us with a bloody rifle. We had to run for us lives. She was shooting at us good and proper."

"So, if that happened why were you there today? I mean, why go back?"

"Well, because she's a nutter and I want to watch her. She's always doing something daft. She takes that old car out and drives about like a lunatic, tearing up and down them roads and up on the rough. I don't know how he puts up with her, that bloke. Mind, he's not often there, I don't think they do that much farmin' to be honest. He has a few sheep but she brings them in with them dogs and I've never seen him do much else really. I reckon there's something else up there that he does, you know maybe internet business of some sort. Anyroad, it's fun to watch her and there's nowt much else to do round here is there."

"Shouldn't you be at school, or college? How old are you?"

"I'm fifteen. I reckon I've done with school."

"So, you haven't got a job then?"

"Nah, haven't made me mind up what to do yet. I might just go off down to London, sommat like that."

Simon saw in the boy at his table so much of himself at that age. Trying to make a life but with not much future and a thin and feeble past.

"I don't think it's all it's cracked up to be actually. Living in London."

"What do you do then? That warehouse is empty, there's nowt in the yard, the shelves in your shop were bare."

"Me, oh erm… well I run my own business."

"Oh right. What's that then?"

"I'm an investigator." He had spoken without thinking.

"A what?"

Now it was a struggle to keep his dignity, how could he convince someone else of his credentials when he didn't really believe them himself. He swept a hand towards the table with the computer on it. "I investigate things. You know, like a private detective."

"Yeah. Hey cool." Now, he was embarrassed by the look on the boy's face, the gleam of interest in his eyes.

"Well, I've only just started. I've applied for my licence and what have you. I'm going to make the shop into my office, well probably." There must have been something in the way that he spoke and the boy shook his head.

"Right. Oh well good luck with that then."

"Well, that was why I wanted to talk to you really. This case I'm working on." Simon squared his shoulders, went and brought a small pile of the record cards to where they were sitting. He wrote Fuzz's name on one, tried to look serious and as though he knew what he was doing. "Well, I think that farm may have something to do with what I'm looking into right now. That's why I thought you might be able to help me." As he spoke, he saw the error but it was too late.

"So, you'll pay me then?"

"Pay you? What for?"

"If I help you?"

"Well no, I just thought you could tell me about the woman."

"Yeah, but that's like me being an informer or sommat, so you have to pay me."

He had to step back from this hole before it was any deeper. "No, that wasn't really what I had in mind. I just thought you could tell me about her, as a favour you know."

"Nah. Not happening. I tell you about her, you pay me."

"But how do I know that any of what you tell me is worth anything?"

"If you're investigatin' her then it must be worth sommat."

"Forget it, we're going round in circles here. It was just a thought that was all. You got a curry and a beer out of it so we'll call that it, shall we?"

"Tell you what though, I could keep an eye on her and you could pay me for that couldn't you? Like an assistant."

"No, no I don't want an assistant. Look all I wanted was to find out what you knew. You've told me, she's a nutter who shoots things, she drives about like a lunatic. Do you have any idea how long she's lived there?"

Fuzz held out his hand.

"Oh, for shit's sake." Simon reached into his pocket and pulled out a ten pound note. He handed it over.

"Been there years. It was empty for a while, when I was a kid, then they bought it and did it up a bit, about 2009, sommat like that. We used to go up there a fair bit back then, but once they moved in we had to stop. That's why we went to the barn that day, because we were used to it and that."

"Right, okay then. Well…" Simon stood up from the table and reached for the dishes. "I'd better get on. Thanks, Fuzz."

"So, do you want me to keep on watchin' her then?"

"No, there's no need. I don't even know whether she has anything to do with what I'm looking into."

"What is it?"

"It was somebody who was killed up there, an accident. Some people want to know more about it."

"Oh, that lass, was it?"

"Sorry?"

"That lass, that Melanie?"

"Yes. But, how did you know, I mean, what made you think that?"

"Well, with her walking that way all the time and that, everyone knows about it."

"But, how did you know it was there?"

"Like I said, we used to be up there all the time and then when they moved in so were she. Always on that road, back and forth."

"Did you know her?"

"No, she's older than me, well she was. She was in school with my cousin though. He said she were pretty fit and a bit loose, you know."

"Loose?"

"Yeah, you know – up for it."

"Right. I see. Your cousin doesn't know any of her friends, does he?"

"Might do, but he's gone. Joined up last year, don't know where he is right now."

"And you don't know any of them?"

"Only that Fiona, she went out with my cousin for a bit. She's working in Leeds now – with a vet."

Chapter 22

Once Fuzz had left, Simon called Gloria.

"Do you want to go out for a quick drink? I have some news."

"I'm in the middle of some stuff actually. Do you want to come here? Give me an hour and then come down."

"If you're sure. What are you up to?"

"I'll show you when you come down."

"Fair enough."

He tidied the flat, re-read some of the notes he'd made earlier and added what he had learned in his conversation with Fuzz. It hadn't been much really but the important thing was the lead to Melanie's friend and the boy had agreed to get in touch with the infamous Jazzer who apparently would have even more information. He really didn't have much more to go on and sometime soon Charles Clegg was going to call and want to know what he had found out.

He locked up the flat and walked down to Mill Lodge, taking the car was still not his natural choice. He hoped that they could go out for a drink after all and anyway, there was always booze on offer when he was with Gloria. That was another thing niggling in the back of his mind. He ought to be more help to her, he was using her again and not giving enough back. Although she was talking to him, helping and going out and about more, there was still a shadow in her eyes when she didn't know he was watching her.

He knocked on the bay window of the dining room. He had seen the shadow of her moving about inside as he walked up the path.

She was dressed in her jogging pants and a sweatshirt, her hair piled on the top of her head. She was in work mode and he was pleased to see her looking so animated.

"Come in."

She leaned away as he tried to give her a hug. "No, don't, I'm filthy."

"What've you been doing?"

"Come and see." She had to thread her way between the furniture piled in the hallway, chairs and tables stacked haphazardly beside the walls. "I was just giving this place a lick of paint."

"Nice. The same colour though?"

"Yes. We always did it the same colour. When people come back for a second or third stay they like it to be just as they remembered. It gets a bit boring but we have to keep the punters happy after all."

"So, are you opening up again?" She didn't answer straight away, she looked down at her feet, glanced around the small room and then turned to face him directly. "I thought I might sell."

Speech alluded him. There were many things he wanted to say but he couldn't find the right words. He wanted to simply say, "Don't," but couldn't explain why it was so important that this place stay as it was, that she be here, as she was. It wasn't even fair for him to feel that way but the idea that such a change was possible, when he was just beginning to feel settled and anchored, shocked and actually scared him.

There were a few moments of awkward silence. Gloria didn't say any more, she watched his face, assessing, judging and then she gave a brief nod and turned away.

She passed along the hallway and into the flat. It was clean in there now, the way it had used to be. This at least was reassuring. He had to say something, the atmosphere was changing, becoming uncomfortable. "So! You might sell? I had no idea that you were even considering that."

"I haven't been able to think about the future for a while now. Then yesterday I was walking around inside, remembering – you know – and I just thought that perhaps the best thing would be for me to just start again. I enjoyed this place, when it was me and Dave. Then after he died I had come to quite like it again and it was easy, in a way, just to keep on going but..." She shrugged her shoulders and then moved to lean against the mantelpiece. "Well, I don't know if I can face opening up again. The regulars will all know about what happened and I don't want to answer questions about it and... new people." She paused. "To be honest, it struck me that some visitors might come because of what happened and I don't want to look at every guest and wonder if they are really just ghouls."

"I hadn't thought of that."

"Well, no, why would you? This isn't your business, is it?" She swept a hand in front of her. "This is mine."

He wondered if she was doing it to hurt him, shutting him out deliberately.

"Is there something wrong, Gloria? Have I done something wrong?" As he spoke, he hoped she didn't think him as self-interested as he sounded to his own ears. She looked at him and shook her head.

"No, it's not that. You haven't done anything. If it hadn't been for you I'd still be sitting in my own stink, slowly drinking myself to death. No, it's just that this place feels like a whatsit – oh that bird – round your neck?"

"Albatross?"

"Yeah. That's it. I tried to imagine the summer, you know, the new season, opening up and waiting for the guests and it just doesn't seem possible. I don't think I want to do it, it's just – I don't want to be here anymore."

His mouth had dried. Until that moment it hadn't been so clear to him, but he knew for certain that if she wasn't here, he didn't want to be either. He couldn't say that to her, it wasn't fair. She was fighting demons of her own and, although he was winning his own battles, he understood the turmoil.

"Can I help?" She shook her head quickly and then turned to look at him.

"Although, actually, yes why not. It won't take long and I'm only doing that one room. Then I'm going to get a valuation. Yeah, go on. Why don't you come down tomorrow? I bet we could finish it in one day between the two of us."

"Right." It wasn't what he meant, but if she just wanted an extra pair of hands with the painting – well, he could do that as well.

"Now, let me get us a cuppa and you tell me your news. You have some news?"

"Yes, I do."

Chapter 23

"I went back up to the farm, I wanted to have another go at speaking to someone."

"In your new car then?"

"Yeah, it was a bit hairy to be honest. I need to get more practice, driving on my own." He cringed inwardly, that wasn't right, he didn't want her to feel he was pushing her away. "I didn't want to put you at risk again, Gloria. I didn't want to expose you to that nutcase with the gun." She nodded, made a small noise, dismissive. He carried on. "Anyway, there was nobody there, well not in the house at any rate. But there was this kid. A boy came running from behind the barn and insisted on getting in with me."

"How do you mean insisted?"

"Well, he didn't give me any choice, you know?"

"No" – she shook her head at him now – "how could he make you let him in? Doesn't it have locks then, this new car?"

"Yes, of course it has locks. Gloria, what is it? What's the matter?"

She closed her eyes and when she opened them, he was shocked to see the glint of tears.

"I'm sorry. I'm just in a foul mood. Ignore me, really, carry on."

"No, wait a minute. Are you sure I haven't done something? You're so annoyed."

"No, I'm not. I'm not annoyed. Oh well if you must know it's my mother's birthday today. I just keep thinking about it all, everything that happened and I can't change anything. I feel bad."

There was nothing to say, he stood up from his seat on the settee and went across to kneel before her.

"I'm sorry. I had no idea."

"No, of course you didn't. Why would you? And I shouldn't feel guilty, it was him, Peter, that went wrong but it's just been playing on my mind all day."

"Of course it has, I'm not surprised. Is that anything to do with selling this place, all of that?"

"Probably a bit I suppose. But it makes sense really, doesn't it?"

He swivelled around so that he was sitting beside her, on the floor, and he laid a hand across her knee. "But what will you do? Where will you go?"

"I should think I'll stay around here, or maybe go back to Leeds. If I do manage to sell, I should get enough to buy a little place, to live in, you know. Then I could get a job I reckon. Not sure what yet but there's stuff in pubs and cafés for a start. Later I could try and get something better, admin – like I used to but I'd need to update my skills a bit."

"Will that be enough though, after running your own place?"

"Don't know until I try, do I? You need to be thinking about yourself anyway, what you're going to do. After this stuff with Charlie Clegg." He should tell her now, about the licence application, about his plans, but he just couldn't lay himself open to the risk of it all falling apart and her being disappointed in him.

He took the conversation back. "Anyway, this kid. Fuzz he's called."

"Oh right, a skinny lad. Really blue eyes and short spiky brown hair. About a foot shorter than you probably. Nice looking really, a dimple in his cheek."

"Yeah, that sounds about right. You know him then?"

"I know his granny, she used to work in the old people's home, until she retired. Nice woman. He's not a bad lad but he can be a bit wild. Phillip, that's his real name, Phillip Farnworth. He was a lovely little boy but I think he got in with the wrong crowd. Follower rather than a leader is Phillip."

"Like me then?"

She didn't say anything but gave a sort of grin and a nod.

"Like I was when I was his age at any rate."

"Lived with his Gran last I heard. I think his mum had some mental problems, depression or something. She never married his dad. Anyway, what has he got to do with all this?"

"Well, turns out he knows the veterinary nurse. No, that's wrong. He knows somebody who knows her. Somebody called Jazzer? God, where do they come up with these names?"

"Oh that one, Jazzer, he's a nasty piece of work. His surname is Jasper, so that's where that's from. David, I think he is. Yeah, David Jasper."

"How come you know all this?"

"Well I've been around here a while and I've had a few women work for me, cleaning and what have you, I used to have a couple in the kitchens as well, until I gave up on the dinners. People talk and you just have to listen."

"Hmm. Well anyway, apparently it's possible that Jazzer knows where Fiona works. I gave Fuzz my number and he's going to ring when he finds out.

"Well, that's a move in the right direction anyway."

"It's information for Charlie. Makes it clear that we've been doing something."

She smiled at him now.

"We? You found this out."

"Yeah, but well, I think of it as we."

"Do you?"

"Yes, of course I do." And that was it, the darkness left her eyes and she grinned at him. Without trying he had found a way through and as she got up to go to the kitchen to start something for dinner, he felt his nerves settle for the first time since he had seen the furniture piled in the hallway. It would be okay. It had to be, because this was his one chance. If this all fell apart, he didn't see any other way forward.

Chapter 24

"Have you thought exactly what you are hoping to get from this girl?" Gloria was serving up the bolognese and pasta, they had red wine and the atmosphere was relaxed. She smiled at Simon as she pulled her chair out from under the edge of the table and sat opposite him.

"Well, it's just general information really. I reckon if I can start to understand her a bit, the girl who died, then maybe it will give us some sort of clue…"

"Clue to what? Just what did you think you might find?"

"A clue to whether or not there could be more to it than meets the eye, more to it than just a horrible hit and run accident I suppose. Originally, I thought maybe it was just another driver, you know, maybe before Colin and Colin just drove past and didn't see, something like that anyway. But now after all that's happened, with the fire at my place and that phone call, it just seems much more – oh I don't know – sinister. I honestly still can't see any other way to deal with it. I can find out exactly what time she left her friend, from the horse's mouth as it were, what mood she was in. At one time, I wondered if maybe she'd done it deliberately – thrown herself in front of the car – but in that case, surely he would have stopped. I know I'm going round in circles but Charlie Clegg is so convinced that Colin didn't drive drunk and then just leave her. I can't believe that there was anything deliberate. I mean, for a start, if you were going to do that would you use a car?"

"Yeah, I would."

"What?"

"Well, if I was going to try and kill someone, it'd be a good choice. It happens nearly every day doesn't it, and most of the time it is what it seems to be. The only difference with this was that whoever did it, didn't stop. That happens as well, but often because the driver is drunk, as they said in the court case or they have something else to hide, drugs I suppose or – well yeah, that it was deliberate. See, if you wanted somebody dead, it works."

"Bloody hell. That's been staring us in the face all along, hasn't it? If it wasn't a hit and run accident…" He lifted his hands, palm upwards. "But, in that case?"

"Yes, in that case who and why?"

"I suppose the obvious answer is Colin Bliss. There was all the evidence on his car and the CCTV and so on. Perhaps this hasn't really been a miscarriage of justice but simply Colin covering up what he did deliberately and taking the easier way out. Oh no, come on, who would want to kill an ordinary young girl, a student? It's ridiculous."

"That could be why Mrs Clegg told you to leave it alone. Maybe she knows, maybe even Maureen Bliss knows."

"But then, why would Charlie Clegg want to open it all up, why not just leave it and wait it out. Do you think it's possible that the rest of them know and he doesn't? No, he might be an old bloke but he's got all his chairs at home, that just doesn't work for me."

Gloria was shaking her head. "No, me neither. So, is it back to square one then?"

"I don't know. I don't think so though. There was something else, something that Fuzz said after I met him."

"I know what you're thinking. You're thinking of the woman at the farm but it's just too obvious, you're jumping to conclusions. Just because she shot at us… Oh what am I saying, she shot at us! There's no, 'just'."

"Yes, but according to Fuzz she shoots at everything and we're not the first people. But Melanie wasn't shot, was she, so it's irrelevant."

"Bloody hell, what a tangle." They sat in silence, eating the rich sauce and nibbling at garlic bread. "Hey, lovely meal by the way."

"Thanks." But they were lost in their own thoughts and the food became secondary to the puzzle and on Simon's part the need to succeed at this. He made a decision.

"I applied for a licence."

"What, shit you haven't been driving illegally have you? I just assumed you'd passed your test."

"No, no a licence to be an investigator." It was obvious from the expression on her face that Gloria hadn't a clue what he was talking about.

"Okay, I know it sounds a bit daft. Well yes, it is a bit daft. But anyway, I've done it. That whole thing, when I came back, sorted things about Sandie."

She nodded but the frown line between her eyes deepened.

He paused, feeling stupid and embarrassed. "Because of all that meant to me, and then Charlie asking me for help, well, in a nutshell I want to be a private detective, I applied for the licence for it. I paid and that, but it could come apart because of my record."

"You haven't got a record. You were cleared completely."

"Yes, I know but they need to know where I lived for the last five years."

"So, when did you do all this?"

"Only last week." He waited for her to laugh at him, to shake her head and tell him he was an idiot.

"Hey, well good for you. I mean, really, I see that there could be problems. I would have thought you'd need to be somewhere better than here. Leeds maybe, or Liverpool and – to be honest it's an odd idea. Still I suppose with the internet and so on – why not, I suppose. Ah, the car, that's why you needed a car."

He nodded.

"I thought that maybe if it all worked out, I could open the shop up as an office. Is that stupid? Am I being daft, Gloria?"

"Yeah, probably – but what have you got to lose?"

He couldn't sit still, he jumped up and dragged her into his arms.

"I was scared of saying anything. I thought you'd laugh at me. I was embarrassed and, quite honestly I wasn't even sure myself and here you are saying all the right things. You're brilliant. Do you know that, Gloria, you truly are brilliant?"

Chapter 25

He didn't go home that night. The next morning, she made them bacon sandwiches and then they dragged out the paint and brushes and spent four hours brightening up the dining room. The talk was casual and easy, about the colour scheme, the cleaning up afterwards and then mutual congratulation as they carried the tables and chairs back into the room, which smelled of paint and furniture polish. "It looks good, Gloria."

"Yeah. It does, doesn't it?" He stood behind her and wrapped his arms around her waist. He nuzzled her neck. "You've got paint in your hair. I reckon you need a shower and I should give you a hand to make sure you get it all out." She laughed and took his hand and pulled him with her through to the bedroom.

Afterwards, when they were dressed and sitting in the newly decorated room sipping their coffee, she leaned across the table and took his hand. "This is nice, thanks, Simon. Thanks for coming back and for helping me through this." She raised his fingers to her lips and kissed them. "I feel really good for the first time in months."

"I'm glad. Are you still thinking of calling the agent, still thinking of selling?"

"I am yes, but I'll give it until next week. Oh, there we go, is that your phone?"

"Yes, it's in the other room. It'll be a sales call, it always is. I'll leave it. Do you want to stay in, go out for a walk?"

"Yeah, let's have a walk up on the hills, it's stopped raining for now at least. We should go soon though, the weather could turn again. I'll go and sort out my stuff. You need to get your boots. Shall I drive you up to the flat?"

"Great."

He collected his jacket from the lounge and pulled his phone from the pocket. There was no message but the text alert was blinking. "Hmm that's odd. There's only you and my dad ever send me texts and that's not his number." He opened the message.

At the farm. Pls cum Fuzz.

"What is it?"

"Well, it's a bit odd. I'm not sure I understand it." He held out the little handset and Gloria took it from him.

"You don't recognise the number?"

"No. What's that *pls cum?* What does that mean?"

"It means 'please come', don't you know text speak?" She was laughing at him until she saw the worried look on his face.

"Shit, it's that stupid lad, isn't it? He wanted to help, said he could keep an eye on that woman. I told him no – but…"

"Oh God, come on, get your coat. I suppose we're not getting a walk after all. Shall I drive?"

Simon nodded. "Yes, I think that's best. Me and wet roads aren't getting on that well at the moment."

She turned away from the end of Mill Street and onto the main road. The surface was slick but she was confident and Simon sat back in his seat looking down at the phone in his hand. "Do you think I should send a message back? Should I tell him we're coming?"

"Well, I suppose so. I wonder what the hell is going on."

"I've no idea. He was only supposed to be asking his mate about the veterinary nurse. I told him not to go back up there. I told him specifically. I don't like this. I don't like it at all."

"Me neither but, Mr Private Detective" – she turned to grin at him – "I guess you're just going to have to get used to this sort of stuff, aren't you?"

"I don't want him getting into trouble though, Gloria. It's not funny really, if he's gone and got himself into a mess because of me I'll feel awful. I don't want people hurt because of me."

"Hey, come on – we don't even know what's happened yet. He's probably just being melodramatic; you know what kids are like. It'll be fine."

They turned onto the moorland road as the rain came back and the clouds lowered. The sky turned black and in the distance lightning bounced on the top of the hills. They could feel thunder in the air. Gloria had her lights full on now and the wipers were struggling to sweep aside the flood on the windscreen.

"If he's just got us out here on some wild goose chase, I'll have his bloody guts for garters." She was trying not to sound angry but when Simon looked across her knuckles were white where she gripped the wheel and he saw tension in the set of her jaw.

He took in a deep breath and tried to calm himself, tried to convince himself that this was indeed all just a silly kid's drama.

Chapter 26

"Don't drive all the way up to the junction. Park over there." Simon pointed to an area of flat grassland at the side of the road.

"I don't think so, not in this rain. That looks boggy to me." They were creeping forward now through a torrential downpour. Along the road they had passed several cars pulled onto the verge as the drivers waited for the worst of the squall to blow through. Visibility was down to just a few metres. Small branches from the tough little moorland trees scuttered across the carriageway and the car rocked and swayed as the wind caught it.

"We should stop anyway, this is dangerous." Gloria was leaning forward peering through the rain-washed windscreen. "Over there, look, it's gravelly, we can stop there."

"Right, good." She turned slowly onto the scree and the tyres slipped and spun on the loose wet stones. As soon as she was far enough off the road for safety she pulled on the handbrake and switched off the engine. Simon leaned into the back to reach for his jacket.

"What the hell are you doing? You're not getting out in this."

"Well, I can't just sit here, can I?"

"But it's mad, you can't see, the wind alone is bad enough without the sodding rain."

He twisted back and forth on the seat. "But, Gloria, what if that lad's hurt or something, it won't improve leaving him in weather like this."

"Simon, you haven't even got a proper waterproof, you're wearing trainers for God's sake. That would be stupid on a good day. You can't set off up that road dressed like you are. It'll pass in a bit, it can't last like this. Just sit tight. Let's face it, it must be half an hour since you got the text. We don't know what his problem is, or even if there is one really. If he is hurt or something, he's in dire straits by now anyway. It won't help for you to get into trouble as well. Just wait. Look, it's brightening already, over there to the west."

He knew she was right, and although his legs jigged up and down with frustration and he constantly wiped at the condensation forming on the windows to peer through at the grey wetness all around them, he waited. He took the phone from his pocket and stared again at the text message.

Gloria spoke, trying to ease the tension, "I think I've got an old waterproof of Dave's in the boot, once the rain eases we can have a look. It'd be better than what you're wearing, we should have gone to the flat, got your stuff."

"It's too late now. You're right though, the cloud is lifting a bit, I think the rain is easing. We'll just give it a couple more minutes, then drive a bit nearer and walk across the field. I don't want to go down that road and announce our presence. I have no idea what's going on but it's probably best, if the woman's around, that she doesn't see us."

"Look, we can't go across the field. You can't anyway, not in those shoes and I'm not doing it on my own. Here, get the spare anorak from the boot and we'll walk up the road as far as the junction. The car's safe here, there might not be anywhere further up. This is better, I know you're worried Simon, I do understand." She knew there was more to his worry than just concern for Fuzz, knew that the guilt about his sister would never leave him and it brought with it fear of letting people down. "You know I'm right. Come on." She slammed the car door and took a few steps up the sloping road.

He dragged on the thin plastic coat and a woollen hat that had been in the pocket and together they bent into the wind. Gloria was more surefooted in her hiking boots but it was still hard going. It was impossible to talk and they trudged on as the clouds scudded overhead showing the odd incongruous small patch of blue. Wild and wonderful he had called it and any other day, with the proper equipment, Simon would have been in his element, now all he could think of was the slight figure of Fuzz hammering on his car window.

Once they reached the turn off for the farm, Simon pulled Gloria behind a small stretch of broken dry-stone wall. Out of the worst of the wind it was strangely calm and they took a moment to just breathe and recover from the climb. "I think we can get round the back of the barn if we cross this field." He saw her look down at his feet. "They're soaked already, there's no point worrying about it now. The anorak is good though, I'm not cold, are you okay?"

"Yeah, I'm fine. It's pretty wild though, isn't it? She grinned at him. "Do you still think you love it like this?"

"Normally, yes – I do. Once I know that lad's okay, I'll be happy. Well apart from wet feet." He smiled back at her briefly. "Are you ready?"

"Yeah, but exactly what are we going to do? He just said he was at the farm, we don't know where or anything, do we? He might even be inside the house."

"Well he mentioned the barn yesterday so I thought we could go round the back and have a look in there first. If he's not there I don't see we have any choice but to knock on the door to be honest."

"Yeah?" She opened her eyes wide and grimaced.

"You don't have to come if we do that."

"Don't be daft, of course I'm coming, it's just that I still remember that bloody gun."

"Me too. I reckon we can just tell them we're worried about our friend in this weather, something like that anyway. I don't see how she would recognise us without the car."

"Good point. Come on then let's get on with it." They followed the broken wall along the edge of the field until it ended at a dilapidated wooden gate and then they paused again to catch their breath. The rain had blown away and the sky was pale grey with puffs of darker cloud, a warning that the deluge could start again whenever it pleased.

"Right, if we go down that dip and turn right it should bring us out behind the barn on the far side from the house. There is a side door, I noticed it last time we were here. Just where that Land Rover was parked. That's where I think we should head and hope it's not locked."

The car wasn't there and the small side door hung open. Rain had blown into the barn and dirty puddles of water were filled with bits of muck and dry leaves. The bales of straw filled up one corner along with piles of the usual detritus to be found in such buildings. Some old machinery, rusting and in pieces, was scattered across the dirt floor. There was a blue tarpaulin heaped against one long wall, it was filthy and holey, and lay in a hump. As Simon leaned towards it, his heart pounded. He lifted the corner and found, not the broken, bruised body he had been dreading, but an old pile of sand and a couple of rusty shovels. He blew out a breath.

Gloria had been working her way down the other side, kicking aside old planks of wood and bits of metal. "It's a shit hole isn't it. I don't think they use this for anything much. I know farmers are untidy but this place looks abandoned." She stopped and bent forward. "Oh bugger."

"What, what is it?" She stood and held her hand high in the air. It was a blue waterproof jacket. "You're going to tell me this is his, aren't you?" Simon stormed across the littered floor, he reached out and fingered the dirty sleeve of the coat.

"It might be. It's the same colour as the one he was wearing. Oh hell."

Gloria put her hand into the pocket and nodded her head.

"Phone. It's only a soddin' phone isn't it. It's smashed." She was peering at it now in the dull light, poking at the button on the side. He reached for it. She shook her head as she handed it to him. "It's no good it's completely dead, the case is cracked. I don't think there's any hope for that."

"Oh God. What do you reckon?"

"I have no idea, Simon, no idea at all."

Chapter 27

"Leave the coat, it's evidence. We shouldn't have touched it really. Bring the phone though, maybe we can get it to work." Simon was heading for the door. "Where's that bloody Land Rover?"

"Calm down, Simon. Stop and think. Just hold on a minute."

"Okay, okay, but he's not here, we have to find him. Listen, is that a car? Can you hear a car?"

"Yeah. I think so. It's getting nearer. Oh great. Now what?"

Simon ran to the door and looked down the lane that led to the main road.

"It's coming down here. It's not the Land Rover, it's a red saloon car. Quick, go back out to the field."

As they peered from behind the corner of the building the car drew up to the front door of the farmhouse. The driver, in a green waxed jacket and denim jeans, climbed out and ran the few steps to the front door. He used his key and then they heard the door slam as he disappeared inside.

"I'm going to go back down the field a bit, over the wall and then walk back, along the drive, give him the chance to see me. He has just driven up, he didn't pass us so we need to make him think we just arrived, we need to give it a couple of minutes, we can't just appear at the door now. Back to the original plan. Are you coming with me?"

"Or what?"

"Well, you could go back to the car. Wait for me…" The look on her face stopped him and he reached and took hold of her hand. They ran along the field, at one point she tripped and fell to her knees. Simon pulled her to her feet and they pushed on. The broken wall had collapsed completely at a point halfway between the car and the house and they clambered over the slippery, moss-covered rocks and stepped out onto the muddy pathway.

They peered back at the cluster of buildings; they could see that one room downstairs in the house had a light on inside. "Those dogs don't seem to be there, do they?"

"No. Everything points to the woman being off somewhere else. If that bloke has just arrived, the house must have been empty; so, Fuzz is not in there, is he?"

"This is bloody stupid. We don't know what we're looking for. Look, tell you what, first of all try calling that number back. If he's still here somewhere we can collect him and it's all done. We're not really sure that was his coat or that this is his phone, are we? Those anoraks are common as muck. He could be back at his gran's by now and we're up here in the wet and cold." Simon took his phone from his pocket and dialled. They waited, both staring at the small grey handset. "Hiya, Fuzz the Buzz here." There was a brief pause and then a tone as the answering service cut out. Gloria looked down at the phone they had picked up in the barn. She hadn't expected there to be any sound and it had lain dead and silent in her palm. "So, either his phone is flat or turned off, which is odd because he's not long ago sent that message or" – she nodded her head just once downwards – "this is his phone."

"Is there no way we can find out?"

"Does it really matter?"

"Oh come on, who are we kidding? Of course it's his phone, it's the only explanation." He didn't need to say anymore, they both knew that a teenager would never voluntarily be separated from their phone.

* * *

"Back to the farm. It's the only answer, but actually let's just drive up there. That woman didn't seem to be around, the dogs weren't there. We'll go and knock on the door and then, I guess I'll just wing it with that bloke."

"Great plan." With the humourless huff of a laugh, Gloria turned and stomped off through the puddles. Once back at the car they stopped to wipe the mud from their shoes and shrug off the wet jackets.

"Look up there, by the barn, coming across the field, isn't that the Land Rover?" Simon stretched out a hand, pointing back the way they had just come.

"I think so. Now what shall we do?"

"Well I reckon we have no choice but to carry on and talk to her."

"Great. Just what I wanted."

"You don't have to come if you don't want to."

"Stop saying that. I'm here, aren't I?"

"Sorry. Look there she is, she's going to the barn, there's no sign of Fuzz though. There, there she's got the coat. She's heading out the back."

"Shall we keep on? Still go down there?" Gloria thrust the key into the ignition and then raised her hands in frustration. "This is turning into a bloody farce."

"Look, we need to get down there anyway. Just carry on, eh?"

She snorted with frustration and pulled away. "Right, fine."

"I'm sorry, Gloria, but I don't know what to do for the best and I'm just worried sick about him."

Chapter 28

The man who answered the door was tall and rangy, his hair was thinning and receding. His face, frowning now at the unexpected intrusion, was tanned and a little weather-beaten. He had been handsome but his jaw line was softening and broken veins around his nose witnessed a familiarity with booze. He glared down at Gloria and Simon where they stood at the bottom of two stone steps, and then glanced up the road towards the gateposts. "Sorry to bother you." Simon held out a hand as he spoke but the gesture was ignored. "I'm Simon Fulton and this is my colleague Ms Bartlett, we wondered if we could speak to your wife?" It seemed safest to keep as close to the truth as possible. Even though he didn't recall seeing this man in the town centre that was no guarantee that he didn't know who Simon was. The scar on his face and the pictures that had been in the paper might well generate a spark of recognition.

The answering voice was gruff but the accent wasn't local. "Why do you want to speak to Lily?"

"There was an accident, on the main road." As he spoke, Simon felt Gloria tense beside him, but he continued. "A week or so ago, an elderly chap ran off the road."

"What's that got to do with us?"

"Well, Mr erm…?"

"Coleman."

Simon nodded.

"Right, Mr Coleman. We are looking into it, insurance and what have you and a witness thought that maybe someone, a woman from this farm, may have seen something?"

With a shake of his head Coleman stepped back and began to push the door closed. "We know nothing about any accidents. We've seen nothing."

"But if we could just speak to your wife?" Simon had reached out with his hand and laid it against the wood of the door.

"She's not here. Probably out on the tops with her sheep. She saw nothing." As he spoke, he had pointed backwards beyond the wall at the side of the house. He pushed harder now at the door. "I've nothing more to say. If you'd leave, please."

They couldn't stay now that he had asked them to go and without another word Coleman simply slammed the door closed. Gloria and Simon turned and walked back down the puddled lane towards where they had parked the car.

"Friendly sort," Gloria muttered as she plipped the key to unlock the doors, "Not, local. I didn't recognise him at all. Doesn't look like a farmer, his hands were too clean and soft-looking."

"Yes, that's what I thought," Simon replied. "Spends plenty of time outdoors though, he was tanned and it's not from sunbathing, not at this time of the year. Unless he goes abroad."

"Well, maybe a walker, a golfer, that sort of thing. Anyway, it's pretty irrelevant. What do you want to do now?"

"I'm fairly convinced Fuzz is not there. The bloke was unfriendly but I got the impression that he was on his own there."

"So, we have to go and see if we can seek out the wife I suppose. Wherever the hell she was going, 'Up top with her sheep'."

"We can't just drive around. She could be absolutely anywhere." Simon slid into the passenger seat.

The weather had been calmer for a while but, as they turned away from the farm road and out towards the higher hills, the clouds lowered. Rain spattered in wild bursts against the car and the wind buffeted them side-on making it more and more difficult for Gloria to hold to her line on the road. Visibility dropped again and they were forced to slow to little more than a walking pace.

Gloria mused aloud, "She's not on the hills with sheep, not in this. The sheep will have found shelter."

"Well, if he really knew where she was, he wasn't going to tell us, was he? He didn't seem too concerned though."

"Perhaps he's used to it, her just being out here on her own. We can't go off road, you know that don't you. This car will go a little bit on the rough but not in this weather and not when it's soaked like this."

"Perhaps I should have bought a four-wheel drive instead of that poncy thing I did get."

"Yeah. Probably a better idea. Mind you, there's no saying you're going to have to do this every day is there? Won't you be chasing cheating husbands and insurance frauds and stuff like that? All sounds very 'towny' to me."

"I hope not. I suppose I'll be able to decide for myself, won't I?"

"Don't know, depends whether it's just for the sake of it or to make a living."

Simon fell silent, he realised that his idea of working for the truth would sound rather worthy and idealistic and in fact that might not be what it would be about; it was a depressing idea.

Gloria glanced across at him. "Anyway, that's not for now is it. For now, we just need to find this daft lad and make sure he's safe."

Simon leaned forward, peering through the windscreen.

"We can barely see past the edge of the road. She's crackers out here in this." As he spoke, the glow of headlamps grew in the rear-view mirror and pools of water from the carriageway flew up and around them, and a car sped past rocking them like a boat in a swell. As it raced by, Simon jerked in his seat. "That was him, wasn't it? Wasn't that Coleman?"

"Well it was a red car, whether it was the same one, I wouldn't like to say."

"Can you follow it?" His voice was tight with tension.

"Not the speed it was going. It's too dangerous. Shit I can hardly see anything. I swear the rain is heavier."

"You're right, you'll have to pull in, if we run off the road we're in a real mess."

Gloria took a hand from the wheel, pointing forward. "I can see the lights ahead. It's stopped. What should we do? It's turning."

"Can you follow it, do you reckon, now it's slowed down?"

"I'll try, but this is crazy, you know that, don't you?"

"Just do your best and if you can't manage it, we'll have no choice but to get the police."

"But we've nothing to tell them. We have no proof that Fuzz was at the barn, not now she's taken the coat, and they won't be impressed with a text message that doesn't say anything much. Bloody hell, we've screwed this up good and proper and if Fuzz is in real trouble, it'll be our fault." As she spoke, Gloria glanced at Simon and wished she hadn't voiced her thoughts. His face was deathly pale and his jaw was clenched so tightly it looked painful. "It'll be okay, we'll find him. We won't give up until we find him." She reached across and touched his hand where it was bunched on his knee. "We'll find him, Simon." There was no answer and she knew he was in a dark place that only he could access.

Chapter 29

By now, the worst of the storm was passing. The clouds broke and dispersed, and like a sudden miracle the lowering sun shot golden beams onto the wet moorland. Saturated grass shone in the glow and if they hadn't been trying to follow the other car, Gloria would have had time to wonder at the beauty of it. As it was, she concentrated on keeping the red bead of the taillights in sight, without getting too close.

As they approached the top of the rise the other car turned left down a narrow track. They drove on past, pulled in beside the wall and Simon flung open the door to stand and watch as Coleman drew to a halt, walked a few yards away from his vehicle and, shielding his eyes from the blowing spots of rain, peered down into a dip. He clambered back into his own car, turned carefully on the narrow road and drove out, turning right and heading back the way that he had come. Once they were sure he wouldn't spot them with a glance in his mirror, Gloria turned onto the sheep track and bounced and splashed slowly in the direction Coleman had been looking.

The low stone building was so much at one with its surroundings that they could easily have missed it, if they hadn't seen the Land Rover.

Gloria turned aside behind a clump of gorse, carefully rolling forward on the slick grass. They slid out into the cold wet air. Bending low they skirted a group of spiky green bushes to look down on the dilapidated old hut. The roof sagged and the door hung ajar, one small unglazed window made a square gap in the wall showing only the blackness inside. Gloria turned to Simon and lifted her shoulders in a questioning shrug and he in turn could only shake his head in bewilderment.

"I wonder if she's got that gun. And where are the dogs?" There was fear in her voice and Simon reached out and put a hand on her shoulder.

"Do you want to stay here while I go and try to see what's going on?"

"No, I bloody don't. Waiting here would be worse than being there." She pointed down to the hollow where the sun glinted now on the rain-sheened slates of the old roof. "Just, for God's sake, be careful."

Sliding and skidding in his rubber soled shoes, Simon led the way across the path and over the knobbly land so that they would arrive at the rear of the ancient dwelling, out of sight of the single aperture.

By the time they reached the flatter land of the clearing they were wet through and muddied to above their knees. Gloria reached out to Simon to grip his freezing hand – he was soaked to the skin despite the old anorak, which was no longer properly waterproof.

He lifted a finger to his lips and she grimaced at him in irritation. A small area of land had been levelled outside the front door and behind, a cut had been made in the slope of the hill. They had veered towards the rear and were now level with the edge of the roof. The huge blocks of stone which had been used to make the walls negated any chance of hearing anything inside from the rear. Simon pointed to the left of the building and with a nod from Gloria they both crept almost on all fours along the edge of the embankment. They slid on their backsides to the lower level and pressed against the wet walls.

The dogs sitting in the back of the car spotted them and set up a cacophony of barking and yelping, scratching at the windows and leaping from the rear seats into the front and then back again.

Simon shifted his position on the rough ground and a loose rock under his foot rattled against more gravel sending a small avalanche behind them to splash into a puddle at the edge of the clearing. The clump of feet on the earth inside the place sent them scrambling back along the walls of the shack. It was the worst possible place for them to be, trapped between the walls and the slope and with no way to climb back up to the top of the hill. Simon bent and picked up a couple of fallen rocks, he passed them to Gloria and then found more for himself. They backed away around the rear corner like rats in a maze.

They could hear Lily calling out to the dogs, heard the door grate along the ground as she emerged and crossed the clearing, splashing in and out of lying water, muttering and cursing as she stormed over to hammer on the car windows. "Quiet, quiet down."

Grabbing Gloria by the back of her jacket, Simon moved along the wall taking them towards the front of the hut. Gloria reached to clutch at his coat and he turned quickly to nod at her but gave her no idea what he had in mind. He bent now at the waist and peered along the front wall. Lily was still talking to her dogs, trying to get them to settle, oblivious to what they were trying to tell her. With a sudden spurt, Simon grabbed Gloria's hand and dashed for the entrance. He swung her round in front of him and pushed her inside the dark, noisome place and then grabbing the heavy old door he dragged it closed behind him. As it slammed shut, he heard the yell of surprise, swiftly followed by the pound of feet. There was an iron handle fixed to the door and he wrapped his hands around it and leaned backwards into the room, Gloria wrapped her arms around his waist and together they fought to hold it closed as the skinny woman on the outside tugged and pulled at it, yelling and shouting with anger. "Hey boy, you better let me in there. This isn't going to help you. Open this door boy." Gloria glanced around and in the dim light from the window space she could make out the prone shape of Fuzz, lolling against the wall in the corner.

"Fuzz, it's Fuzz. Hold the door."

"What, no, I need you to help."

But she had already gone. Simon braced his feet more squarely, leaning back and praying that the ancient iron handle was as firmly set in the door as it seemed to be.

Gloria ran to the boy, he pushed away from her sliding along the bottom of the wall until he was under the little window.

"Is he okay?"

"Ger'off, bloody well ger'off."

"Well, I think so. He's tied up somehow." She had come back now to hang on to the handle but the pulling and dragging had stopped and she hissed towards the boy who was scrabbling and wriggling on the floor. "Fuzz, cut it out. Just shut up a minute." They heard the rattle of loose rocks and then the scrape as the barrel of the gun was pushed across the bottom of the window space. The blast, when it came, was deafening, enclosed as it was by the old stone walls. She fired and shot pinged and bounced from the rear wall. She dragged the gun back. They heard the mechanical clicks and rattles as she reloaded and then she fired again into the space. Fuzz had frozen now in fright and they heard him panting in the darkness.

They saw the dim oval of her face as she tried to look inside. "You can't stay in there for long boy. I'll be here waiting." With the threat ringing in their ears they listened to the slam of the car door as she took up position to sit and wait in the dry and the warm, leaving them in the dark dankness with a bound boy and nothing to protect themselves with save a few round rocks.

Chapter 30

"Why the hell does this door open outwards?" Simon demanded of no-one in particular.

"What? Why does that matter?"

"It means I can't wedge it, can I? If I let it go now it's probably going to swing open, at least a bit and then she'll see."

"Well, I think it is so that the weight of snow doesn't push it open, something like that. Anyway, there's nothing to wedge it with, so you'll just have to hold it I guess."

"Check on him, will you?"

Gloria crossed the hut again and knelt on the damp floor. "Keep still, Fuzz. Let me get you loose. Are you alright? Are you hurt anywhere?"

"No, not really but I reckon I banged my head."

"I've had enough. I'm just going to ring for the police. She won't shoot at them, will she? I mean of course she won't, so that's the only option. Anyway, even if she does, that'll solve the problem in a way. You just hold the door. We can't fart about here like this. Shit, shit, shit."

"What, what's wrong?"

"Well there's no bloody signal is there, of course there isn't. Why did I think there would be? Bugger it all to hell."

"Is he alright?" Simon was trying to simultaneously hold the door and lean to where Gloria was using the light on her phone to examine Fuzz.

"Yes, he is. I've got him free. Fuzz, did you hear me, are you alright?"

She was answered by a stream of muttered expletives.

"Ha, I guess he is then."

"Simon, what are we going to do?"

"I'm going to try and see, I'll have to open the door a bit." He released his grip and the heavy old wood swung outwards a couple of inches. "I can just about see the Land Rover, she's got the window down and the gun pointing this way."

"She's not going to shoot us though, is she? I mean people don't shoot people, not here. Not in Ramstone." He didn't answer her because, as she spoke her voice lost conviction and he knew that she had gone back in her mind to the room above the betting office where her brother had a gun pointed at Simon and hate in his eyes.

"What the hell is happening?" They heard Fuzz fumbling about in the darkness.

"Just sit tight, Fuzz, it's okay."

"Bloody hell, my head's pounding. Who are you? Who the soddin' hell is that? Gloria turned her phone light towards her face. "It's alright love, it's alright. It's me, it's Mrs Bartlett, Gloria."

"What are you doing here? Where is it anyway? You haven't got any aspirin have you, my head's pounding?"

"I have love but they're back in the car. What happened to you, can you remember?"

"I fell. I was in the barn – oh yeah. I was helping this bloke. He's a private eye, like on the telly."

"You weren't. I told you to leave it. You weren't helping me."

"What the hell is going on here? Oh never mind, my head's killing me."

"Don't worry, once we're out of here we'll get you a doctor. Do you hear me?"

"Aye, I hear you, but honest to God it really is pounding and I'm bloody freezing."

"Oh, I know love. Here, wrap my jacket round you."

"Can't we just go? Have you got your car? Will you take us home?" As he spoke, she sat beside him and she wrapped her arms around him. She was a little shocked that he didn't pull away. "You're shivering, here, snuggle a bit closer to me – Simon?"

"What's going on?" The boy was sounding petulant now and pushed away a little. "Let's go, come on. My Gran's going to be after me."

"We can't go just now, Fuzz. We have to wait for a bit. Can you not remember how you got here?"

"It's a bit of a blur. I remember I fell. Out of the loft."

"So, it wasn't her, she didn't hurt you?"

"Who?"

"The woman from the farm?"

"Well I reckon it was her fault. I think I conked out for a minute and she stuck me in her car and brought me here."

"We thought you'd been kidnapped, or something."

He shook his head and then groaned and lifted a hand to his eyes.

"For Pete's sake, can't we just go?"

"We can't. She's outside with a gun."

"Who is?"

"The woman from the farm. She's been shooting in through the window and now she's outside with a gun."

"Shit."

Chapter 31

"Right, this is bloody pathetic. It's only a sodding woman with a shotgun anyway. I'm going to go out there and sort this, we can't just stay here. Once it's safe, Gloria, you should be able to get a signal for your phone outside, it'll be the hill and the thick walls that are stopping it."

"No, Simon!" But it was too late. He took a breath and yelled out as he pushed open the door. There were no words but just howling noise to distract and shock the woman in the car. He had hoped that the crash of the door, the suddenness of movement and his shouting would catch her off guard. He hadn't planned much beyond simply escaping the dark little hut and making something happen.

As it thumped backwards the sagging door jammed against humps on the rough ground and so instead of a straight gallop across the space between him and the car, screaming like a banshee, he collided with the heavy wood which unbalanced him and took him to his knees. He scrabbled now on all fours, trying to stand but slipping and splashing in the mud and puddles. Still he pushed on, unable to see which way he was heading but loping as fast as his ungainly position would let him. He was aware of a loud crack somewhere in the back of his mind but there was no pain, no loss of power, so he pressed on.

By the time he reached the Land Rover door he was almost upright. His strange clumsy progress had been partly what saved him. Lily had her gun pointed at waist level at the door and as he fell and scrambled on all fours, she had struggled from her position in the car to tilt the long barrel down towards the galumphing figure. He could hear her shouting, was aware of Gloria behind him thundering across the clearing as he reached out and grabbed at the end of the barrel. The crack as she fired the second round filled his ears and he recoiled in shock as it was snatched from his grip. The woman by now was screeching but he was deafened and didn't hear either her or Gloria who was yelling "no" over and over.

Lily pulled her gun inside and in a jerking, hiccupping jolt, with the wheels spinning wildly and spitting grit and stones behind her, she sped up towards the muddied road and out across the moor.

Simon fell back onto his behind and watched as the car sped away. Gloria crouched beside him, reaching out, feeling at his arms and legs, peering at his face. "Did she hit you, are you hurt?"

He knew she was speaking and had an idea what it was she was asking but the ringing noise drowned out all other sound. He shook his head and poked fingers into his ears. He held his nose and swallowed hard but nothing helped and he decided the only thing he could do was wait and hope there was no permanent damage. He looked down at his legs. His trousers were soaked through and filthy, there were tears around the knees and the seam had given way near the hem but there was no blood, not enough to worry about at least. He held up his arms, "I'm okay, it's okay. I'm not hurt. Are you alright, Gloria?" She nodded at him and took hold of his hands to help him to stand.

"Shit, Simon, don't you ever do anything like that again. You bloody idiot, what were you thinking…?" She stopped because he was grinning at her now and pointing at his ears, shaking his head and she understood that her words stood no chance of reaching him. She turned away and stomped back across the clearing.

Inside the hut, Fuzz had pushed himself up into a standing position but he was braced with a hand on the damp wall. "Is he dead, did she shoot him?" Gloria couldn't tell whether the look on his face was excitement or dread. She gave him the benefit of the doubt.

"He's okay, she missed him. She's gone. Are you okay there? Let me give you a hand. We can just ring for an ambulance now and they can take you out of here. I'm not sure you should be walking about."

"No, I'm grand. My head's still splittin' but I'm okay I reckon. I don't want no ambulance anyroad. My Gran'd have kittens."

"Come on then, let's see if we can get back to the car. I'm sick of the sight of this bloody place."

They staggered and scrambled back to the car. Simon and Gloria walked either side of the still wobbly Fuzz, he stopped a couple of times and swayed, holding his head and groaning but eventually they arrived and Gloria laid him in the back seat with a blanket over him.

"So, Simon, you need some clothes. Fuzz needs to see a doctor and a lift home when he's ready. I don't think you should be on your own. You'd end up climbing the walls, going over it and over it and, anyway, we really need to decide what we're going to do about that mad woman. I'll take you to the flat, you get your stuff and then we'll all go back to my place. I'll sort us out some tea while you get a shower and then we can talk." Neither of the males spoke, Simon nodded, Fuzz smiled, warm and safe and with someone else making the decisions for him, he was happy and by the sound of it there might be food later. Gloria glanced around the car and sighed, "Right then, that's sorted." And she drew out from behind the gorse bush and drove off down the road in the direction Lily had gone just a short time earlier.

Chapter 32

Gloria glanced across the table at Simon and shook her head. Not much earlier Fuzz had been lying on the damp floor of the hut up on the moor shivering and complaining about his head and his aches and pains. Here he was now scarfing down a second sausage sandwich and knocking back glass after glass of coke. She had stopped asking if he was alright. Even Simon who was bruised and grazed and walking stiffly, was reaching out for another round of thick white bread, Cumberland sausage and brown sauce. She had managed a small one but every time she thought of Simon careering across the wet grass and that woman shooting at him, she felt her stomach roil and thought she might have to run for the bathroom.

"Okay, that's enough football I think." She interrupted the inane chatter and the two guests at her table turned to her. Simon frowned.

"Are you okay? You look a bit pale and you've hardly eaten anything."

"I'm fine. A bit shaken up to be honest but fine. I need a drink." She saw the look on his face and stopped. "Later anyway. But look, we should get the police; it's stands to sense. The bloody woman has shot at us twice now and she…"

"She what?" Simon finished his sandwich and wiped his mouth with the paper napkin.

"Well, I was going to say she knocked Fuzz out but I don't know that she did. You just fell, didn't you?"

"Yeah, I was watching her changing the tyres on that car, fiddling inside the bonnet and so on. She was clambering about underneath it one minute and then throwing sticks for the dogs and stuff. She carries guns with her all the time. That's one thing that I did notice, seen it before. It's like the bloody wild west, like a cowboy film. I bet she hasn't got licences for any of them either. Anyroad, she comes into the barn all of a sudden, I nipped up the ladder into the hay loft, sent that text. She saw me though, and she's yelling at me to come down and I remember starting down those steps. I had my jacket in my hand and I suppose I just got tangled up and went arse over elbow all the way down. I've got a bloody great bruise on my back, where she was poking at me, and the egg on me head. I'm black and blue to be honest, I could see in the shower. Nice bathrooms up there Mrs Bartlett, better than my gran's anyroad."

"Thanks… so then she took you to the hut and tied you up?"

"Yeah, she went off on one something shocking when she found out I didn't have my phone. Tied me up and left me. It was proper scary to be honest, for a bit like. I thought she was just going to leave me."

Simon nodded at them both. "I suppose she wanted to get rid of the phone so it couldn't be traced. She's not completely daft then." He didn't verbalise the rest of the thought. If she was so keen for the phone to be out of action, just what had she planned for this kid? "I told you to keep away, didn't I?"

"She was pointing a gun at me, she tied me up, she scared the shit out of me."

"I know, but you were in her barn. She's weird, I'm not saying she isn't and she shouldn't have taken you away, Fuzz, but at the end of the day, it's her farm and she could argue we were trespassing."

"So, no point getting the police, is that what you're saying, Simon?"

"Oh, I don't know, maybe we should. Trouble is, I think at this point it could work against us. If the Colemans decide to, maybe they could have us barred from going up there and then we really are stuck. But, after what's just happened…"

"No." They turned to look at Fuzz who had pushed back from the table. "No, I'm not talking to the police. I'm just not."

"But Phillip, you were hurt, you were frightened. If we hadn't found you, if you hadn't sent that message, well…" Gloria didn't want to say what they were all thinking.

"I'm not going to though, Mrs Bartlett. My gran'd skelp me. It's going to be bad enough when she finds out I've lost my phone. She'll flay me, I'm not going to speak to them. Even if you call them, I'm not telling 'em nothing." The boy shook his head, his eyes were alight with rebellion but there was excitement there as well. It chilled Simon to the bone, he didn't want this lad involved and in spite of all his efforts it just kept happening.

"But all of this, as upsetting as it is, doesn't necessarily have anything to do with the hit and run, does it?" Gloria began tidying the dishes as she spoke.

"Oh, I don't know. She's just so odd, and her husband, he was unpleasant. Then there was the day Charlie had his accident and Michelle said that she saw a woman watching. Maybe it's nothing more than just wishful thinking but I can't get past it."

"So, what should we do?"

Fuzz interrupted, "I can keep watching her. I can go back up there tomorrow. I'll be more careful and hide better."

Simon snapped at him. "No, I honestly don't want you doing that. No, what we need now is to find a link between her and Melanie. Have you heard anything from your friend about the veterinary nurse, Fuzz?"

"Depends."

"How do you mean?"

"Well, it depends on whether I'm helpin' you or not."

Simon glanced across the table to where Gloria simply shrugged her shoulders. "Okay, look. You find out anything of use and I'll pay you for the information. But, and this is a big but, you don't go hiding and stalking people and what have you. Talk to your friend, see if we can go and meet this Fiona and then we'll see."

"Sick!"

"What?"

"You know, sick – like excellent. Cool, brilliant."

"Oh right. Good. Now, I think you should be getting home, do you want a lift?"

"Yes, please, but can Mrs Bartlett take me. I want to get there in one piece."

"Oh fine. Fine. Is that okay, Gloria?"

"Yes, no problem. Maybe you can clear the dishes for me. Then when I get back I am having a drink. Are you staying here tonight?"

"Ooh, are you two at it then?"

"Nothing to do with you. Come on, does your gran still live at the top of Bradford Road?"

"Aye, she does. See ya, Simon. Oh by the way, I know who you are now. You're that Tommy Webb, aren't you? The one with the dead sister. It's okay, I don't mind."

Chapter 33

It didn't take long to deliver Fuzz to his gran's house. As he swivelled on the seat and clicked open the door, Gloria laid a hand on his arm. "Fuzz, don't forget what Simon told you. Don't go poking your nose in and getting into trouble. Simon could have been killed today and then how would you have felt?"

"I was trying to help though. I like him Mrs Bartlett, I think he's cool. I mean he looks dead hard with that scar but he's not really, is he? Are you and him together then?"

"I like him as well but it's complicated, he has a lot of anger locked inside and sadness and guilt."

"He didn't do it though, did he? They said, he didn't kill his sister, it was that Peter... oh shit. I'm sorry."

"It's okay, don't worry about it, and listen, Fuzz."

"Yeah?"

"Call me, Gloria, you make me feel old calling me Mrs Bartlett all the time. Say hello to your gran for me, will you? Behave, and remember what we said, okay?"

"Yeah. Thanks for the lift and the sarnies and, well you know, the rest of it." She lifted a hand to stroke his hair but thought better of it and simply grinned at him. "Go on, bugger off." She watched as he strolled up the path, the hunch of his shoulders and the swagger already back in place. She felt a lump rise in her throat as Fuzz turned at the door to raise his hand to her.

When she turned into the driveway of Mill Lodge, she noticed Simon had closed the curtains. The light glowed cosily behind them.

She turned off the lights and locked the car. The road was quiet except for a dog barking somewhere in the distance and an owl out on the lonely hills. The curtain moved and Simon's face peered out at her and then he lifted a hand and waved. It was time to go inside.

"Was he okay?"

"Yes, he seems to be. Incredible really but that's youngsters for you. I watched him going up the path and it struck me, my brother was like him once. Desperate to break out, but then when he broke, he went the wrong way and lives were ruined. There's nothing much we can do for them, is there? The Fuzzes and the Jazzers, they have to find their own way." She sighed. "How are you?"

"A bit sore here and there but I'm fine."

"So, where the hell does this all leave us?"

"I just don't know. I've been trying to get it all straight in my head. Part of me thinks you're right and I've been jumping to conclusions but it just seems that the farm and that woman are there all the time. The first accident, Charlie's crash and, oh, I honestly think that there has to be a connection."

"I did have one thought. It was when I was driving back and I had a little giggle to myself about Fuzz wanting me to drive him home." She laughed now at Simon's raised eyebrows. "Well, to put it bluntly, I am a better driver and that's a fact. Well it is, isn't it?"

"Yes, yes, you're right, but I don't see..."

"Well that woman is a crazy driver, or so it seems to me. But do you think it could be quite simply that she hit Melanie and she got away with it and that's why she's gone a bit loopy. Maybe she is just terrified of being caught out."

"What, you mean just an accident? But in that case why not come forward at the time? Why not get help? I mean it's a sad fact that people have accidents, but they don't all run away, do they?"

"No, but some do and it was dark and late and she could probably, well I say she, but whoever, could probably tell right away that the girl was dead. Maybe she just freaked out, ran away and then chance put Colin Bliss in the frame, the police were satisfied and that was that."

"If that is the case, and I have to say I can see a lot of sense in it, then where does that leave us though? Colin is still in jail for something he didn't do and that's what we are supposed to be sorting out. The other thing is, why did Mrs Clegg tell me to leave it alone? She can't know and if she did, surely, she would want to shout it from the rooftops. Unless…"

"Unless what?"

"Well unless there is something between the two of them, Beryl Clegg and the mad woman."

"Oh, bloody hell, stop now. I thought I had an answer but it's just opening up more questions. Here, let's have a whisky. "Oh, don't look at me like that, I think I deserve one after the day we've had." She walked to the cupboard and poured them both a hefty measure, then she sat beside him on the sofa and let her eyes gaze unfocused on the flicker of flames in the fireplace.

"Will you stay tonight?" She hadn't meant to ask but she needed him and, at the end of the day, if you needed something you usually had to ask for it.

He kissed the top of her head. "I'd love to, thanks." And it was settled, for this night at least.

Chapter 34

Gloria turned over in bed expecting Simon to be there, still sleeping. But the smell of coffee drifted through from the kitchen and she could hear him moving around her flat.

She put on her dressing gown and went into the living room just as he was bringing her a hot drink. "You're up early."

"Fuzz rang. He's fine by the way, he seemed surprised that I even bothered to ask. Anyway, his mate has come up with the name and address of the veterinary surgery that Fiona works at. It's about an hour away on the outskirts of Leeds. I thought we could go straight away this morning, if you want to come with me that is?"

"Yes. Right, give me about half an hour. It's only what, nearly eight – I don't imagine they open much before nine. Maybe we should ring first and make an appointment to see her – do you think?"

"If we're there, face to face it might be easier to persuade her to talk to us, if she needs persuading that is. Maybe she won't. I really feel that I need to move this on. It's a while now since I spoke to Charlie and I don't want him thinking I've stopped trying. I thought I might ring him later and it'd be great to have something properly to report."

"You're not going to mention about the mad woman then?"

"Not sure, I'm still struggling with what all that means."

* * *

They waited until the traffic thinned from the morning exodus between Ramstone and the surrounding towns and the drive was easy. Gloria gave Simon instructions on how to use the Sat Nav. "You really need to have one of these. When you have to go places that are not familiar, they're a Godsend. You can use your phone but I reckon these are more reliable."

"I thought I was keeping up to date with stuff. Inside I mean, with the classes I took." He started to laugh and she realised that it was the first time she had ever heard it. She felt herself grinning in response.

"What, what are you laughing at?"

"Well, the thought of them teaching us how to use a Sat Nav – in jail." He couldn't carry on. The laughter stole his ability to speak. She began to giggle and soon they were roaring until their eyes watered.

"Oh God. My stomach actually hurts. Oh, come on now, let's concentrate, we must be nearly there." He laid his hand on top of hers where it sat on the gear lever. "There, that's it there. Barclay and Howarth Veterinary Practice. You can pull into the car park round that corner."

"Yup, got it. It's big, isn't it? Of course, there's a lot of money in animal health these days. The time when you just let them get on with it are long gone. There's health insurance and everything." She pulled on the hand brake and glanced around.

"I'll stay here in case anyone needs the parking place. If I have to move, I'll just cruise round the block."

"Great."

* * *

It had been years since Simon had been inside a veterinary surgery. One of the dogs from when he'd been a boy had needed something and he'd gone along with his dad. It had been smelly and grubby and though there had been posters of happy-looking animals on the walls the atmosphere had been odd. There had been a young girl sobbing in the corner with her distressed father gently murmuring, the other people waiting had been embarrassed and uncomfortable. He hadn't enjoyed it and had never gone again. This space though was bright and clean, the young woman behind the counter wore a uniform and the atmosphere was calm and cheerful. He was followed in by a young woman hefting a cat in a plastic carrier and he stood aside. "It's okay, I'm just making an enquiry. You can deal with this lady if you like."

"Aw thanks, shouldn't be long. I'm just dropping him off, it's his big day." She giggled. Simon smiled and nodded and tried not to think too deeply about what was in store for the kitten.

While forms were filled and instruction about aftercare and times for collection were discussed he spent the next few minutes flipping through brochures about flea infestation and the benefits of castration. He was relieved when the cat was taken away, its plaintiff meows disappearing into the interior of the building.

"Thanks for waiting. What can we do for you?"

"I wanted a word with one of your nurses. She doesn't know me but I was given her name by a friend and I'm hoping she might be able to help me with some enquiries?"

"Is it about a lost pet?"

"No, sorry – I'm working on behalf of a client – I'm an enquiry agent and it's about a crime some years ago."

"Oh crikey, right. Do you have a card?"

"Card?"

"Your business card or do you people have ID like the police? I've never met a private investigator before."

"Oh right, I see." Something else he would need to deal with. For now he'd have to try and blag his way through this. "To be honest my licence hasn't arrived yet. I have only just set up, you know. I'm waiting for my cards to come through, no point until I have my licence number." He had no idea whether or not he would have a number but then again neither would the young woman in front of him. She didn't look quite as impressed now as she had a few moments ago. "If it's a problem I can go and get my colleague, she's waiting in the car…" He left the rest of the sentence unspoken, hoping to give the impression that his 'colleague' had a card or licence.

"No, no, it's fine. Who is it you want to see?"

"Fiona Carpenter. I believe she works here?"

"That's right. She's out in the recovery room at the moment. If you'd like to take a seat, I'll call through for her. Who shall I say?"

"Simon, Simon Fulton." It was obvious that he was going to have to be more organised, more professional. "If she's too busy I can call back, make an appointment."

"No, it's fine. Better now to be honest. Once surgery starts she won't be able to get away." And with that the receptionist picked up the phone. In a couple of minutes the door in the rear of the room opened and a young woman came towards him, her hand outstretched.

"Hello. I'm Fiona." She reached up and swirled her long ponytail into a bun on the top of her head, pinning it in place with a tortoiseshell comb.

"Thanks for seeing me. I won't keep you long I hope."

"I'm on my break now, do you want to come through to the coffee room? I can make us a drink."

Once they were settled in the little kitchenette with cups of instant coffee between them on the small table, Fiona folded her hands on her lap and tipped her head to one side. "Now then, Mr Fulton, what can I do for you? I can't imagine how I can be involved in anything to do with a private detective."

"I want to talk to you about something that happened a few years ago. A friend of yours was killed."

"Oh." Her eyes widened and she raised a hand to cover her mouth. "Melanie. You want to talk to me about Melanie?"

"Yes, if that's alright."

"Shit. I knew this was all going to come back again one day. I meant well, I never imagined it could do any real harm."

Chapter 35

The girl's big brown eyes brimmed with tears and for a moment Simon wasn't sure what to do. To reach across and touch her would be wrong, he knew that, but if she were to cry he couldn't simply sit and watch. She swallowed hard and blinked the tears away. She shook her head and then looked straight at him.

"I know it was wrong. I started out with the best intentions and before I knew it, she had me knee deep in lies and trouble. I just felt sorry for her mum and dad, that was all. They had no idea you see, it would have really upset them, well I know in the end they were devastated anyway but it would have been worse, much worse. At least that's what I kept telling myself."

What he said next would be terribly important, if this was to be the breakthrough he'd been hoping for. He smiled at her. "Sometimes we do things for the best reasons and it gets out of hand. The thing is though, maybe now is a chance to make it right. You won't have to worry about it anymore. Maybe it's time to just let me handle it and sort things out."

He wished that Gloria had come in with him, this was a time when her empathy and insight would be invaluable but he needed to keep up the momentum. Catching the girl off guard could be about to pay huge dividends, if he could just handle this well.

"I don't know though. It's not just me, is it? It's others, her mum and dad, even people here, people I work with.

"It was horrible afterwards, I knew what I'd done was wrong but it would have happened anyway. Once I finished college, I just tried to put it behind me, tried not to think about it anymore. It's always been there though, guilt, in the back of my mind. It's spoiled what should have been brilliant. We were really close, me and Melanie, she shouldn't have made me do it but she was my friend and when you're friends, well…" she shrugged and shook her head. "I suppose they're getting divorced then? Is that how come you know about it? That's what you do isn't it, private detectives, you help people to get divorced?"

"I'm just gathering information at the moment, that's all."

"I always told her he was no good you know. He was too old for her, she said it was exciting but he never took her anywhere or anything. He bought her a couple of things but they could never go out for meals, nothing like that. It was stupid. It was all about sex really and even then it was a bit grim, in cars and stuff, never even in a hotel. Then of course he wanted to break up with her and she got into that bloody awful mess. She shouldn't have been on the moors that night but he'd said he wanted to talk to her. She should have told him to go to hell, then maybe she wouldn't have been there on the road to get run down. She would have been with me, I was still in town, I went for a drink. It was my fault really, all my fault. She met him because of me." Again her eyes filled with tears and she brushed them away. "Look Mr erm…?"

"Fulton, call me Simon."

"Okay, Simon, I have to go and help in surgery now, I can't do that if I'm in a state. Can I have some time to think about this and then meet you somewhere away from here, when I've decided about it? I could lose my job if everything comes out, and just saying I didn't know any better or I wasn't really sure – well it won't wash, not now I'm here and I'm trained and everything. I love my job. I need time."

"Of course you do. I'm grateful for anything you can tell me, I'm sure we can sort this out. Let me give you my number. Do you have a bit of paper?"

"Have you not got a business card?"

"Not on me no, sorry."

"Oh right, well. Here, you can write on this." She handed him a small notepad from her pocket and then stood up and ushered him out into the waiting room. The receptionist glanced up. "Are you okay, Fiona?"

"Yeah, I'm fine."

She glared across the room at Simon as he turned at the door. "Why is she upset? What have you said to her?" He struggled to answer but Fiona came to his rescue.

"It's fine Molly, just fine. I'm okay really. Mr Fulton hasn't done anything wrong. I'll call you, Simon. Later today. After work."

"Thanks. Sorry." And he slipped out through the door and jogged across the car park.

"Well, anything?"

"Yeah, but I'm not sure what. I'm really confused now. She's going to ring later and if I meet her again, will you come as well? I need someone else there in case she starts crying and anyway I need you there because this is all so bloody complicated and I need your input. There's definitely something off about it all but I can't for the life of me think what. I think maybe the girl was having an affair with Colin Bliss. I think that seems like the best possibility right now. Will you come with me later, is that okay?"

Gloria turned to face the front and busied herself with the business of pulling out into the junction. She didn't want him to see the grin of pleasure that had spread across her face. After a while she spoke. "Okay, yeah, I can do that. No problem. Back to my place now?"

"Actually, could you drop me at the flat? I want to make some notes while this is still all fresh in my mind. I'll come down later, in my car if that's okay, and I can get some driving practice in as well. Oh yes, and do you know where I can get some business cards printed? Huh that's bloody ironic isn't it, me an ex-printer and living up the hill there. Ah well."

"Yes, I think we can order some online. We'll have a look later, when you come down."

Chapter 36

Simon opened his drink and took a gulp before he remembered he'd planned to drive later. "Sod it." He poured the frothy beer into the sink and tossed the can into the recycling and went back to the fridge for a coke.

At the little desk he jotted down what he could remember of the conversation at the vets. He read the words over a couple of times but they didn't help. Apart from the fact that there had been some collusion and subterfuge on the part of Melanie and Fiona, it was still a fog.

Usually in this situation he would head out for a long walk and give his brain space but if he took the car out, he could get some driving in. He'd park further away from Ramstone; he could walk in a different area from his usual one. He'd go up to where they'd picnicked when they were young.

He changed into his walking gear except for the boots, he wouldn't be able to drive in those. He folded his shirt and trousers and put them into a backpack ready to change at the hotel if Fiona rang while he was out. Downstairs he checked the locks in the shop and then went through the routine, backing out into the road and securing the yard.

He was disgusted to find that he'd forgotten the chain and padlock on the big gates and they had slipped through the metal eye and lay in a heap on the pavement. It had been a stressful day yesterday and when he'd collected his stuff, he'd had other things on his mind. He had to be more careful about this stuff. When he'd been a kid people used to leave their doors unlocked, if they were only going out for a short while. He wondered if his dad still did that.

The thought of his father reminded him that he owed the old man a visit and he had promised him a drive out in the car. He felt a jolt of regret for the ease of a few weeks ago when life had seemed a bit slow and dull and he'd still been trying to decide what to do with himself. Charles Clegg would be waiting for a report as well. He tutted with frustration as he turned the car around and headed out of town. The hills would calm him as they always did and surely in a while he'd learn how to take all this in his stride. He had lost the knack of organising time, it had been done for him for so many years and since his release, until recently, there had been no need. Well, he would just have to re-learn – like the driving.

The sun was battling with puffy clouds that rolled over the tops of the hills, it was breezy and cold and perfect. He didn't go far – just up to the waterfall where there was a little gravel parking place and, once he was out in the quiet, he felt his nerves begin to unravel. He pushed the niggling thoughts aside and concentrated instead on the singing of the wind in his ears and the ripple of the short grass stretched out either side. The weather would be wet later, nimbostratus was blowing in from the horizon and here and there in the distance grey streaks of falling rain smeared the view. He would walk for an hour and then head back to Mill Lodge.

He passed a couple of other hikers, they nodded at each other and stomped onwards. Up at the top of the waterfall he sat on the edge of the cliff. He had done this ever since he'd been a child. His mum had hated it, that had been one of the reasons for dangling his legs out into the void, watching his trousers grow dark with spray. He'd go up to the graveyard at the weekend, sit with Mum and Sandie for a while, tell them what he'd been up to.

"So, Mum, what about all this then?" He spoke aloud into the silence. "There's something off about it all, isn't there? That girl, she was lovely but scared and upset. I hope I don't get her into trouble. We're all connected aren't we, one way and another." He had to stop, he was suddenly overwhelmed with emotion and longing for his long dead mother. He threw a small pebble into the waterfall, watched it tumble towards the pool at the bottom and then vanish with all the others he had thrown in over the years. This was his place, he hoped Gloria didn't move away because she was his best friend, and he'd come to rely on her just being there.

He walked around the top of the cataract and across the flat stones in the stream and then followed the path to the humped bridge and back to the car park. The sky was darkening and he could smell rain in the air. He changed out of his boots and brushed the back of his trousers, so he wouldn't get mud on the car seat, the influence of childhood again, it made him grin.

He'd go the longer route back to town, it was more challenging, steeper and with sharper bends. All good practice. The comments from Fuzz about his driving had stung and it was time to get to grips with it. He'd been a decent enough driver when he was younger, a bit too fast probably, a bit reckless certainly, but he mustn't turn into a middle-aged ditherer. Gloria was confident and proficient on the road. That would be enough for him and it would just take time.

There was no other traffic about and he settled into the rhythm of gear changes and the feel of the wheel sliding through his hands. The road was deserted in the early afternoon and he let the speed creep up a bit, he felt the twitch of the rear on a couple of corners, the first time it made him slow but the next time it happened, he grinned. The empty moor stretched out either side of the narrow carriageway, a small ditch on one side ran with water and the odd sheep cantered away as he past. The speed crept up a little more and at the next bend he slewed across the tarmac, small stones flew from under the wheels and spit onto the grass. He fought a little against the pull of the centrifugal force. He should slow.

The next corner came up faster than he'd anticipated, there was a clump of gorse growing out of the sloping edge. As he feathered the brakes a ewe with a young lamb scrabbled out from behind the shrub. He stamped on the pedal. Rubber screamed on the road as he swerved away from the panicked animal. She turned and ran off with her youngster beside her, the rear of the car went light as the grip of the tyres loosened. Frantic, he pounded on the brake and glanced down in disbelief as his foot hit the floor and still the car sped on. He stamped again, and again, the next bend was flying towards him and as he turned, he felt the tip as his nearside wheels left the road. The steepness of the hill was increasing and he stomped over and over on the useless brake pedal. He should change gear, he should use the engine to slow the car but his hands were locked to the wheel, "shit, shit, shit." He couldn't breathe, the next bend was coming up and he knew he wouldn't make it but he didn't have a clue how to react. He spun the wheel, thumped with his feet again on the pedal and time slowed into the silence as his car left the road and shot into the ditch, rolled and rolled again and slid for yards on the roof before coming to a shuddering halt in the rain.

Chapter 37

Reality returned suddenly. Sound was the first thing to come back, small thuds of soil falling from the upturned vehicle and the hiss and fizz of hot machinery in cold rain. There was no great pain anywhere, at first he was relieved and then wondered if that really was a good thing. He moved his hands and fingers. He was upside down, held by his seat belt and the air bags had deployed. He flexed his arms carefully to pull aside the thin white fabric, then looked upwards towards his feet. They didn't feel trapped as far as he could tell but they were wedged against the underside of the misshapen dashboard and steering wheel. It was hard to breathe because of the angle of his head, crushed towards his chest. He shifted carefully, slightly. If he unfastened the seat belt his lower body would surely fall and if his back was injured the consequences could be ghastly. He should sit still, wait. Someone would come in a little while. He sniffed, surely a smell of petrol was to be expected but it panicked him even more. His heart pounded and dizziness overcame him briefly. He tried to take a calming breath but his lungs were restricted by his position. *"Okay, I'm okay."*

Rain pounded on the upturned floor of the car and he could see it streaking mud down the windows and the shattered windscreen. That was good, that would wash away the spilt fuel, his fear of it igniting was growing with every minute. He mustn't panic. Surely there were safety cut outs – things like that. It was okay, he was going to be okay. A flash of lightning outside forced a yell of fright from his throat, melding with the roll of thunder. He had no idea how far he'd slid from the road and the sudden, squally storm could reduce visibility to just yards, anyone passing might easily miss him. He couldn't sit here for hours. He began to shiver.

He tensed the muscles in his thighs and calves, moved his ankles. This brought on the first stab of pain, maybe the adrenalin had held it back, maybe it was just the fact that he moved more but there was a problem with his right ankle and foot. He tried again to move it and cried out this time as sharp fire hissed the length of his leg.

He closed his eyes for a moment to shut it all out, calm his breathing and gather himself. When he'd been stabbed in jail, his face and stomach slashed, he had felt no fear. He hadn't cared at all that he might die but here, on this deserted Yorkshire road he wanted to live and he wanted to come out of this unbroken. Life had more value to him now and he wasn't letting it slip away without doing all he could to survive.

The rain was a deluge, it blew in from somewhere on the damaged vehicle, cold on his face and soaking his clothes. As far as he could tell, he wasn't bleeding much from anywhere but he was shivering and getting colder by the minute.

He tried again to shift and hissed with the pain from his ankle but he had to move through it. He tensed his legs, his lower back and then reached for the buckle on his seat belt. He drew in a deep breath and pushed his body hard against the seat. He released the lock and felt the strapping loosen but kept it taught pulling it into his body. Despite the cold, sweat popped out on his forehead as he began to ease himself slowly down and back, sliding against the seat fabric. His foot screamed at him but he gritted his teeth and pushed a little more. When he had moved a few inches, he was able to bend his left leg and twist it round so that he could brace the foot flat against the dashboard. He released his grip on the seat belt, just a little, just enough to move back a bit further. Gasping and grunting with the pain and effort he pushed with his left foot and managed to drag his injured leg free. It was surely only his leg that was hurt because if his neck or back had been damaged, this movement would have been impossible. Carefully he let the tension on the seat belt go and slid back as far as he could. The roof of the car had stood up well to the accident and now that his legs were free, he was able to move reasonably easily. He pushed against the door but it wasn't going to give and with his injured leg it was impossible to get into a position where he could apply more pressure.

He shifted and slid until he was able to breathe normally; resting his right leg against the passenger seat he reached and pushed his hand into his trouser pocket and slid out his phone.

He pushed the first button on his call list and waited for her to answer. "Simon. Hello, are we ready? I'll meet you outside, how long do you reckon?"

"No, erm, no, Gloria. There's a bit of a problem my end."

"Right?"

"I'm stuck up on the moor, on the road from the waterfall."

"Oh bugger. Okay, do you have AA membership?"

"No, but I'm not sure that's what I need right now, Gloria, I've had a bit of a prang actually."

"Shit, are you okay? I mean is anybody hurt?"

"I seem to have a problem with my leg but actually, at the moment, I'm stuck in the car. Do you think you could call somebody to get me out?"

"How do you mean you're stuck in the car? I don't understand."

"Well, it's upside down right now and…"

"Shit, shit. Oh God. Where are you exactly, do you know? Oh, bloody hell."

"It's okay, honestly, I've hurt my leg but I'm okay, well except I don't know how to get out. I'm about quarter of a mile from the Old Cross Junction, do you know the one I mean?"

"Yeah, yeah. I'm coming. I'm ringing the police and the fire brigade and I'm coming."

"Okay, yeah that's good."

"Don't hang up, just don't hang up. I'm using the other phone. Stay on the line."

"Yeah, right. Gloria?"

"Yes?"

"Thanks."

Chapter 38

She was there almost as quickly as the emergency services. The police held her back, made her sit in her car out of the weather and wait. When she saw him strapped on a back board, his head steadied and cushioned by pads of foam, she couldn't hold back the tears. She ran through the rain to grab his hand and was overwhelmed with relief to see that he was conscious and managed to smile at her.

"Sorry, Gloria."

"Bloody hell, Simon, you scared the shit out of me."

"I know, sorry. To be honest I pretty much scared myself." The paramedic put his hand on her arm.

"We need to move along love, won't do him any good being out in this rain. Are you going to follow us to the hospital in your own car? That would make most sense, means you can get home again later. He's okay, we'll look after him."

"Yes, okay. Yes, I can do that."

"Great, I reckon the police would be grateful if you could give them some details as well, his name and what have you."

"Oh yes, yes right I can do that. Shall I do it now?"

"Yes, why don't you, then once he's all settled, we'll get off. Leeds infirmary, head for the A&E, we'll probably see you there in a bit."

"Thanks, thanks so much."

"Go on then, give him a kiss and let's be off."

And she did. She turned away and wiped at her eyes as the ambulance pulled onto the carriageway. The rain had eased and in the grey light she could see his car, wrecked beyond all recognition now that they had cut away pieces to extricate him. She wrapped her arms around herself. It was so strange, first Charles Clegg and now Simon. It was all drama and worry and she didn't want it.

"Sorry?"

She hadn't noticed the policeman coming up beside her.

"Are you alright madam?"

"Yes, yes of course I am, it's just a shock isn't it, this?" She waved a hand in the direction of the mangled metal.

"It is, but it seems that he got away with it pretty lightly, all things considered. Is he your husband?"

"No, he's a friend. Yes, just a friend."

"Will you be able to give me some personal details?"

"Yep. Quick though, because I want to get to the hospital."

* * *

They made her wait, sitting on a hard plastic chair, watching fractious children and bewildered pensioners shuffling and sighing and wishing it was over. By the time she saw him again, Simon had been dressed in a hospital gown, his small cuts and abrasions were cleaned and he was on a trolley waiting for his leg to be x-rayed.

"How are you feeling?"

"A bit shook up but okay really. Just relieved. I was scared, I thought it was going to go on fire."

"What happened?"

128

"I lost control I reckon. I'm a stupid sod, and then when I tried to brake, it just didn't."

"How do you mean?"

"Well, it's a bit of a blur in a way. But I remember struggling with the wheel and pumping and pumping on the brake and it just didn't work."

"You were probably just skidding on the wet road." He shook his head. "Well, that's odd. Have the police been in to see you?"

"Briefly."

"What did they say?"

"Not much, they asked me for my version and then said that the car would be taken away and they'd be back in touch. I have to let the insurance company know what happened."

"Did you tell them you lost control?"

"I said the brakes failed. That's what it seemed like to me. I don't know what the insurance people's reaction will be. I didn't have a no claims bonus anyway so what the hell. Anyway, first thing is to tell them."

"I'll do that for you. Where are the papers?"

"Oh brilliant, they are on my desk, you know the table in the corner with the notice board over it. I hadn't even had time to start a file for it all."

"Don't worry about that now. Are they keeping you in?"

"I think so, just overnight, observation they said, they don't think this leg's broken but there's ligament damage or something."

"Okay, well look I'll go and find your insurance stuff, I'll make sure everything's okay at the flat and then I'll come back later."

"Brilliant. Oh, yes, while I was in the cubicle downstairs Fiona rang. I didn't tell her what had happened, I just said I couldn't make it today. She's going to ring back tomorrow. I gave her your number, is that okay?"

"Yeah, whatever. That doesn't matter at the moment, it's you that matters." As the radiographer wheeled him away, he gave her a wave and a grin and she knew he would be okay, but his comments had unsettled her. He wasn't the best driver and conditions had been poor but it all sounded wrong. She turned and walked down the corridor.

Chapter 39

When she next saw him, Simon was propped against the pillows in his bed on the observation ward. He was pale and bruised but still grinned at her when she walked up to the bedside. "So, what's the verdict then?"

"Leg's not broken. I've got some torn ligaments, tendon damage and soft tissue damage. I've got to use crutches and keep my weight off it and I have to wear a thing like a plastic boot to keep it still."

"Well, that doesn't sound too bad."

"No, though they did say that sometimes a straightforward break is easier to deal with. Anyway, I've got some pills for the pain and they reckon I'll be able to go home in the morning. The doctor wanted to know about the other cuts and bruises. The ones that I got up at the hut on the moor. He gave me a funny look when I told him I did those yesterday, that sent him off on another tangent – did I have blackouts or dizzy spells, did I ever lose feeling in my legs and feet. I had to waffle a bit, said I'd fallen when I was out walking. He was on the ball though."

"Are you any clearer about what happened today?"

"I've gone over it time and again. I know I was driving a bit fast, I hold my hand up to that but those brakes failed. I'm convinced of it now. I recall distinctly stamping on the pedal over and over and trying to remember what I was supposed to do. I don't think rolling it in a ditch was quite the right thing." He gave a forced laugh.

"No, it bloody wasn't, you scared me stiff. What are you going to do?"

"How do you mean?"

"Well, you've only had the car a few days so the garage must have screwed up somehow. I mean brakes don't just fail for no reason. I assume that they did some sort of service on the car before they sold it and surely they would have checked it all over."

"Okay, but what would make them fail? I haven't a clue."

"I had a look on the internet while I was waiting. She held up her mobile phone. Apparently it's generally loss of pressure caused by a leak of brake fluid. In old cars that can be wear, rusting brake lines or something, or problems with the brakes themselves. But the garage should have checked all that and it's not an old car anyway. So, it seems that the best possibility is a leak somewhere. Again the garage must have been at fault, you know if it was leaking and they didn't notice."

"So, what are you saying?"

"I think you should probably have a conversation with the insurance company about it. Oh yeah, I let them know the car was busted. They said you could have a rental car for two weeks. I left that open because of this..." she waved her hand towards his injury. "That brings me to the next thing as well. You can't go home, not on crutches, up and down those stairs. Come back and stay with me."

"Blimey, a lot to think about. Thanks, I'd really appreciate it if I could stay with you for a day or two at least. I'm going to have to think about the other stuff, the brakes and what have you, I mean how would we be able to tell now?"

"I think we should leave that to the insurance company. It could make a difference to your settlement if they can prove it was the garage at fault. I'm going home now and I'll ring Fiona and arrange a meeting for next week sometime. God, I feel like your bloody secretary." She smiled as she spoke and leaned to kiss him quickly. "I'm so glad you're okay, Simon." She turned away, and coughed. "Right – I'll ring in the morning and find out what time I can collect you. See you tomorrow."

"Brilliant. Thanks again for all of it."

* * *

It was dark by the time Gloria walked back into Mill Lodge and she moved through the ground floor turning on the lights and closing curtains.

She picked up the landline handset and read Fiona's number from where she stored it on her mobile. "Hi there, Fiona, my name is Gloria, I'm working with Simon Fulton." She frowned to herself, when did she become his colleague?

"Oh right, hello."

"He's asked me to apologise about today. It was unavoidable I'm afraid and he wondered if you would mind meeting up with me, maybe tomorrow in the morning? I can do very early if that would be alright?"

"Before work you mean?"

"Yes, is that terribly inconvenient?"

"No, not at all, I have to take my dogs out anyway."

They arranged to meet for breakfast in a small café just off the main road. Gloria replaced the handset and caught a glimpse of her face in the hall mirror. She stood for a moment staring back at the reflection and then spoke into the silent house. "Now what the hell are you doing, stupid woman?"

Chapter 40

It was a bright morning, although there was a chill in the air, there was a promise of spring – the early leaves were unfurling and spikes of daffodils pushed through the flower beds. Gloria paused to have a look at them as she walked down her drive. They made her smile. She left Ramstone heading towards Leeds and her meeting with Fiona, hopeful but nervous. She still wasn't sure what they thought they would learn but Simon was convinced there was something.

There weren't many customers in the little café and only one young woman on her own. She was dressed in a uniform of smock and dark trousers, Gloria smiled at her and the girl raised her hand in greeting. Contact. "Hello, Fiona isn't it?" She was surprised as she took the girl's hand to find that her palm was moist and there was a tremor in the slender fingers. "So, you want coffee? Anything to eat?"

"I wouldn't mind another drink please, but tea. I had a piece of toast earlier."

"Oh come on, let me treat you to a nice Danish or something." The tension eased a little as the younger woman grinned back.

"Go on then, one of those maple and pecan ones. I try not to have them too often, they must be really bad for you but – yes, why not?"

"Well, I don't think you need to worry about a few calories, you're lovely and slim." She had to be just a friendly older woman if she was to have the girl relaxed enough to confide in her. At the end of the day she didn't really have any right to come asking questions. Charles

Clegg had an agreement with Simon not her, and even then she was unsure how much weight it really carried.

She walked to the counter and placed her order and then carried the tray back to the corner table. "Simon couldn't come. Actually, he probably wouldn't want me to tell you but he's not well. Really not well, it's not just 'man flu' but anyway he's in bed."

"Oh poor thing. He's nice, I liked him, he seemed kind. Have you worked with him for long?"

"I've known him for a while now, about a year I suppose. Yes, he is nice. He really wants to try and get to the bottom of what happened with your friend. Such a shame." That was enough now. Gloria fussed with her coffee, buttered the thick piece of toast and waited.

"I've worried about this ever since it happened. Ever since Melanie died. I was just waiting, waiting for someone to find out that I lied. I meant well, as I told Mr Fulton, I didn't want her mum and dad to be any more upset. I tried to talk her out of it, over and over but she was stubborn and once you start lying it's really hard to get out of it isn't it."

Gloria nodded, she squeezed her lips together, nodded again.

"They thought she was with me all the time. Her dad was a bit strict, so she always told them she was with me. I backed her up, made excuses. I wish I hadn't. It was her lie and I shouldn't have let her make me a part of it. I don't know if it would have made much difference in the end but that's what I did. Said she was with me."

"And where was she really? When you were lying for her, where was she?"

"With him, every time she was with him. She would leave college with me, sometimes she would have a coffee and then she would go and meet him. In town now and again, here and there but most often up on the hill. She went on about how he would be waiting for her, parked in a layby and they would have sex in his car. He sometimes gave her stuff, bits and pieces you know, and she was besotted with him.

"I told her he was too old for her. He was married and she knew that. I don't know if he told her he was going to leave his wife. I don't think so to be honest, and no matter what I said, Melanie just kept on, over and over she would walk up onto the hills. All through the summer when it was light and I didn't worry quite as much, and then as the nights got dark she still went. I pleaded with her not to go in the winter, I said he should take her to a hotel, something better than his car in a layby or now and again at his house when his wife was out, and that was really nasty wasn't it? Sordid, you know. But Melanie was afraid to make waves. She'd always been under her dad's thumb and so it was the same with him. She didn't want to rock the boat she said, she was terrified that he'd drop her."

The girl fell silent for a moment and sipped at her tea. She pulled a tiny piece from the end of the pastry and pushed it into her mouth. "Of course then he said he'd had enough. Said he was going to be faithful to his wife, she hadn't been well, he didn't want her upset. A bit late by that time if you ask me but, anyway, Melanie went to pieces didn't she. That was the worst part, she was desperate and I couldn't do anything with her. Then she suddenly stopped talking about him."

"When was this?"

"About Christmas time. I asked her to my birthday party and she said she couldn't come because she was going to be meeting him. I asked her about it then, how come they were still together you know." Gloria nodded, she wished she had thought to turn on the recorder on her phone but she was just going to have to remember all this.

"Anyway, when I pressed her on it, she told me that he couldn't leave her because of what she knew." She stopped again and hid her face in her hands for a moment. "If I tell you the rest of it, you have to promise that you won't ever mention my name. I told Mr Fulton I could lose my job, my whole career. Do you promise?"

"I won't mention your name." As she said it, Gloria's gut clenched, a promise was a promise and she couldn't and wouldn't break it to this lovely young woman who was crying freely now. She handed her a tissue. "Go on."

"She was blackmailing him. Not for money or anything like that but just so he wouldn't break up with her. It was because of what I'd told her. Because of me. I introduced them really, one day when I had to see him about some research I was doing. She went with me for the walk. It was for my dissertation. One of the lecturers had put me in touch with him. You see, I had weekend work where I am now, at Barclay and Howarth, and they had promised me a job when I graduated. It was so lucky – I couldn't risk upsetting anyone there. But then I worked out what was happening. If it hadn't been for that I would never have known. It seems so selfish now but at the time I just didn't want to mess up my chances, you know. I told her what I thought was going on, what he was doing, and then she used it to blackmail him. To be honest that was one of the reasons I kept up with the lie, and afterwards, after she was dead, I still had to keep my mouth shut. I should have said something, I know I should and it's too late now and I suppose I'm guilty because I've known about it and never said anything to anyone, not even now. I'm a selfish coward if you want to know and what happens to me is my own fault."

"So, you introduced her to Colin?"

"What?"

"The man she was having the affair with. Colin Bliss?"

"Colin Bliss!" She shook her head violently. Her eyes had grown wide and horrified. "I thought you knew; I thought it was because of his wife. A divorce. It wasn't Colin Bliss. That was the whole point, I knew she wasn't just walking home that night, I knew why she was where she was. It wasn't Colin Bliss; she was on her way to the farm."

"The farm?"

"Yes, Melanie was having an affair with Coleman. Patrick Coleman up at High Hill Farm."

Chapter 41

The women stared at each other in silence until finally Fiona took in a deep breath. She looked down at her hands which were clasped together on the table beside the uneaten pastry. Her knuckles stood out white and shiny. Gloria resisted the urge to reach across and touch her, to try to soothe this poor young woman who was so distressed.

"I thought you knew it was him. I would never have said anything if I'd realised. I just thought it had all come out because they were getting divorced. Shit, what a bloody idiot – now look what I've done. Oh yes, I'd seen him up there, Colin Bliss, that's how I figured out what was going on. That and some other stuff, I poked my nose in where it didn't concern me and found out more than I bargained for. But she wasn't having an affair with him. No."

"It's okay, really, it's alright. We didn't mean to mislead you."

"No, no, it's my fault. I jumped to conclusions. Stupid, stupid." Again she hid her face in her hands, shaking her head from side to side. When she next looked up, she glanced at her watch. "I have to go in a few minutes and now I'm confused and scared."

"Don't be scared, please don't. I made you a promise. However, you haven't told me what it was that you were so worried about, have you?" Fiona shook her head, she was losing her, Gloria felt her pulling back. "Would it help if I told you what it's about?"

"Maybe. I don't know, yes maybe."

"Okay, Simon is working for the family of Colin Bliss." And she talked about the sick wife, Colin's wish to leave things alone and Charles Clegg's desperate need to find the truth. She didn't tell her about the accidents or the fire or phone call insisting they leave it alone. She didn't tell her any of the things that might frighten her even more.

"Okay, well I suppose it's all too late now anyway and I'm sorry about Colin's wife, that's very sad. You already know Melanie was blackmailing Coleman so, what the hell. She gulped back the last of the tea which had cooled, the milk forming an unpleasant film on the surface. She grimaced. "I need time to think. I'm not messing you about, honestly but it's complicated, there's other people involved and it'll cause trouble. I've got to go. I don't want to be late, we've got a busy day today and I need to go."

"Will you meet me again?"

"Yes, I will and I'll tell you what I know, as much as I can anyway. I need time to think it all through. I might even have to warn some people about what's going on. I'll see you here again if you like. Not tomorrow, I'm going away for a couple of days. I'll see you next week. Monday or Tuesday. I'll call you."

"Okay. Great. But, perhaps it's best if you don't mention it to anyone else, just for now at least. Hopefully next time Simon will be able to come and between us we can work out what's best. Will that be alright?"

"Yes, he can come. But, for now I need time to think, to decide what to do. You don't understand." She paused, her face creasing into frown lines not yet set in the young skin. "Still though, she did get run down, didn't she? Even though it was because she was in the wrong place at the wrong time, that Bliss bloke did run her down." And with this final parting comment she threw confusion on top of puzzlement and left Gloria frantically searching for a piece of paper and a pencil so that she could jot down some of what had been said. In the end she scribbled bullet points on a thin paper napkin.

She folded the notes into her bag and then ran out to the car park in time to catch a final glimpse of Fiona Carpenter, far off, striding down the road towards the veterinary clinic, her shining ponytail swinging as she walked.

The trip back to Leeds to collect Simon was a nightmare, she hit the road at the height of the morning commute and by the time she reached the infirmary she was frustrated and irritable. The caffeine in the coffee had jangled her nerves and before she went up to the ward to collect him, she bought a bottle of water from a machine and stood outside the door gulping at the cold drink and clearing her mind. Letting it all settle.

He was sitting in a chair beside the bed and looked stronger. The bruises on his face were dark blotches and as she walked across the shiny floor, he pushed himself upright using one of a pair of crutches. She saw him wince. "Are you okay?" She reached towards him.

"Yes, I'm okay. I ache all over to be honest and some of the bruises are pretty impressive but I'm okay. I'll be glad to get home. I can't rest here. Did you find my clothes okay?"

"I did, in fact you are surprisingly tidy – you know, for a bloke."

"Ah well, training." She nodded, acknowledging the reference to his time in jail.

"I suppose so. Some good came out of it then." He grinned at her.

"I have some news for you. Go and get dressed and do whatever you have to before they'll let you escape. There are some chairs in the corridor. I'll see you outside and then I'll fill you in on the way home."

* * *

She carried the thin plastic bag holding his spoiled clothes and walked slowly beside him as they made their way back to the car park. "You getting the hang of those things then?" She nodded towards the crutches.

"Yeah, they made me practice. It's not too bad once you're used to them. Bloody leg is throbbing though. They said I should keep it elevated. Shall I sit in the back so I can prop it up?"

"Yeah, here you go."

As they pulled out into the main road, he leaned forward. "So, what's this news?"

"Tell you what, let's wait now until we get home. To be honest I'm only just processing it myself and I think it'll be better to do it when I'm not trying to get through this bloody traffic. I'll just say that I took a chance and went and met Fiona this morning, before I came to fetch you and she's pretty well messed up any ideas that we had. But I've been thinking about it and actually it does make some of what has happened seem a bit more logical, in a way. Anyway, you just sit back and relax we'll be home soon. Bloody hell there's another one."

"Another what?"

"Oh, take no notice. Since that time on the moors I go to pieces every time I see one of those old Land Rovers. I know I'm just being daft but they freak me out a bit now. There was one this morning and I nearly missed my turn off I was so busy watching it."

He didn't speak, she glanced quickly at him in the mirror but he was laid back against the seat with his eyes closed and his mouth slightly open as he began to snore gently.

Chapter 42

"You can stay in the disabled access room, if you'd rather?" Gloria had to hold back a giggle at the look on his face. "Only kidding, actually no – only half kidding. That shower might be easier for you to use than the one in my room."

"Yes, to the shower and, I'd rather not, to the room." He put down one of the crutches and hopped across the living room to where she stood grinning at him. He wrapped an arm around her and she felt him sway and wobble and drew him towards her, to stop them from falling.

"Sit down, you daft sod, you'll have us both on our arses. Now, do you want tea and do you want anything to eat?"

"I'd love some tea but I'm not hungry. I'm dying to hear this news though."

"Okay. I won't be a minute. Later we need to go up to the flat and get some more of your stuff, did they give you any idea how long you're going to be on those crutches?"

"I have to go back next week. Will you take me?"

"Of course."

"Then it's supposed to be a few weeks, all being well. They said the more care I take the quicker it'll heal."

"Okay then, will you stay here until it's all better?"

"That would be really brilliant. Thanks. Yes, please."

"Right – tea."

* * *

"Now then. I don't know how you feel about me going to see Fiona but it just seemed like the right thing to do."

"It's fine, really it is. I hated putting her off and you solved that. Was she able to tell you anything of use?"

"I think it's best if I just go through it. I have to say I was pretty shocked. Hang on." She ran through into the hall to fetch her handbag and pull out the paper napkins. She spread them out on top of the little table, smoothing them with her fingertips. She pulled a cushion from the settee to the floor, so that she could sit closer to him.

"Right. First of all, and probably the most mind-blowing thing–" She glanced up to make sure she had his full attention. He nodded at her to continue.

"You were right about Melanie having an affair."

"Ah!"

"Yes, but before you get too smug…"

"What?"

"It wasn't Colin Bliss. No, it was with the farm bloke, hang on" – she peered at the scribbled notes – "Patrick Coleman – that's his full name. We didn't know that, did we?"

"No, we didn't. Shit, he's a lot older, isn't he? Blimey, what do you reckon she saw in him? I mean, he was going to seed a bit, wasn't he?"

"I have to agree but don't forget this is a few years ago and if it's all true he's had quite a bit on his mind. Plus, that wife of his – she's bloody odd."

"Good point. So that's why she was up on that road."

"Apparently, it had been going on all through the summer and the winter as well. But that's not all of it." She recited the rest and as she shuffled the flimsy sheets of paper together, she glanced up. He was scratching at his hair and shaking his head.

"Blackmail?"

"That's what she said."

"And this never came out, not at the time?"

"Well, it's as she said. They started lying and couldn't get out of it. It was wrong of them of course but that poor girl has suffered enough I reckon. She only did it out of friendship and just imagine all this time dreading that the truth might come out."

"It does complicate things. Although…"

"What?"

"Well, does it? From what she has told you there were truths hidden, yes, I accept that. But it seems as though it is still very likely that Colin Bliss ran her down."

"I suppose so."

"We need to be careful. Think this through before we tell anyone about it. We need any more information she can give us. When are we seeing her again?"

"Next week. She's gone away for a few days."

"Right. Well it's Tuesday now, so tomorrow I'll ring Charlie Clegg. I'll tell him we're still working on it. It'd be nice to know how he is anyway. Then we'll put our heads together about all this and write out some questions."

"Yeah. I should be careful talking to Charlie though."

"How do you mean?"

"You keep saying we! He doesn't know about me helping you does he… What's that noise? Did you hear something. Outside. Sounded like the bins."

"No, shush."

"There, there it is again. It's probably the fox. I'll go and see. No, don't try and get up. I won't be a minute."

"It's a bit early, isn't it? He usually comes when it's dark."

"Oh, the little beast's been getting really bold. Won't be a minute."

Chapter 43

"Was it the fox?"

"Nah, nothing I could see anyway. Couple of people out in the road, just the usual. I could have sworn I heard something though. The small gate was open. I do still get people looking for rooms so maybe it was that. They go away again when they see the state of the place."

"Have you decided what you're doing, about selling?"

"I had the agent round. He said it would be easier to find a buyer if the hotel is still open and operational. So, it looks as though I'll have to keep it going for now anyway, or rather get it going again. I've got a bloke coming next week to give me an estimate for painting the outside and doing the garden."

"How do you feel about it now?"

She shrugged and glanced around. "Well, I'm feeling better generally, so I reckon I'll accept my usual return visitors if they call and then I'll take it slowly. I already have the Parsons. They come with their disabled daughter for a week every year. I didn't want to let them down because she gets anxious in new places but she's used to Mill Lodge. I usually give them two nights babysitting as well so they can have some time to themselves. They'll come."

He fought to keep the smile of relief from his face. He didn't want to put pressure on her but if she was taking bookings at least the next few months would feel more settled.

"How about we go up to the flat soon as we're ready, then we'll order some take away, I have a yen for Indian. I'll grab my notes and stuff and we'll try and get our thoughts in order so that when I ring Charlie, I sound as though I know what I'm doing."

"Yep, works for me. Are you sure you want to come? I could go and bring your stuff."

"I'll come, you're doing enough. I can't have you running around after me."

The light was beginning to fade and the streetlamps threw little puddles of orange onto the damp pavement. A car turned into the gates of the old people's home but it was the only sign of life, Mill Street was calm and quiet.

Gloria helped Simon into the passenger seat of her little car. "Are you sure you don't want to go in the back again?"

"No, it's not far and I've had my pain killers, I'll be great."

"Bum."

"Sorry?"

"I said bum. I've got a warning light."

"Petrol?"

"No, not petrol. It's a new one, I've never seen it before. That one there."

"Right." She glanced at him and gave a quick laugh.

"Yes, not much point asking you is there? I wonder if I should chance it. Sometimes these things are just... Oh pass me the handbook, will you? It's in the glove box."

He rattled around for a while, took out a packet of mints and a couple of old receipts and then he finally found the manual. She took it from him and ran her fingernail along the edge of the pages, "Warning lights, warning lights. Ah here." There was silence for a minute and then she pushed the book towards him. Her finger pointed to the tiny image in the middle of the page. He heard her gulp and glanced up to see that her expression was serious and in her eyes was a flicker of fear.

"Brake fluid warning light," he read out. "Hmm just as well you didn't chance it..."

She reached across the small space and curled her hand into his. "Simon, do you think it's a bit odd though? I mean you said you thought your brakes failed or am I just being silly?" She glanced nervously over her shoulder out into the quiet street. "I'm worried."

"Okay. I see where you're going with this but it's got to be a coincidence, surely. We still don't know for sure what happened with my car and these things" – he patted his hand against the interior of the door – "well, they do go wrong, don't they?"

"Yes, I know they do but this has never happened before and I have it serviced regularly."

"Well, there we are then. You said so yourself with my car, the garage could have screwed up."

"That's ridiculous, two garages making similar mistakes. What if that wasn't it at all, what if it was something more, deliberate?"

"We don't know yet what's wrong with it. It could be nothing; it could be the light malfunctioning. Look, let's not jump to conclusions. Do you always use the same people?"

"Yes, that's why I don't believe they screwed up. I've used them for years and they are really reliable."

"Call them, see how soon they can get here and then once we know what's going on…"

"What?"

"Well, erm... well, then we can panic." He laughed, trying to make the worry lines disappear from her face and the doubt vanish from her eyes. It didn't work. She pulled out her mobile and used speed dial to contact the garage, told them her problem and arranged for the mechanic to call on his way to work early in the morning. "Come on, let's go in and have a drink. There's nothing else we can do tonight." For once Simon didn't feel any compunction in agreeing with her. He felt as though he needed something to settle the fizz in his nerves and calm the thoughts that had begun to tumble through his mind, not least the image of the chain and padlock from his yard, lying on the pavement when he had left on the day of his accident.

Chapter 44

They stood side by side in the drive peering down at a pair of overall clad legs poking out from under the car. It didn't take long before Carl wriggled and slithered along the concrete and with the ease of youth uncurled to stand in front of them, wiping his hands on a rag. "Good job you didn't take her out Mrs Bartlett."

"Oh right, was there a problem then? Only my friend wondered if maybe it could just have been the light going wrong." The young man glanced at Simon with a look of disdain.

"No, there's a problem alright. It's your nipple."

"Sorry?" In spite of herself, Gloria felt colour rise to her cheeks, she knew it was a technical term but this lad was so young. Fortunately, he saw no double entendre in his comment. "Yes, it's loose and let the fluid drain."

"Oh right, gosh that's worrying. I didn't know they could do that."

"They can't."

"Sorry? But you said…"

"They're designed not to come loose. That'd be dangerous, them rattling loose. No, you don't get that."

"But I don't understand."

"Well, it's been loosened. Some bugger has been under there and undone the bleeder."

"Are you sure?"

"Well, I didn't see them do it, did I? So I couldn't stake my life on it, but if that came loose on its own that's the first time I've ever known it happen."

"Was it dangerous?"

"Aye."

"Would the brakes have failed?" He was a taciturn young man and she clenched her fists with frustration at trying to draw the information from him.

"They would aye, eventually. It'd depend. You could probably go out and down into town like, braking gently and they'd maybe feel a bit spongy. But then, any real hard braking – well that'd be it."

"It?"

"Aye, you'd have no brakes. It wasn't missing the bleed nipple, so you had seepage but hard braking would pump it out, the fluid. There'd a been no way to tell from outside. Good job you were on the ball with that warning light. He glanced at Simon again, raised his eyebrows. We'll need her in. We need to replace the brake fluid and bleed 'em properly now. I'll organise the tow truck to come. Do you need the courtesy car?"

"How long will it take?"

He sucked at his teeth in the manner of mechanics the world over.

"We're busy, but seeing as it's you I reckon I could drop her off on my way home. I'll get Jack to come with me, drive my car. He turned and indicated the shining vehicle parked at the roadside. Another young man sat inside, when he became aware of the attention he grinned and raised a hand.

"That would be brilliant, I think I can manage for today without a car." She turned to Simon who nodded in return. His face was pale and she could see his jaw clenched tight with the effort not to speak, not to give anything away. Not until they were on their own would it be time to acknowledge the shock and disbelief.

"Right you are, Mrs Bartlett, I'll get that sorted. We'll put it on your account, shall we?"

"Please."

He backed away a few steps and then stopped again, looked at Gloria and spoke quietly, "Mrs Bartlett."

"Yes, Carl?"

"This is bloody odd, I'll take some pictures and write a report. I haven't messed about with it too much specially. Fingerprints and stuff, you know. You might want to consider talking to the police. This is nasty, it's probably vandalism but it's not funny and whoever did it has a bit of a knowledge of motors. I'll leave it until lunchtime. Give you a chance to think on it. Then if I don't hear from you, I'll have to get going with fixing it." And with the final oblique comment he turned and strode away.

"Thanks, Carl. Thanks very much." Her wobbling legs wouldn't hold her much longer and with Simon hobbling behind her on his crutches, Gloria only just made it back into the hotel, down the hallway and into her own flat where she flopped onto the chair beside the fire. When he joined her, she looked up, her face was drawn and she had to swallow hard before she was able to speak. "So, what are we going to do? We have to consider the police, we just have to."

He puffed out his cheeks and lowered his head. "I don't know – I really don't know. On the one hand, yes of course. You were in danger, God that gives me chills but on the other hand..."

"On the other hand – what sodding other hand? You heard what he said, they can't come loose on their own, somebody loosened them. What about you? What about your car? Don't you see?"

"Yes, of course I do, I'm not stupid. But what are we going to tell them? If we go to them and just say we think someone has been tampering with our cars – well I don't know what their reaction would be, probably just give us a crime number. On the other hand, if we tell them about the shooting, the things up at the hut – all of that stuff – maybe even what we know about Melanie's death, the blackmail." He paused and raised his head to look at her.

"I just don't know how they would react to that either. It would mean you breaking your promise to Fiona and it would mean that I would have let Charlie Clegg down as well. Going to the police with it all is going to stir up a shit storm."

"Bloody hell, Simon, isn't that what we've got already? Look, I know I've said it before but why not call Ian Prentiss. He told us both, anything we needed to talk about, any problems, just to call him. See if you can talk it over with him, ask his advice."

Simon was shaking his head violently; he laid a hand on her arm. "Stop, stop, Gloria. That's not the way, I know what he said but all of that was to do with Sandie, with Peter. He's not my tame policeman. Anything I tell him will be on the record and you know he'll tell me to back off, to leave it alone. To put it bluntly, if I want to do this stuff I can't just go to the police every time I think there's been a crime – oh that sounds stupid, I know it does but, do you understand me? Yes, I will probably go to the police in the end, maybe even to him because at least I think we can trust him, he won't have an axe to grind, he'll listen and there is definitely a stink around all of this, but I need to have something concrete to give him or it won't make any difference to Colin Bliss. He'll probably just hand it on and then it'll all become drawn out, they won't care about Maureen Bliss, she'll be collateral damage. Do you see, we could risk all that we've done ending up meaning nothing?"

They sat in silence for a few minutes. Simon chewed at the corner of his nail. She had never seen him do that before and it unnerved her more, seeing him stressed and tense. She wished she hadn't shouted at him. Eventually he spoke. "Look, we still have to wait to hear about my car. Carl is writing a report on yours, why don't we wait until we've spoken to Fiona and then make the decision. If we have no other choice, we can take it all to the police at the same time, if that's what we've decided. Before that I want to speak to Charlie Clegg and perhaps tell him what happened. Maybe even suggest to him that he have his own car examined."

Gloria gasped. "Of course. I hadn't thought of that. His car! It crashed on a winding road and he couldn't work out why." Simon nodded and again started to nibble at his thumb.

"Carl said it was vandalism, but we both think it's deeper than that, don't we?" Gloria couldn't speak, horror had stolen her voice, she nodded at him and then reached out to take hold of his hand, to stop him gnawing at his nails and because right then she needed a hand to hold.

Chapter 45

"Hello Mr Clegg, Simon Fulton here. How are you?"

"Mr Fulton, Good mornin' lad. Aye, well I've been better but I've been worse as well. I'm driving us both mad hanging around. I'm going back into work next Monday. Give Beryl the run o' the house again. What can I do for you lad?"

"I wanted to let you know I'm still working on things."

"I didn't doubt it. You said you'd help and I reckon you're a man of your word. You don't need to keep reassuring me, don't you worry about that – though I do appreciate it."

"I have made some progress anyway. I am pretty convinced now that there were things that weren't as they seemed. But, I am not sure at this point whether it will help Colin. I have a couple of questions though, if you've time."

"Nothing but time at the moment, fire away."

"Have you remembered anything more about your own accident?"

"My accident? Well, no, but I don't understand. What does that have to do with anything?"

"Maybe nothing but please bear with me. I wondered if you had the car looked at, by a garage or anything."

"Heck no lad. That car's long gone now."

"Yes, I know it was written off but…"

"Gone for scrap."

"Oh."

"Aye, no bugger else were injured so the police weren't that interested. They tested me for drink and drugs of course but there was nothing to find, so that was that. I had it shifted myself, well my manager did, I was laid up of course."

"Okay. Well, it was just a thought. Where was it kept?"

"Kept?"

"Yes, while you're in work, is the car locked up or whatever?"

"Oh, I see. Well it depends, doesn't it, I don't spend all day at my desk. That's not my way, so sometimes it's in the yard, sometimes I leave it at home altogether and have a lift in."

"And that day, the day of your accident?" He heard the expiration of air as Charles Clegg blew out his cheeks, thinking.

"I don't know as if I can remember. I was in the office that day, but I did go out for a bite at lunch time, went to a couple of appointments, so it'd be in the car park in town. Is it important lad? I mean what is it all about?"

"It was just an angle I'm following up really. Don't worry about it please. I'm glad you're feeling better. I'll be in touch."

"Aye right you are lad. Bye." Simon replaced the receiver and looked across to shake his head at Gloria.

"So, we'll never know about that then?"

"I don't think so, no. As far as Clegg and the police are concerned that was all just an accident and it's done and finished. It could have been interfered with in town but sounds as though that was pretty public, so it's unlikely anyone could mess about with it. No, that's not going to help us, but it's a hell of a coincidence if that was an accident. We're going to have to go back up there you know. At some stage we are going back to the farm and we'll have to speak to that woman. There's not much more we can do right now, not until we get more information from Fiona on Monday."

"Monday or Tuesday she said, but I'll ring her Monday and try to hurry things along. Do you want me to sort out somewhere for your papers and your computer? I've got a spare desk I could put in there by the window, that way you could work with your leg on the stool."

"Brilliant. I'll make some notes and I want to go over some of the newspaper reports online again. It's really a lot of killing time but the more familiar I am with it all, the better it feels. I thought I'd have a shower; shall I use the disabled room?"

"Yep, that's fine, it's all ready for you."

* * *

It was a frustrating weekend. The repaired car was delivered and on Sunday they drove back towards the waterfall to look at where Simon had left the road. It told them nothing they didn't already know. They stopped on the way back to Ramstone for a drink in a pub. There was a coal fire in the corner, a fat black cat taking up one of the bar stools and the atmosphere was calm and cosy. As she looked around, Gloria wished that they were there simply having a weekend outing and they were going back to ordinary lives on Monday. But for months now there had been nothing ordinary. Simon took a big gulp of his beer and smiled at her, the scar down his face puckering at the corner of his mouth. He wasn't really handsome, although his grey eyes were unusual, his dark hair thick with no sign of grey yet and it had the hint of a curl where it was growing long around his neck. She tried to imagine what he'd looked like before the injury. The undamaged side of his face was smooth, the skin clear and there were just the beginnings of laughter lines around his eyes, the hint of furrows on his forehead. He was okay looking, just that. He was damaged, there was no doubt of that. But still, he was good and decent and he was kind. She smiled back at him and raised her glass of wine in salute.

* * *

On Monday, they were up early and constantly checking the time.

"Was she back at work today?" Simon asked.

"She didn't say so specifically but I think so. I wonder if I should ring before nine, catch her early?"

He shook his head. "Leave it for now eh. I reckon it would be better to let her ring us. Let's give her a chance to do that. Maybe even leave it until after lunch. I don't want to scare her away."

"Yes, you're right. So, let's fetch the rest of your stuff and check on the shop. We'll go batty sitting here staring at the clock."

* * *

"Good afternoon, Barclay and Howarth, how can I help you?"

The receptionist sniffed as she spoke, her voice thick and hoarse.

"Oh goodness, you've got a shocking cold."

"How may I help you?" Gloria turned from the phone to pull a face at Simon. She pushed the button to activate the speaker and mouthed the words, *a bit grumpy* at him, he grinned, remembering the snappy reaction of the receptionist when she thought he had upset Fiona Carpenter.

154

"I wondered if it would be possible for me to speak to one of your nurses?"

"What is it regarding?"

"It's personal. I'd like to speak to Fiona, if she's free." There was a long silence punctuated only by quiet sniffing and then a muttered conversation in the background. The next voice they heard was a man. "Who's this speaking please?"

"My name is Gloria Bartlett, I'm a friend of Fiona's." She grimaced across the table, acknowledging the exaggeration. Simon nodded his approval.

"I am sorry, Mrs Bartlett, it's not possible for you to speak to Fiona."

"Can you tell me when she'll be free, Mr...?"

"Howarth, I am Ken Howarth. I am really sorry, Mrs Bartlett. Fiona isn't here today. She was in a walking accident at the weekend."

"Oh, I am sorry, is she in hospital? Is she badly hurt?"

"She was killed, Mrs Bartlett. I'm afraid Fiona died over the weekend. I am sure you will want to contact her parents but could I ask you, if possible, to leave it for a day or two, they are, as you may well imagine, distraught, as are we here in the practice."

"I... I don't know what to say. I am sorry, I am so sorry. Oh, God that's awful."

"I hate to have to break such distressing news about your friend on the telephone. Is there anything else I can do for you?"

"No, no that's all. That's all, thank you."

Tears streamed down her face as Gloria replaced the handset and flopped back on the dining chair. "Simon, what have we done? Is this our fault, what have we done?"

"An accident, he said it was an accident. Don't jump to conclusions. We don't know this was anything to do with us."

"Don't we – truly? We have to stop it now. We have to leave this alone and go to the police with what we know."

The room was quiet save for the click of computer keys and Gloria occasionally blowing her nose as she cried quietly. "Here, here it is, Simon. Up near Scarborough. It hasn't got her name but it says a veterinary nurse from a practice near Leeds with a promising career. It has to be her. It says that they think she was walking her dogs along the cliff edge and slipped over. The alarm was raised when the dogs returned to the car park without her but with their leads still attached. Ah, it's awful, they went back to the car and just sat there waiting for her. Of course, they'd be well trained I suppose."

"So, it was an accident. She just slipped and fell."

"There's going to be an inquest. There's no date set yet. Do you think we should go to the police, Simon? Surely we should."

"But if it was an accident, what could we tell them?"

"Oh, come on, you know as well as I do that this was no accident. She was a young, fit woman, it was a fine weekend. She didn't slip. It says here that she was an experienced hiker."

"Even experienced walkers have accidents."

She let out a groan of exasperation and pushed away from the desk.

"You can't do this. You just can't go on and think we can continue to stir up trouble. We're out of our depth here, for Christ's sake, Simon, people are dying."

"I know. I know. But maybe you're putting two and two together and coming up with five. What happened was a long time ago, she's come to no harm up to now. We haven't even told anyone what we're doing. How can this be because of us? Tell me how?"

Without looking at him she stomped through the room and he heard the bedroom door slam. Simon hopped across to where she had left the computer open and read the report in the paper. He knew she was right, no matter how much he tried to rationalise what had happened, to try and convince himself it was coincidence. He knew she was right. What he didn't know was how they should deal with it.

Chapter 46

Gloria threw together a meal for them, huffing and clattering about in the kitchen and then they turned on the television so that they didn't need to talk. After an evening of mindless channel-hopping they eventually gave in and went to bed. Neither of them spoke about the dead girl or their angry words.

They were both subdued and quiet over breakfast the next morning. "So, what are we going to do?" Gloria picked up their empty plates and stood beside the table. "It's out of hand, Simon. I know you meant well, I know you meant to help and I understand why, but this! A girl is dead, we've been shot at, you could have been killed in the car. Don't you see, there is evil at work here, real evil and we can't handle it. We've no idea what's going on and we're out of our depth. We have to hand it to the professionals."

"The professionals, oh yes, well I've had plenty to do with the professionals, haven't I? In spite of everything that happened last year I don't think I'm one of their favourite citizens, am I? It'll take a long time for them to forget that I showed them up for sloppy work, taking the easy way out. Honestly, do you really think that anybody is going to listen to us, to me? Okay we were shot at. In both cases we were trespassing." As he spoke, he counted off the points on his fingers.

"My car went off the road, that happens and I'm a crap driver. We don't know what happened to Charlie Clegg's

157

car and nobody can find out now. Poor Fiona is dead and we don't know exactly where or how. Do you want me to go to the police and say something like 'Hello, remember me, you put me in jail for something I didn't do? Well now, I'm pretending to be a private detective to see if I can make it work and you know that girl who fell off a cliff, well I think that was because of me. She'd been talking to me about another girl who was run over years ago, and you already have a bloke in jail for that.' Is that what you want, Gloria? How far do you think we'd get before they said, 'Well thank you so much for coming in and if we need to talk to you again, we'll be in touch'?" He leaned away from her now and lowered his head onto his clenched fists.

"I know your faith in the system is non-existent, Simon, don't you think I have doubts. My whole life I was tied up with illegal stuff, first my dad and then him and my brother together. I know it's often far from perfect but it's what we've got. Okay, so you want to do something to help people, I think it's great and maybe in time it'll all work out but I reckon this is too big, too nasty. It's not a place to start dipping your toe into this pool."

"I've been over it and over it, all night. The only thing I can think of is to find out just what happened and then... then we can go to the police, maybe even Ian, but I see it as a last resort. When we've nowhere else to turn. I want to wait, I want to do what I did before, prove who is guilty and what exactly they've done. This has gone beyond Colin's wife now, beyond helping Charlie Clegg, this has gone way beyond that."

She snatched up the dishes and spun from the table and he could hear her crashing about in the kitchen. Simon grabbed his crutches and hobbled over to the window. The small figure walking up the drive turned as the curtains moved and Fuzz raised a hand in greeting. "Fuzz is here, Gloria. Shall I just let him in?"

"Oh great, that's all we need. Yes, I suppose so. Can you manage?"

"I've got it." He hopped through to the hallway and opened the front door. "Hiya, Fuzz, what are you doing here?"

"Shit, Simon, what have you done? Is that from up at the hut?" He gestured towards the bulky plastic splint. "I thought you said you weren't hurt?"

"No, I pranged my car. Rolled it."

"Wicked." Simon couldn't help but smile.

"Well, I don't know about that, I'm lucky to have got away with just this." He wagged his leg. "Anyway, are you coming in? I need to sit down."

"Yeah. Thanks." As they walked down the hallway, Gloria called a greeting from the kitchen.

"Go on into the living room, I'll be there in a minute."

* * *

"So, what have you been doing?" They were gathered around the fireplace; Fuzz lowered his eyes for a moment and coughed nervously.

"Don't be mad, okay. I know you said I shouldn't get involved but it was me that got kidnapped and I was that brassed off about it. I was mad that she made me scared and she gave me that filthy headache and then in the end she just buggered off and got away with it."

"Oh, for heaven's sake. What have you been up to now?" Gloria leaned forward in her seat as she snapped at him.

"I just went up to the farm. I wanted to watch her, that loony. I wanted to see if she was still carting that bloody big gun around. I thought she might have got rid of it. I thought maybe we'd scared her, well Simon, when he got in her face like that."

"And?"

"Well it was dead boring. I was up there off and on all weekend and nothin' happened." Simon glanced across the room. Gloria had clasped her hands and was wringing her fingers together.

"She wasn't there, was she?" Simon felt his heart begin to pound; he felt the excitement build as the suggestion of a lead was dangled in front of them.

"Oh she was there. She was there all right. Messing with them sheep and the bloody dogs, tinkerin' with her car. Nothing else. Just that."

"She was there? She was at the farm? How often did you go? How long were you there?" Simon was struggling to keep his voice even, he didn't want Fuzz alerted to the importance of what he was telling them, he didn't want him to embroider the truth to keep their interest.

"I went on Saturday, hung about a bit and then… well… I just went off. When I came back the car was gone but then, it was back. So, I reckon she went to Tesco or sommat."

"So, she was there for part of the time? How often did you see her, how do you know she was there?"

"She was in and out both days like I said. But she didn't do nothing interesting. She still had the gun but she was just messing about, farming stuff I reckon, then off for a few hours, probably shopping and then back. Anyway, I thought I'd come and see you and see what you're doing and if you wanted me to do owt else?"

"No, I told you already. Thanks for coming but there's nothing for you to do and you should keep away from the farm, keep away from that woman."

"Actually though, Fuzz, if I give you a few quid would you wash my car for me?" At the promise of money, the boy's crestfallen face brightened. "It's been in the garage and it could do with a clean, he can't do it." She flapped a hand towards Simon, raising the boy above him in usefulness and making him grin.

"Aye, I'll do that." Once she had sorted out the buckets and cloths and connected the hose, she left Fuzz in the drive and re-joined Simon in the flat.

As soon as she walked through the door he asked her, "How long do you reckon it takes to get up to Scarborough?"

"Depends on the traffic of course but at this time of the year I reckon round about two hours."

"He wasn't there all the time, was he?"

"No, but it would be two hours back, that's a big chunk of the day and that's just the driving. Anyway, it's meaningless really because we don't know just when Fiona died."

"No, we need to look on the internet again, see if there are more details by now."

Fuzz finished washing the car and wandered back into the hotel. "What ya doing?" He leaned over the back of Simon's desk chair to peer at the computer screen. Simon reduced the newspaper web page he'd been reading. "Just research, nothing exciting. Fuzz, when you were up on the moors, in between spying on the woman at the farm, what were you doing?"

"Oh, this and that."

"But there's nothing up there to do is there?"

"Well, you know."

"No, tell me?"

"Well, if you must know I was watching birds. And don't laugh."

"I wasn't going to. Do you do that often then, watch birds?"

"Aye, sometimes. My cousin and me, we used to go. This was afore he joined up. I still go sometimes, it's not gay."

"Did I say it was?"

"No, but I don't tell many people. There's some big birds up there, really big sods and they hunt. Anyroad that's what I did."

"So, you can't say exactly when she went out and when she came back."

"No, she came back just afore I went home. It was getting dark and I was meeting the lads, and she just went in the house and slammed the door."

"Was she on her own? Did you see him at all, the bloke?"

"No, his car wasn't there at all, all weekend. He's not there that much though anyroad. That's nowt new. He's no sort of a farmer. I've only seen him in that Land Rover now and then. Mostly he's in the red car. It's smarter is that one. It's only if the weather's really bad that he takes the other one out."

"Thanks. You've been helpful, Fuzz, but I don't want you to go back again, okay?"

"Well, I reckon it's not up to you to say, I'll please myself." And with that he left the room and Simon could hear him in the kitchen scrounging toast and tea. He clicked on the bottom toolbar and re-opened the screen that told him that Fiona had died on the Saturday between the time when she was seen leaving her car at around noon and the late afternoon when the dogs were spotted waiting for her. In spite of the horror of what he read, there was a quiver of excitement in his gut. It must be her, it had to be Lily Coleman. But why, and even more importantly, how could he prove it?

Chapter 47

Simon was frustrated. He wanted to get out and walk, and knowing it would be weeks before he was able to do that again, he felt confined and irritable. He'd tried sitting at his desk, making notes but he couldn't concentrate.

As if she had read his mind, Gloria appeared at his shoulder with a jacket in her hand. "I've put some cushions on the bench in the back. It's not that cold and we can have coffee out there."

The air was thin and sharp and the green and brown hills were painted against an endless clear blue sky. Simon felt the frustration begin to lift and his nerves settle. For a while they sat in silence, it was Gloria who broke the deadlock. "Okay, so, what do you think? Lily wasn't at the farm when Fiona was killed but, Simon, how did she know where the girl was? She would have had to have been watching her, following her. I'm flip-flopping now between the conviction that it was a deliberate act by someone, maybe Lily and it just being a rotten accident. We could go to the inquest of course."

"But we can't speak. We can't start throwing out accusations, can we? You're right, if it was Lily and it was all connected, then she must somehow have known that we were talking to Fiona, she must have been watching us. Have you seen her, since the incident with Fuzz?"

"I don't know, I'm not even sure I'd recognise her to be honest. Every time I've seen her, I've been in some sort of panic. Apart from that, you had your accident the day after didn't you, and I've been a bit preoccupied, then..." She stopped for a moment. "I did see that Land Rover, when I went to meet Fiona. Do you remember I mentioned it because it spooked me a bit? It can't have been her... Can it? Really, do you think she's been following me around? That's really scary."

"Let's assume the worst just for a minute. Let's imagine that she is watching us. We'll think about why later but anyway, we know that she's a nutter, that's already been proved. So, if she was following you and saw you at the vets and in the café, then why would that put Fiona in danger?" As Gloria gasped and covered her mouth with quivering fingers, Simon reached and laid his hand on her leg. "I'm not saying it's your fault, it's not your fault. Whatever happens, you mustn't ever blame yourself. Okay, do you hear me, Gloria?" He raised a hand to her face and turned her to look at him. Her eyes swam with tears but she nodded and murmured her understanding. "So, Fiona told you that Melanie was blackmailing the bloke at the farm. We must find out more about that. If Lily is trying to hide something, then we have to find out what. Maybe it will lead us to the next stage. The trouble is, with Fiona gone, we'll have to work it all out for ourselves."

"Right, so you're going to hobble up there and hop around, are you?"

"Shit." He thumped at the splint and rubbed his hand through his already dishevelled hair. "Trust me to screw things up by being stupid."

"How, how have you been stupid?"

"Driving so bloody fast that I couldn't even keep my sodding car on the road. That's pretty stupid."

"But, Simon, it wasn't that, was it? There were no brakes."

He shook his head.

"It won't sink in, will it? The fact that somebody could actually be doing this stuff deliberately just won't make sense. Oh, hang on." He reached into his pocket and pulled out his phone. "Simon Fulton."

"I want to meet you, Mr Fulton."

"Mrs Clegg, is that you?"

"It is. I want to meet you today. There's a café by the bus station. I'll see you there this afternoon. About half past two, is that alright?"

"Yes, my friend will be with me."

"No, you – just you."

"But I'm on crutches, Mrs Clegg, it's tricky for me to get about."

"Just you. Half past two." As the phone went dead, he looked across to where Gloria was watching him, frowning in puzzlement.

"She's not as friendly as her husband, is she?"

"No. I wonder what this is all about. Will you take me down, drop me off?"

"Yes, of course. I'll hang around in the car park by the fountain. This is odd, isn't it?"

"I don't even know what she looks like. I suppose I'll have to get there early and let her find me."

"I shouldn't think it'll be busy that time of day, it's after the lunch rush, but yes, at least if you're there early she'll have to make the first move. I wonder how she'll know it's you though?" He raised a hand to his face where the long scar snaked down his cheek.

"You could have it fixed you know. They can do marvellous things these days."

"Nah, if I did that how would strange women in cafés recognise me?" She smiled at him. "Good point. Come on, let's go in. I'm getting a bit cold now and I've stuff to do. The decorators are coming in the morning to talk about the repainting outside."

Chapter 48

He chose a table in the corner but near the window so he could keep an eye on the road outside. When he spotted the thin woman striding towards the door, he had no doubt about who it was. The blue coat was obviously good quality, her ash blond hair was beautifully cut – even he could see that she was expensively turned out. She was out of place here in the dingier side of the town but as she walked into the fuggy little café she nodded across to the woman at the counter and he heard her call over. "Just a filter coffee please, warm milk." She glanced around the half a dozen patrons and when her eyes lighted on his, he gave her a small smile.

He stood to pull the chair away from the table, she was the sort of woman men would do that for. "Mrs Clegg, it's nice to meet you. How is your husband?"

"Better, thank you." Before there was time for any more conversation the waitress brought the coffee.

"There we are, Beryl. Are you okay?"

"Fine thanks, Cath. Your mum any better?"

"Not really, but then at her age what can you expect?" As the woman went back behind the counter Beryl Clegg smiled her thin smile.

"Oh yes, they know me round here, Mr Fulton. Charlie and I have done well. I expect you've had a look online, seen our place?" She raised an eyebrow and waited for him to nod at her. "Aye, but I'm from round here. My mum lived just a couple of streets away until she died, never would move even though we tried to get her to come out to us. Charlie is from just outside town. A bit posher than me." She laughed, just once, it sounded forced.

"Anyway, as I say we've worked hard, especially him and we're enjoying the benefits. But he's not like me, Charlie. For all he's a hard businessman, he's soft inside. He trusts people, he's not daft, couldn't have got where we are today by being daft but he always sees the best in folk. He's as straight as a die and chooses to believe most other people are as well. Oh, it's nice, it makes him what he is but now and then it's done him a disservice. He's lost accounts because he's trusted the wrong people, lost money as well. Me, well as I say, I grew up round here. You have to have your wits about you. Anyway, that's enough, I'll not mess about. I'll say what I have to say."

She took a drink from the thick white mug, her painted nails and soft, slender hands a strange counterpoint to the workmanlike tableware.

"It's hit him hard, what's happening with his sister. He can't deal with it. He's panicked at the thought of losing her. I understand, of course I do, I love him, we've been together a long time. But this business with Colin…" She paused again and her brow creased as she thought about her next words. "There are things that I've kept from him, things I hold close. I know things that would break his heart. I don't want that. Nothing is worth that. Our Maureen wouldn't want it either. There are reasons she's not visiting her husband in that bloody prison and it's not all to do with losing her hair and being as thin as a lath. Men don't notice things like women do, if there's laughter and jokes when we're together then Charlie assumes everyone's happy. He doesn't notice undercurrents, atmospheres. He assumes most marriages are like ours. They're not. There are things I don't discuss with Charlie and because of that I need you to just leave all this alone. I want you to tell him it was as they say, that Colin ran that woman over, it was an accident. When all is said and done, he's paying – they both are. Life has a way of taking what it's owed, some people call it Karma, I call it comeuppance, it's all the same."

As she grew more passionate her accent thickened and he could hear the streets in her voice. "Leave it and I'll pay you off. Go and find somebody else to help."

"Have you heard about Fiona Carpenter?"

"Aye, I have. The poor girl. They were silly girls. They should have concentrated on their hairdressing and dogs and cats, but I was sad to hear about her. Mr Fulton, I'm sure you don't want to see Charlie upset. Will you leave it?" As she spoke, she lifted her leather bag to her lap and took out the chequebook. "What do we owe you for your trouble?"

"No, I'm sorry, we've already had this conversation on the telephone. Things have moved on since then. I admit this started as me just wanting to help someone I thought of as a distressed old man, but it's gone beyond that. There's something wrong here and, as you say, Charlie is a decent person. I think he would want me to continue. With the things that have happened I don't think he'd want me backing off. Put your cheques away, Mrs Clegg."

And with that he stood from the table, threw a couple of pound coins down on the hard top and hobbled out of the café with as much dignity a man on two crutches could muster, leaving her fuming – the steam from her coffee curling lazily in front of her.

He was sweating with the effort of heaving himself along by the time he reached the little town centre car park. Gloria climbed out to open the passenger door for him and help him inside. Not until he was settled did she ask the questions that were buzzing in her mind. "What was it all about then? What was she like? Is she nice? Did she tell you anything useful?" He held up a hand.

"She's not somebody I would choose to make a friend off, no. She didn't actually tell me anything and from the conversation I knew she wouldn't and didn't want to give her the chance to refuse. But I'll tell you this, we're not wrong about this being rotten, and no way am I letting it go now. She wanted me to. Tried to pay me to leave it. We're on our own and we're going to have to be careful what we say to Charlie, but I have a horrible feeling this is going to end in tears."

"Shit."

"Yes, quite. I don't see we have any choice now about going to see Colin Bliss, in jail. I know I've been cowardly about it, I should have insisted right at the start, but it's time to get down to brass tacks. There's no other way."

"Will you be okay with that? I mean it's going to be tough for you."

"I don't know to be honest, not until I try."

"I'll come with you."

"You don't have to. It would be just as hard for you, what with Peter and all that."

"Aye well, it won't be the first time I've been to one of those places. I'd like to think it'll be the last but I'm beginning to believe that, hanging around you, I could be wrong." And with a quick glance in the rear-view mirror she pulled out and turned onto the Bradford Road and headed back to the hotel. She didn't look at him but she felt the tension in the man beside her and knew that he was battling with demons only a few people would understand.

Chapter 49

Simon hopped into the kitchen where Gloria was busy with the evening meal. "I've sent a message to Charlie Clegg. I didn't want to phone in case Beryl answered. I've asked him to arrange for us to go to the jail."

"Right. Well from my experience that's unlikely to be quick. Could be anything up to a couple of weeks depending on Colin's visiting orders and how efficient the administration is."

Simon nodded before he continued, "In the meantime we have to go up and look at the farm, at least I do and you, if you're up for it. D'you know, if only Fuzz was a bit older, he would have been useful, with me like this. He seems to be pretty good at watching, doesn't he?"

"Aye he does but he's a boy and I don't want any more youngsters in danger. It's bad enough when it's us but I would never forgive myself if he got into trouble again."

"Well, we're just going to have to manage. I've got binoculars at the flat, do you have any?"

"Yes, somewhere. I'll fish them out. What are you thinking?"

"For now I just want to watch. If Melanie was blackmailing that bloke, then he must have been up to no good. It's a couple of years ago and he might have stopped, whatever it was, especially since she died. It must have been something to do with that place though, as Fiona said it was because of her going there that the affair started. Gloria, we must be due for some sort of a break, surely.”

“Okay, so tomorrow I’ll see the painters in the morning and then we’ll get up there and just find someplace to sit so we can watch. It sounds to me as though it’s going to be a complete waste of time but there we are, what else is there? I hope it doesn’t bloody rain. Come on, this is ready and it needs eating straight away.” She turned around and walked in front of him, carrying the bowls to the table.

* * *

It rained, it was cold and dreary and they almost talked themselves out of spending time up at the farm. “Really, Simon, it’s probably a waste of time. We could do better trying to find out about Fiona. I’d like to go to the funeral. It’s going to be really miserable up there on the hills.”

“Look you don’t have to come, I’d rather you didn’t to be honest. Why don’t you take me up there and you can leave me?”

“Leave you, where the hell am I going to leave you, with that bloody leg and this weather? You do say some stupid things at times.”

“Oh come on, there’s sure to be somewhere to shelter. I’ve got my good waterproofs and I’ve got a tarp in the warehouse. I’m only going to watch after all.”

“No, don’t be ridiculous. We’ll sit in the car. I’ll make a flask. It’ll be great fun.” She pulled a wry face as she spoke. “If the rain gets any heavier, we won’t be able to see anything anyway so I’ll keep my fingers crossed for a downpour. Right, I need to get a move on, the men’ll be here any time.”

She leaned to kiss him. “You’re a pain in the arse, do you know that? I don’t know why I have anything to do with you. I think you drag trouble around after you.”

He didn’t answer but he reached a hand to her and curled it around the back of her neck, pulled her down towards him.

170

"Okay, stop that, I've got people due any minute." She went into the bathroom laughing as he struggled to the side of the bed and began to drag on his clothes.

* * *

"So, you know this car can't go off road, don't you? It's pretty low-slung, it grounds."

"Yes, I know, you already told me that. Look, follow the track up that way." Simon pointed to a narrow sheep trail on the opposite side of the paved road that ran past High Hill Farm. "We can swing round to the other side of the rise and we should have a pretty good view from there."

"If the rain clears. Honestly, we can only just see the buildings from here. We're wasting our time. We could be nice and warm at home."

"We'll give it a couple of hours."

"What are we even watching for?" she huffed.

"Shit, Gloria, I don't know. It just feels as though we should be doing something, anything, and watching that woman feels like something. If we can just get any idea of their comings and goings, well, maybe we can follow her or something. I just want to feel that we're taking some sort of action. I'll go spare just sitting in the house waiting for Charlie to get back to me."

"Oh, alright. So, a couple of hours. We'll watch the front door. Nobody is going to be coming in and out in this weather. This is stupid."

"A couple of hours, then I'll buy you a drink at The Oak."

"Okay. Done."

"Here, can you pull off the track here?"

"A bit I think, but not too far. I don't want us getting stuck. Huh that'd be good wouldn't it. We get stuck and have to go to the farm to get them to drag us out."

"Hey, that's…" She held up a hand.

171

"No, no don't even think it. I'm going nowhere near that bloody woman. Right, this'll have to do. Can you see?"

"Yeah, actually it's not bad. I've got a decent view of the barn and the house. The Land Rover is there and his car as well. So, they're both home. There's another car. Just at the end of the drive. Do you see it, green, quite big?" As he spoke, Simon pointed down across the little valley.

"Yes, hold on. I always have trouble focusing these bloody things. Ah yep, got it now. Oh."

"What?"

"I've seen that car somewhere before."

"Where?"

"I'm trying to remember. It's that sticker on the back, oh where, where? It's recently, where have I been? Oh, hang on, the car park."

"In town?"

"No, not that one. No, the one at the vets. When you went to see poor Fiona. Do you remember I waited for you in the car park? I'm sure it was that one. It's got a funny sticker on, a bit like the medical one doctors use, that snake thing. Can you see?"

"Yeah. I see it now. Well, that's odd. See, see I told you it wasn't a waste of time."

"Well, maybe. How long has it been?"

He glanced at his watch. "About ten minutes."

"Oh right, seems longer."

There was no birdsong today, just the occasional sputter of rain on the windows and the click of cooling metal. Now and then a car would pass on the road below them, flinging up water from the puddles. They watched the farm and occasionally put down the glasses to give their eyes a break. It was boring and Simon began to believe that it was in fact a complete waste of time and that they should call it a day. Gloria started to fidget, "Listen, I need to go and find a bush."

"What? Oh, oh right."

"Back in a bit."

There was no movement at the farmhouse, the small flock of sheep that had been brought down to the field, probably for lambing, wandered aimlessly back and forth. The two dogs roamed the yard and then eventually plodded back to their kennel and settled inside, out of the weather.

Simon reached to turn on the engine to warm the car interior, his feet were beginning to freeze and his fingers were stiffening with the cold. As he turned the key he glanced around. She'd been gone a while, surely she hadn't needed to go far, there were little wind-blasted shrubs in a clump a few metres away and out here, there was no chance of her being overlooked.

He rolled down the window. "Gloria. Are you okay? It's bloody freezing, you need to get back in here. We'll open the flask, have some coffee. Gloria?" He waited a short while and then swung open the car door.

"Hey, are you okay? How long does it take for God's sake? Gloria." The tiny snake of disquiet grew into worry and he grabbed his crutches and, using the door frame, heaved himself out onto the slick grass.

"Gloria, give us a shout, will you? Are you okay?" He moved away supporting himself with the walking aids but even then he had to touch his injured foot to the ground.

"I can't walk on this stuff, Gloria. Hello?" There was nothing and he felt his insides clench as he stopped at the rear of the vehicle and then carefully limped onto the harder surface of the sheep track. He reached the clump of bushes, still calling for her, still not hearing an answer.

When he saw the red and blue hump of her waterproof behind the spiny branches he cried out in panic. As fast as he could in his disabled state he moved across the pebble-strewn trail. As his feet hit the wet grass again, his crutches and the plastic boot lost what little grip there was and he crashed to the ground, yelling in pain as his injured leg twisted under him. He pushed to his hands and knees and crawled desperately towards the bright flash of colour.

Chapter 50

He stretched out and pulled the coat towards him. "Gloria. Where the hell are you?" The ground was hard and rubbly, the grass too cropped by sheep to show any signs of passage. He pushed himself upright, holding his throbbing leg away from the ground as much as possible but when he began to topple, he had to toe touch to keep his balance. The injury to his ankle shot pain through the damaged nerves, sending snakes of fire to his hip. It brought tears to his eyes and he dashed them aside in his desperate need to see. "Gloria?"

"I'm here. I'm here. Simon, it's okay." He spun towards the source of her voice to see her staggering towards him, dishevelled and muddied, her hair tumbled around her shoulders and smears of mud and muck on her clothes. She reached him and he lurched towards her. "Oh bloody hell, don't do that. What happened?"

"I don't know. I don't really know. I fell." She pointed to where the land dropped away sharply into a deep ravine. "I was there, over there and I was okay but…"

"But what?"

"Well then I wasn't, I was rolling in the muck and feeling stupid."

"Why is your jacket here?"

She shrugged at him. "It's a bit long and oh, it's a girl thing. Come on let's get back to the car. You look awful. I hope you haven't buggered up that leg."

"You look a bit rough yourself and you're filthy." They wrapped their arms around each other and with Simon hopping and leaning on her they started back towards the sheep trail, picking up his crutches as they passed.

Once back at the car, Gloria stripped off her trousers. "I'm not getting all this mud on the seat."

"Oh right." Simon glanced down at his own clothes.

"Hang on." She reached into the back and dragged over a folded picnic rug. "Here, sit on this, I can throw it in the washing machine when we get back."

"Hey look."

"What?"

"Get your glasses. Isn't that Lily? She wasn't in the house after all. Isn't that her? See coming down that sheep track?"

"Where? I can't see. Oh, hang on. In the green jacket, yes, yes, I think that's her. Daft bitch, out in this weather."

"Yeah, and that other car is going. Hang on. No." As they watched they saw the tall figure of Patrick Coleman raise a hand to his wife. She walked towards him and they had a short conversation. He patted her on the shoulder before she passed through the yard and into the house. Then the two men went to the back of the green car, opened the hatch and Patrick reached in, taking out a pile of white boxes. They carried them between them to the steps and then went back for more. After shaking hands with the stranger, he turned towards his home balancing the second load before him. He never once looked back as the green car drew into the yard, swung through the space and then headed back down the narrow drive and onto the main thoroughfare and onward in the direction of Ramstone.

Gloria and Simon lowered their glasses, glanced at each other and shrugged.

"Well, I have no idea whether what we just saw meant anything" – Gloria was already reaching for the ignition key as she spoke – "and to be honest, I don't care. I need a shower and some clean clothes. I've had enough of this crap, I really have." And with that she pulled slowly away from the rough ground, onto the dirt track and ultimately onto the road behind the car that had just left the farm.

She drove in silence for a while and Simon, struggling with the ache in his ankle leaned his head back against the headrest and closed his eyes. After a while she glanced across at him. "Simon?"

"Hmm."

"Would you think I was mad if I said that I thought I was pushed into that hole?" His eyes shot open as he turned to look at her.

"Pushed?"

"Well, I've been going over it and over it in my head and I just have this feeling. I was fine, not wobbly or anything. Okay, it was a bit close to the edge, but I was more bothered about, you know, getting down behind the bushes to be honest. It's just that it was all so sudden. I was about to put my jacket back on, you see I was steady, on my feet, standing up and then… oh, I don't know, it sounds stupid… take no notice. I'm just feeling embarrassed that's all. It shouldn't have happened, I'm not normally so clumsy and it was so fast, I think it's befuddled me a bit. One minute fine and then the next rolling into the muck. That's how accidents happen though isn't it? A moment's inattention. No, take no notice."

They pulled into the drive and she helped him to struggle back into the house. "I'm going into the shower."

"Yeah. I'm going to take a couple of those painkillers and sit here for a bit. It's okay, I'll take these dirty things off first." As he began to pull off his wet trousers the phone twittered and he dragged it from his pocket.

"Ah, well, at last some good news. We can go and see Colin next week on Friday. Charlie says he doesn't have many visitors and he's already spoken to him. Huh, probably an illegal mobile, otherwise that's pretty darned quick. Anyway, good. At least that's one thing that's gone right. Are you okay, Gloria, only you look a bit shaky?"

"I'm fine. It's just the fall you know, it's left me a bit wobbly. Anyway, you owe me a drink later, down at The Oak. You promised. Really, I'm fine." She went through to the bathroom and stood in front of the steamy mirror. There were bruises showing on her legs and her side and she knew that she'd be sore and achy later.

She muttered to her reflection, "You silly mare, rolling about in the mud at your age, and don't be ridiculous, of course nobody pushed you." She stared for a moment longer and then shook her head and turned away.

Chapter 51

Gloria was wrapped in her dressing gown and sitting on the settee with her laptop across her knees. "The funeral will be a week on Wednesday. No flowers but a donation to an animal sanctuary, well I'll do that. Half of me wants to go and then part of me doesn't because it's going to be so awful. They are always awful when it's somebody young. I know they try and say it's a celebration of life and they play pop music and wear bright clothes, but it's all pretend, it's still horrible."

"We can go if you like. In fact, if we do maybe some of her other friends will be there, somebody else who might know her and about her 'boyfriend'."

"No, no I'm not doing that. I'm not going to use her funeral as an excuse to try and find out more about this stupid business." Simon held up his hands.

"Okay, okay. Sorry."

"Oh, take no notice. I'm just feeling really shaken up and I wish we'd never got involved in all this stuff. Then I think about her and about Colin Bliss's wife and I want to find out what it's all about and have it sorted. I'm not cut out for this. I'm a hotelier, well actually I'm just a B&B landlady with aspirations. Oh sod it." She stood quickly and crossed the room to the cabinet. "I'm having a bloody drink, I don't care if it's early and I don't care if you disapprove. I'm having a sodding drink. I don't want to go to the pub, I want to stay in where I'm safe and warm and I don't have to look at other people."

"Gloria?"

"What?"

"Pour me a whisky, would you? A nice big one." She handed him the glass and he sipped at it for a moment. "So, you're coming with me, to see Colin?"

"Yup."

"Thanks. I have no idea what his reaction is going to be."

"No, of course you don't. Ah there's your mobile again."

"Hello, Mr Clegg?"

"Aye, it's me lad. I'm not catching you at a bad time, am I?"

"No, it's fine. What can I do for you?"

"I just wanted to let you know, there's been a development this end."

"Oh, right."

"Yes" – the old man cleared his throat – "our Maureen's taken a turn for the worse. They've got her in hospital. She's poorly. Some sort of complication. Listen lad, I don't think we have much time. I can't talk. I can't say any more." And with that he disconnected.

Simon turned to Gloria and shook his head. "Well, that's not good. Maureen Bliss is in a bad way apparently. After all this, we might run out of time anyway. Bugger." He thumped his hand down hard on the desk rattling the pen pots and scattering his index cards on the floor. "No, this can't happen. Not after all this. What's the point if it's too late for them?"

"You said yourself it has become about more than them. It's about Fiona as well now isn't it, and about Fuzz and what happened to him and well… just about wrongdoing and truth."

"What happened to the B&B landlady with aspirations of a few minutes ago?"

"Oh sod off, Simon, and pick those cards up off the floor. We need to move things along, I'm not going to let us fail. If Colin Bliss is innocent, he's coming home and he's coming home in time to see his wife."

"Waiting to see him is going to be frustrating, isn't it? That seems ages away. There must be something we can do in the meantime?"

"We'll go to the funeral. I'm taking that phone call as a sign. What do you reckon was in the boxes, Simon? The ones at the farm?"

"Shit I don't know. Some sheep stuff probably or dishcloths, chocolate, wine, could have been anything."

Gloria nodded slowly. "Yes, but it's odd about that car being there, isn't it? The one from the vets. You see that's another link between Fiona and the farm. A tenuous one I'll grant you, I know I didn't believe it at first, but what are the chances?"

"Tomorrow we'll go back and see if it's in the car park again. We can try and find out who it belongs to, go inside and speak to the receptionists. We can pretend we want to know about the arrangements for the funeral."

"Okay. I can't think of anything else right now so why not."

Gloria didn't sound convinced, so he turned to her, looked her in the eyes.

"You know, after what Beryl Clegg said to me, about all marriages not being like theirs…?"

"Yes."

"Well since then this has been more about Charlie to be honest, you know more than Colin. More about letting him feel that he did his best for his sister. If at the end of the day Maureen and Colin had problems, well it changes things a bit, doesn't it?"

"I suppose. Does it matter really though?"

"Not to me, not anymore. I can't say I'm driven, not like I was with my own stuff, of course not, it would be silly to expect it but I am hooked. I need to sort this out, one way or the other I really need to get to the bottom of it. You know, when I thought about doing this stuff it was a bit of a vague idea, I didn't realise how it would affect me. I am beginning to see why someone would do this and in spite of everything..." He tapped the hard plastic encasing his ankle, "Yes, in spite of everything I really want to carry on, and I really want to succeed and I never thought I'd feel like this about anything again."

Chapter 52

The small gate rattled and Gloria lifted the curtain at the bay window. "Oh, look out, here comes Fuzz. What is it with that boy? He should be out looking for work or back at college. Can you let him in while I go and get some clothes on?"

"Hello, Fuzz, what are you doing here?"

"I was passing."

"Oh right. None of your mates about then?"

"Aye, they're down in the shops, hanging around and that. I was a bit bored to be honest. Can I come in for a bit?"

"Come on."

"I thought maybe Mrs Bartlett wanted the grass cutting or sommat?"

"Oh, I don't think so, Fuzz, we don't normally cut the grass at this time of year and apart from that, she's having some people in, to do the place up a bit you know."

"Aye well, it needs it."

"Hey cheeky. Anyway, sit down for a minute."

"What have you been doing? Have you found out any more about that bloke, that Bliss bloke?" Simon hesitated for a moment. Gloria was right, they shouldn't let the boy become involved, he had to be careful what he said.

"No, not really. We did spend some time at the farm. Nothing happening as far as we could see. Well, Gloria fell but she's okay. There was someone making a delivery. We thought it might be from the vets, but that was all."

"Oh aye, them boxes." Gloria walked into the room as Fuzz made the statement and for a moment there was a tense silence.

"So, you've seen them?"

"White boxes, about the size of the ones that crisps and stuff come in?"

"Yes, that's it. A bloke in a green Peugeot brought them. We thought he might be a vet."

"Oh aye."

"You've seen it?"

The boy nodded.

"Don't think he's a vet though, he never looks at the sheep or nothing. He comes nearly every week. Sometimes it's just one box sometimes it's more, sometimes other cars come, more boxes. Then vans come and pick them up. Sometimes it's one of Cleggs."

"What. Clegg's Haulage?"

"Aye, one of the little vans, not the big trucks."

"How often have you seen them?"

"Oh, loads of times." Simon, rubbed his hands over his face, tried to stay calm, keep his voice even and not get the boy excited.

"I wonder what's in them?"

"Dunno, that farmer bloke keeps them in the house, then the van comes and takes them away. Same drivers every time, Clegg's is a big fat lad with a daft beard. Sometimes he brings boxes an all. Takes them in, brings them out. It's like bloody Tesco. It's like I told you, he must do some sort of business there."

"Ah well." Gloria had joined them, sitting on the settee. Simon could feel the tension in her body and let her take the lead as she changed the subject. "Will you go to Fiona Carpenter's funeral, Fuzz?"

"Nah, I shouldn't think so. I didn't know her really. Shame she fell off that cliff and that but – nah. Funny though, isn't it? Funny they're both dead now. Fiona and Melanie, them being best mates and all."

They gave him snacks and drinks. They let him play a computer game on the laptop, and all the time he was with them Gloria and Simon were itching for him to leave. They wanted to discuss his casual revelation but he was at a loose end and angling for dinner.

"Gran's out tonight, got to see to myself. Probably go to the chippy."

"Right, nice. Not got anything planned for later then?" Simon asked.

"Not really, might meet Jazzer and play pool, might not. If that driver's there, do you want me to ask him about them boxes?"

"No! Sorry, sorry – didn't mean to shout. Frog in my throat. Do you see him often then, the driver?"

"Not often, but now and then. He's casual for Clegg's not one of the full-time blokes. He's not a proper truck driver, just a van driver really. I reckon he goes abroad though, sometimes he has cheap ciggies."

Eventually he left, Simon had promised to go with him one night to the pool hall. He had the impression that he was some sort of trophy for Fuzz to parade before his friends and though that rankled a little, it was only making the promise that eventually persuaded the boy to go. "Will ya come tonight then?"

"No, I don't think so. My leg's a bit sore tonight but one night soon I will. We'll arrange it."

"Sick. Well I'll go then. I'll see ya." And he'd gone, probably to meet his associates and brag about his friendship with the infamous Tommy Webb, for Simon knew that while he stayed in the area, he would always be Tommy Webb to a lot of people.

Simon closed the door behind him and stood leaning against the wood as Gloria walked out into the hall. "Okay. So, does this mean anything? It's just Fuzz, it's just hearsay. Does it tell us anything at all?"

"Well, what is one of Clegg's vans doing up at the farm and Charlie never mentioning it to you?" She wondered. "Although maybe he doesn't see any connection between Colin's situation and High Hill, after all, why should he?"

"Do you think it's possible he doesn't know? Beryl Clegg is involved in the business. According to the website she's a director. I wonder how hands-on she is. He always speaks as though she's a housewife but having met her, I don't really see it. Let's have another look at the Clegg's Haulage site. See if that tells us anything."

"It might be wishful thinking, it probably is but I feel something about this, it feels important."

* * *

For a while they clicked and surfed and scrolled and eventually Simon broke the silence. "Beryl is a director but I can't see anything that puts her in the office regularly or anything."

"No, me neither. Simon, look at this though, did you know about this?"

"What?" He leaned across to where Gloria pointed to a list on the web page. "Maureen Bliss, she's a logistics manager."

"Well, I suppose it makes sense, she is part of the family after all."

"Yes, but it's something else that we didn't know, isn't it? Oh, right, open the social page."

"Okay. Yep, got it."

"Now go to that article about the new depot. The one they opened four years ago."

"Yes."

"Look in the background. Can you see? At the table on the far right."

"Oh, it's him, isn't it? It's the bloke from the farm. The bloke from the farm at a social event with Clegg's Haulage, and sitting at the same table it says Colin Bliss, so that's him. He changed between when this was taken and the pictures that were in the paper, didn't he? Aged a bit, but it's him alright."

Chapter 53

Neither of them slept well. Simon's leg was paying him back for the abuse earlier and as he tossed and turned, he knew he was disturbing her. At four in the morning she got up and made them both a drink of hot chocolate and they sat in the darkened chill of the lounge.

"Do you think we're ever going to get to the bottom of this, Simon? It all just keeps going round and round in my head and, although I know there's something bad going on, I just can't get a handle on it."

"I know, I've gone through the index cards but to be honest they don't really help, it's just words. Bloody Fuzz has given us more help than anything."

"What do you reckon about those boxes? Stolen goods? But what? What do you pinch from a vet?"

"Well, we don't know that it is the vets, though we'll go again later today and see if that car is there. What would you pinch? I don't know, nothing alive obviously. Shit."

"What?"

"God, it's so obvious." He threw his hands in the air as he spoke.

"What, what?"

"Drugs. Bloody drugs."

"How do you mean?"

"Well, they have drugs don't they, so isn't that it? Isn't that just about the only thing that you would pinch from a vet's?"

"Well, maybe, but they don't have drugs like cocaine do they, not the sort of drugs you sell on the street? Apart from that though surely they wouldn't have that many, not in that place. It's not like some huge hospital."

"No, no but wait. Not the vets themselves but the company that supplies them?"

"Oh come on, that's not going to happen, is it? I mean there must be all sorts of checks and double checks. It's a good idea but I just don't see it."

He grabbed her hand. "It's where half the trouble is these days isn't it? Half the crime that you hear about is connected to drugs."

"Yes, but heroin, cocaine, smack, street drugs like E. Not pills for sick dogs."

"Oh, well you've probably got a point, but it was an idea. Anyway, I'm going back to bed, are you ready?"

"Well, I could be. Still not that tired though."

"It's warmer in bed. I can think of a couple of ways to relax."

With an arm around her shoulder for support he hopped back into the bedroom. Once in bed, wrapped in her arms, the injury to his leg didn't bother him very much at all.

* * *

The next morning, Simon took a couple of his painkillers and, as he stood with the two white oblongs in his hand, he remembered the conversation of the night before. On his way to the easy access shower in the disabled room he stopped at his desk and wrote the word DRUGS in the middle of one of his index cards. Gloria had some valid points but the idea had taken hold and wouldn't be shaken free.

By the time he came back into her living area, Gloria was sitting at the table opening her mail. "He comes early, the postie."

"Yes, well we are a business address so we still get the first delivery. I was just looking at this and wondering what to do." She held up the bundle of paper. "It's from the garage, a report on the car, he's done a good job, taken pictures even. He doesn't say it was deliberate but he does insist that he has never been aware of a bleed nipple shaking loose and that the car was serviced recently and, well I guess he's covering his own backside but he insists that it must have been okay at that time."

"Do you want to go to the police with it? It's what he said you should do."

"Yes, but he doesn't know what we've been doing. He just thought it was some sort of nasty vandalism. In fact, he put a little hand-written note in saying that if it was him, he'd be locking the car up at night. He has a point. I'm going to do that in future."

"I suppose I should ring my insurance company. I still haven't had anything back from them about my car. I'll do that after breakfast. Are you up for driving out to see if that car is at the vets?"

"Yes, we've nothing else on. I'm still undecided about going to that funeral. How do you feel?"

"I don't want to go really. We won't know anyone and as you say it'll be horrible. I wasn't allowed to go to Sandie's, I don't know how I'd cope to be honest."

"Okay. I don't need much persuading to give it a miss. I've made the donation though."

* * *

"I'm off down to the shops, Simon, are you coming? Oh, sorry, I didn't see you were on the phone."

"I'm sixth in the queue. I'm getting pretty brassed off to be honest. It's taken forever to get this far, press this button and then the other button, I swear they just want you to give up. I'll give it a bit longer."

"Right. Should be back soon."

The constant reassurance that his call was important didn't help with the wait. The crackling recording of some vaguely recognisable tune irritated him and the advertising of their other services almost had him throwing his phone across the room, but in the end he was number one in the queue. The announcement made him irrationally smug. At last the agent asked him how she could help, he had several suggestions regarding music and adverts but knew it would be a bad idea to start on the wrong foot. "I have my claim number."

"Thank you, if you could just read that out to me? Okay. Can you just confirm your address for me?" He did. "And your contact number? Excellent. I have your record here, Mr Fulton. Your claim is being processed."

"Yes, good. That's good. I just wondered if there was a report or anything?"

"Your car has been written off."

"Yes, well, it was in pieces so that's not a surprise but what about the cause?"

"Sorry?"

"Of the accident. Will I be getting a report about the cause of the accident?"

"Well, according to the records your car was overturned and the damage was extensive."

"Yes, well I know that, of course but wasn't someone going to look at it? Try to find out why? The police said they'd get back to me about it and I haven't heard anything."

"We haven't been asked to do any further investigation, Mr Fulton. Just one moment." Again, his ears were scratched by the sound of violins as his blood pressure rose and he felt the muscles in the back of his neck and his shoulders begin to tense. "Hello, Mr Fulton?"

"Yes."

"I've spoken to my supervisor and according to our records your claim is being processed. There is no request for further investigation as far as we can see, Mr Fulton."

He sighed and he knew she had heard him. "Do you have a crime number?"

"A crime number?"

"Yes, did the police give you a crime number?"

"Well, no. Why would they do that?"

"Usually when a car is stolen there is a crime number. If it was stolen and you don't have one, I'll have to put a stop on the claim."

"It wasn't stolen."

"Oh."

"Why did you think it was stolen?"

"As you were querying the cause of the accident, I assumed that you weren't present."

"I was present, of course I was present. I was driving."

"Oh. But you don't know the cause of the accident? I'm sorry I don't understand, Mr Fulton."

"Okay. Okay look, can you tell me where the car is now?"

"It's been written off, Mr Fulton. I did already tell you that."

"Yes, I know. Sorry, we're not quite on the same wavelength here but can you just tell me where the car is now? I would like to have a mechanic look at it."

"Oh, that's not possible. The car will have been scrapped."

"Okay but where is it? Look, I just want to have someone look at my car."

"Well, the thing is, Mr Fulton, technically it is no longer your car. We are paying you for it and therefore it no longer belongs to you. Apart from that I don't have the information anyway. It will have been taken away. It's probably already been crushed."

"Great. Absolutely great. Well, thanks for that."

"Is there anything else I can help you with today?" He couldn't speak, it was a struggle to disconnect the call without any further comment.

When Gloria arrived back from the shops he was still hobbling up and down the lounge using one crutch and muttering to himself. She took one look, mumbled the word *insurance* and slipped into the kitchen quietly to put away her shopping.

Chapter 54

They arrived at the veterinary surgery later than planned and the car park was almost full. There were several cars with dog cages in the back and now and then a patient would be carried out and stowed away in the rear seat, or even plopped on the passenger seat beside the driver. Almost all the owners were muttering to their pets and many of them stuck hands inside the cages to tickle ears and stroke velvety noses.

"We always had dogs when I was a kid. My dad still has one now. It's big business though, isn't it? Nobody seems to want scrappy mongrels, they're all a bit fancy."

"Yeah. We never had any, I think my mum had enough on her plate with Dad and Peter without adding to the work. Anyway, that car's not here, is it? It was a bit too much to hope for I suppose."

"No, where was it parked, can you remember?"

"Oh, let's see. I was there in the corner and it was opposite, so it was over by the hedge in one of those spaces, maybe the second one along."

"Not a vet then."

"How do you know?"

"Well, if you look there, the spaces in front of the doors are reserved. They have their car registration numbers on those little posts and the names of the vets. MRCVS, that's a vet, isn't it?"

"Right. It was early though, wasn't it? There weren't any patients."

"One came in just after me. A woman with a cat."

"Yes, I remember that. She walked though. I saw her come down the road. There were a couple of cars by the door and two in the far corner but I saw a woman in uniform get out of one of those so again, probably staff."

"Huh, well it's information but I don't know what it tells us really."

"It's the same day, isn't it?" Gloria glanced at the day and date display on her watch.

"How do you mean?"

"Was it a Wednesday when we came before?"

"Yeah, surely it was. Ah, maybe not, I think it was Tuesday. Hmm, good point, should have thought of that before now I suppose. We'll hang about for a bit. Is that alright?" Gloria shrugged in answer and began to fiddle with her phone.

After a dreary hour, it appeared that the surgery time was coming to a close and the forecourt was emptying with no more cars filling up the spaces. "I reckon we're wasting our time, aren't we?" Simon had been struggling to keep his eyes open, the sun was warm through the window and the soft sounds from outside had lulled him. Gloria had had the forethought to bring her book with her but even then he had seen her head nodding a couple of times and she had jerked awake and glanced around guiltily. "We're both a bit jiggered after last night. Tell you what, there's a café down the road, let's go and have some coffee and decide what to do next, eh?"

"Yeah, why not. This feels daft to be honest and we've been getting some funny looks from the customers."

"Patients and clients, I think."

"Oh right. Well whatever, some of them have been peering at us. I don't think we're very good at surveillance, are we?"

"No, probably not." With a little laugh she reached and started the car, pulled forward and turned towards the main road. "Shit."

"What?"

"Well, bugger me."

"What?"

"Look, look – just pulling in." She lifted a hand from the wheel and pointed through the windscreen.

"Oh. Right, now what shall we do?"

"Well, it's going to look bloody odd if I park again. We'll carry on and I'll see if I can find a place further down the road. We won't be able to see though, will we? I'll tell you what. You get out and sit in that bus stop."

"Oh, great idea, because I'm really inconspicuous aren't I, with these bloody things." He waggled the crutches.

"Well, I can't do both, Simon, I can't drive the car and watch the car park. Get out. Go on, go and pretend to be waiting for a bus."

"Then what?"

"I'll try and get somewhere so that I can see you, wave when he leaves, then I'll pick you up."

"This is stupid."

"Yeah, well so was crashing your car and buggering up your leg."

"Oh right, thanks for that."

Once out of sight of the car park, he opened the door and huffed and puffed as he made a performance of clambering out and as she pulled away, he crossed to the bus shelter on the opposite corner. He glanced across as he passed and watched the man they had last seen at High Hill Farm collect a few boxes and his briefcase and enter the surgery by the rear door.

As Simon approached the bus stop an elderly woman vacated one of the flip-down seats. "Here you are love, you sit here." His pride wanted to refuse but the crutches rubbing at his arms and the ache in his injured ankle forced him into smiling acceptance. She nodded towards the timetable, "I'm waiting for the number eight. It won't be long." He smiled at her again.

"Thanks, thanks a lot." He knew that a couple of the others had seen him struggle from Gloria's car and they were staring at him in bewilderment. He glanced up and down the road and tried for all the world to appear to be watching for a bus. He felt ridiculous.

Chapter 55

Three buses came and went, each time the passengers waiting in the queue turned to him, made gestures *'are you getting this one'*, and each time he shook his head and they shrugged or smiled or simply climbed aboard and left him sitting there watching the car park and feeling like a fool.

Half an hour he waited. Gloria had found a space to park and he watched the manoeuvre as she turned so she could see him where he sat. Twice more she moved as spaces closer to the corner were vacated, so that now he could clearly make out her face and her hand as she raised it to wave at him. He didn't wave back, there were people at the stop who already thought there was something odd going on.

The buses obscured his view of the car park and so he didn't see his quarry emerge from the back door of the surgery. If he hadn't spent time packing the boot of his car, they may have missed him completely. Simon stood and raised a hand, the headlights of Gloria's car flashed in acknowledgement and by the time she drew up at the bus stop the green Peugeot was turning into the flow of traffic on the main road.

"That was bloody embarrassing."

"Why?"

"Well, all those women and old blokes wanting to help me get on the bus and giving me odd looks when I didn't move."

"Well, you'll never see any of them again probably, don't worry about it."

"Yeah, thanks."

"Hey, I'm helping you remember, this isn't my idea. I wasn't the one who took this on. I could be at home… doing stuff."

"Yeah. Sorry, it's just all so frustrating, isn't it? I didn't have any idea. When you see it on the TV, it's not like this. I just feel as though we're messing about and getting nowhere."

"I know. Come on, let's stop niggling at each other. We're both tired. If there was nothing behind all this none of the scary stuff would have happened, would it? Mind you I have to say, I'm coming round to thinking that you have to put some sort of limit on it."

"How do you mean?"

"Well, you can't just go on and on, can you? Either we are going to find out what it's all about or we're not. When are you going to call it a day?"

"I hadn't thought… I just thought… well I suppose I just thought that I would find out what had happened and that would be it. I never imagined just calling it off."

"Well, maybe you should give it some thought. I mean are you just going to go on until poor Maureen dies? God, that sounds awful but..." She shrugged and glanced at him. He had no answer for her and she felt a pang of guilt as he began to nibble at his thumb nail, the habit resurfacing whenever he was under stress.

The green car left the town centre and followed the route that would take him back to the farm. Simon hadn't spoken and it was Gloria who broke the awkward silence. "So, what will we do, just drive on past? It's obvious where he's going."

"But I want to know what's in those boxes, Gloria."

"Listen, take my phone. Have a look on Google, see if you can find that logo, the one on the back of his car. Maybe if we know just what he is it'll give us a clue. Do you know how to do it on a smart phone?" He flashed an irritated look at her.

"I reckon I can possibly work it out thanks."

"Oh okay, sorry."

"No, it's me. I'm feeling irritated and frustrated. Listen, what do you reckon? I think he's a rep of some sort. It seems to me that there could easily be a connection there. Colin Bliss is a rep, well he was. What was the name of that company he worked for?"

"I'm not sure you ever told me to be honest."

"I'll Google pharmaceuticals. Shit there's millions."

"Whittle it down. Put in Yorkshire."

"Yeah, I'm doing it. You just watch the car."

"Yes sir."

"Sorry."

"It's here. I've got it – yes." he waved the phone in the air. "Stamforths. It's the same company, I remember now."

"Oh right, at last something coming together. God knows what *It* is but it's coming together. So, what do you want to do?"

"Can you pull up onto that road again, where we were watching before? I suppose we can guess what's going to happen but let's just see."

They didn't bother with the binoculars. Simon left his crutches in the car and they moved to the front to lean against the bonnet staring down, across the road and up to the house and yard opposite. The Peugeot pulled into the same spot as it had on the previous occasion. They heard the horn sound just once.

"The Land Rover isn't there. Thank heavens that bloody woman isn't around."

"Yeah. Doesn't look as though there's anyone home, does it?"

"Well it does all look a bit quiet. I wonder what he'll do?"

"Oh sod it."

"What. What's matter?"

"Down there look, behind the wall. It's only bloody Fuzz, can you see?"

"Oh, that's not good." Gloria muttered quietly, "Stay down, Fuzz, stay down."

"He's been doing this a long time. He's always messing about watching them. He'll be okay." As Simon lay a comforting hand on her shoulder they heard the low rumble, he felt her stiffen. They knew before they turned what they would see but still she gasped as the battered roof of the old Land Rover appeared over the rise behind them.

Chapter 56

"Simon!" Gloria reached out and grabbed at his hand.

It was coming at them quickly, the window was down and they could see the barrel of the rifle jumping against the old door as the car rocked and bounced over the rough ground. The woman inside steered with one hand, oblivious to ruts and hollows as she hurtled forwards.

"Get in the car!" Simon pushed Gloria away from him back towards the driver's door. "Get in the bloody car, Gloria!" But she reached out to him again, trying to pull him with her and her foot caught in a dip in the ground. She fell to her knees with a cry. Simon moved towards her, struggling clumsily on his injured leg. The Land Rover was almost upon them now and Lily fired once. She hadn't bothered trying to aim, knowing it was pointless, but just shot wildly in their direction, bringing clods of earth flying into the air to shutter against the side of their car. "Underneath, get underneath!" Simon pushed out and tried to slide himself and Gloria into the shelter of the car but she was panicked and fought against him. Instinctively she rolled away from the approaching threat and stood and began a crouching run from the meagre protection he had tried to win for her. "No, no, Gloria, come back!" Fear and panic deafened her to his shouts and she ran on, the woman fired again. Simon was struggling to his feet but ducked for cover as the shower of mud and stones flew upwards, stinging his face and clattering against the windscreen. "Gloria. No!"

Before he managed to right himself the four-wheel drive had turned and was in pursuit, they were heading for the clump of little bushes and the steep drop beyond. He tried to follow but encumbered by the plastic boot and shocked by the spear of agony from his injury with each step, he was able only to hobble and hop across the rapidly increasing gap between them. He saw her fall. He yelled out as she threw up her arms in a desperate attempt at salvation and he heard the rattle of rocks and debris follow her down the crevasse. The Land Rover turned and came back for him. It didn't last long, he couldn't run, he heard the crack of the rifle and threw himself to the ground, his head bounced just once on the hidden rock and there was a moment of searing pain before the darkness descended.

* * *

He could hear her sobbing quietly, even before he opened his eyes he was aware of it. Simon tried to move. The discomfort he had felt wasn't simply the result of his awkward position. His hands were tied, his arms stretched painfully upwards from where he lay on the floor and there was a vicious burning in the lower part of his leg. The boot had gone; he could tell immediately that his ankle was no longer supported and immobilised. He tried to keep it upright and still but it wasn't possible, it was twisted and constantly flopped to the side causing shards of pain that took his breath away. He tried to speak but his tongue was thick and all that came out was a gargled sound. He swallowed and tried again. "Glor…" The sobbing stopped.

"Simon?" All he could manage in response was a grunt. The world spun when he tried to move his head and nausea overwhelmed him, cold sweat broke out on his brow as the bile rose into his throat. He groaned again.

"Simon?"

Gloria's voice was mumbled and indistinct and the place they were in was dim and cold. There was sticky residue beside his eyes when he blinked and he assumed it was dried blood. "Are you hurt?" His voice sounded strange inside his own head but he had managed to form words.

"Yes."

"Bad?"

"I don't know. It hurts to move, in my side. I thought you were dead. I can't see, there's a thing over my head. A bag or something." The crying began again.

"Don't, don't cry. I'm okay. We're okay."

"Are you hurt?"

"Yes, but I don't know how much. Shit my head's sore." He groaned again as he moved his foot. "Bloody hell."

"What?"

"It's okay, I'm okay, I think. My ankle, just my ankle, and my head, and my arms." He gave an ironic laugh. "Where are we, do you know?"

"The farm. She brought us to the farm. She stuck this thing over my head while I was still groggy, dragged me up from the hollow, and pushed me in the car. She's bloody strong, like a wrestler or something. But I'm pretty sure that's where we are. Up some stairs. I think the men carried you."

"But there weren't any men."

"They came after, they were chasing her, blowing the horn and careering across the moor. They stopped her." She began to cry in earnest now. "They stopped her." She sobbed.

"What do you mean, they stopped her?"

"She was going to shoot you. She was just going to shoot you where you lay. They stopped her." Simon couldn't speak, his throat was dry and he felt the pounding in his chest echo through his body. Gloria was struggling to calm herself, the crying had quieted and been replaced by the occasional sniffle and her ragged breathing.

"Well, she didn't, did she? Shoot me I mean, so we're okay."

"I thought you were dead. They were puffing and complaining at each other. They were all really angry; she

was screeching at them. I was terrified, and I couldn't see.
I've never been so frightened, ever."

"I'm sorry, Gloria."

She began to cry again.

"I'm really scared, Simon. Are they going to kill us?
They were furious. I think they'll kill us."

"No, no of course they won't. No."

Chapter 57

"Simon, can you hear me? Simon say something. I can't
see you. Say something please?"

"It's okay, we're okay. Just hold on."

"What are you doing, are you alright?"

"I think so, yes, I'm just trying to sit up. I'll be okay in a
minute. Just try and keep calm, love. Just breathe and stay
calm. It's going to be fine. I'm going to get us out of here I
promise you, and then we'll go to the police. We'll hand it
all over to them. Okay?"

She sniffed. "How, how are you going to get us out?
They've got guns. That woman's mad. We can't get out."

"Are your hands tied?"

"Yes, I can't move them, there's something holding
them together." He heard the rattle of metal as she shook
her arms. "I can't get up, I can't move, they tied my feet,
they tied me up and there's this sack, it's horrible, it stinks
and I keep getting it in my mouth."

"Just try and take little breaths. Keep calm, just stay
still, that'll help. It's going to be fine, don't worry, I'll sort
it."

"What the hell is this? What have we done?"

"I don't know but don't panic, okay, I'm sitting up and
I can see you. The sack round your head isn't fastened or

anything. It's just tight over your shoulders. Maybe you could roll it up, if you rub your back against the wall it might slide up."

"I can't. I can't sodding roll it up, my side hurts when I move. I'm hurt, Simon, and they're going to kill us."

"No, they won't, I promise you they won't. I'm not far away from you. We're just fastened to some metal containers. You should be able to move your feet, you can bend your knees, can't you?"

"Yes, I can do that. Stop it, stop whatever it is you're doing, stop it. You're making too much noise. They'll hear you, they'll come back."

"I was just seeing what's going on with this chain, it's just fastened with a padlock and it slides up and down a bit. This thing I'm fastened to, it's one of those trolleys they use in warehouses and stuff. It's full of boxes. There are wheels on the bottom. I might be able to drag it."

"Wheels – just roll it then, that won't make any noise?"

"No, no they're locked aren't they, I can't reach the brake, I've been trying to but it's down the other end from me. I'll have to try and pull it. I'm worried that it might fall though and land on you, I need to slide it away a bit. Ah. Shit, shit, shit."

"What, what's happened?"

"It's okay, I banged my ankle but it's okay. Right, I'm going to do this." Simon gritted his teeth against the pain and bracing with the heel of his good foot and the injured one as much as he could bear, gripping the steel bars of the goods cage as high as he could reach, he rocked it gently pulling it from side to side. His arm muscles burned with the strain of dragging and easing it across the bare boards and sweat ran down his face stinging at the wound on the side of his head, but it moved, it jerked and jinked but it moved slowly away from the wall. Eventually, he was far enough from Gloria to risk more vigorous movement. "Look, this is going to make a hell of a noise, but if they were in the house they would have come by now, I think.

Get ready." He gripped the bars, his hands as wide apart as they would go. One side at a time he jerked and yanked it, left to right, left to right. After just a few feet his muscles were screaming, his injured leg throbbed sickeningly. He used the heel of his good leg to push against the floor, but his wounded ankle wagged in the air and he had to stop after every few inches to rest and get his breath. He was aware of Gloria whimpering in the corner but he blanked the sound of her fear and continued to rock, swaying now, buttock to buttock, side to side, pulling and jerking backwards with his arms, his hands locked around the bars. The thing caught on a board that was standing proud and then broke free suddenly. He bit back the yowl of pain as it smashed against his legs. Inch by inch he fought the thing across the room until, panting, tears of pain blurring his vision, he was close enough to touch her with his foot.

Her voice came to him in a whisper. "Are you okay?"

"I need a minute."

For a while there was only the sound of him gasping for breath, coughing, groaning and then he pushed himself back until he was sitting almost upright against the wall.

"Can you lean towards me do you think? Be careful though. If you've cracked your ribs you don't want to make it worse. Lean this way, to your right. Bend your head down as low as you can bear. That's it, that's it. Okay."

He reached and stretched and gripped at the top of the dirty sack with his teeth. Gloria was panting with the effort, the fabric pulsing in and out against her face, but once she felt the bag begin to move, she wriggled, huffing with pain, but it shifted and gave them heart.

"Hang on, give me a second." Simon had hated to do it but needed to pull back to catch his breath. He could hear her gulping back sobs and it tore at his heart. "Right, this time." She leaned down as far as she was able and he grabbed it again. As soon as it was above her shoulders it slid easily away from her and, as she shook it clear he opened his mouth and let it fall into a heap beside him. He was horrified at her appearance. Her face was bruised and grazed, the wounds livid against her pale skin and her eyes were shocked and wide with fright, but once she sat back against the wall she managed to speak to him. "Bloody hell. That was horrible." She looked around, shook her hands and jangled the chain that was holding her to the trolley full of boxes. "They don't look very strong; can't we just break them?"

"I reckon not, they're not very thick but they're made to be tough. All the joints are welded so we can't shake anything free on there. The bases are really thick so they don't tip over, they're hefty bloody things. I think we've got more chance trying to get the chains or padlocks loose."

She jerked at her wrists. "Ow, ow, ow – bugger. That was stupid." Her voice was stronger now that the sack had been removed and she could see him. "I just don't see how we can get these loose, they're looped round and round and the bloody lock is threaded through the links. What the hell are we going to do?"

* * *

"Mrs Bartlett, Simon. It's Fuzz. I'm outside the window, are you okay?"

"Fuzz!"

"I thought you guys were dead."

"We're okay, we're stuck though. Fuzz, can you call the police? We need help here."

"I still haven't got a new phone. My gran said I have to wait till she gets her pension. I could go down to the pub but it'll take ages and I don't know how long they'll be gone."

"Gone?"

"Yes, that daft woman went off in the Land Rover, screaming and yelling and the blokes went off after her in the green car."

"Where are you now?"

"I'm on the roof of the outhouse. I've been knocking on all the windows and then I heard the racket you were making. What are you doing?"

"We're chained up. Do you think you can get into the house, Fuzz?"

"I'll try. If they come back, I'll go and get the police but I'll have to run back down the road. It'll take me a bit."

"Well, see if you can get in first."

"Hang on."

"No, no." Gloria was shaking her head. "No, run away, Fuzz, just get away. That woman's got a gun. Just go while you have chance."

"It's alright, Mrs Bartlett, don't panic. I'll come in and get ya." And he was gone.

Chapter 58

They sat in the quiet, waiting, listening. Simon could hear Gloria swallow now and then and recognised the same tension in her that had his body taut and his ears straining for the sound of footsteps, but dreading the sound of a car. After what seemed a lifetime, Gloria spoke. "I can't hear him. He's not going to get in. I hope he's just gone."

"No, he won't leave us. He'll try and get in and then even if he can't he's going to call the police. It's okay, he knows we're here. We're going to be fine now."

"Shut up, Simon, listen, I can hear someone. What if it's not him? What if they've caught him as well?"

"No, I didn't hear a car, it can't be them. Fuzz! Here, we're in here." Rattles and scratches and the clomp of his feet on the floorboards outside the room ratcheted up the tension and Simon heard the rattle of the chain as Gloria shivered with shock and tension. "It's alright love, please just hold on." In response, she shook her head and thumped her feet against the trolley in frustration.

"Things like this don't happen to ordinary people, Simon. I'm just an ordinary woman. This shouldn't have happened to me. It's all very well saying hold on."

"I know. I'm sorry." A cacophony of noise, hammering and pounding, made it impossible to talk any more and then with the crack of splintering wood the door flew open, crashing back against the wall.

"God, look at you." Fuzz stood before them, a hammer in his hand. He waved it in the air. "Couldn't find any other way to get in. Not very clever, but it worked."

"Yes, it bloody did. Fuzz, can you see if you can find something to cut these chains?" The boy ran across the grubby floor and leaned down to examine the wire cages. "Are you okay, Mrs Bartlett? Only, you look rough."

"I'm alright I think, but can you get us out?"

"I'll have to go back to the garage; they've got some stuff there. Hold on."

* * *

He brought the tool kit, a great canvas holdall full of clanking metal things and he brandished a hacksaw as he ran back through the door. Simon shook his head. "Not that, there isn't time, it would take forever. I think the best bet is to try and break the locks."

It didn't work, hammering at locks that swung and moved with every swipe was never going to. Gloria shuffled and shifted in frustration as the boy tried over and over to deliver a blow hard enough to shatter the curling hasp. "That's no good. You need to do something else and hurry up. Look, they could be back any minute, Fuzz, leave it, leave it and go and call the police. Just go, run down the road and call the police." He turned to look at her and shook his head just once. With two hands he upended the canvas bag, tools and dirty rags and bits of rope scattered across the floor.

Simon thumped his foot and rattled at the chains. "There, there – grab those cutters." Fuzz grabbed at the pair of wire cutters. He tried, twisting and sawing at the metal with the blades, but by the time they acknowledged they weren't going to do the job, Fuzz was red in the face and grunting with effort. Gloria tried again to send him away.

"Fuzz, please. Please, please just go and get some help." But they wouldn't listen.

Simon peered at the other tools scattered across the floor. "There's nothing there that's man enough. Fuzz, run back down and see if you can find something bigger, something with really tough jaws and big handles. Big bolt cutter things are what we need. They'd have to be really hefty. Perhaps in the barn."

"No, Simon, no, don't make him do that. He's got to go for the police, please." She was shouting with frustration and fear. Fuzz turned to her and then back to look into Simon's face before he ran from the room. "Oh no!"

"Look, Gloria, let's just try. If he goes off down the road he has to find somewhere with a phone. Then he has to convince the police that he's telling them the truth. He's not much more than a kid, they could be difficult with him and then, even then, they have to get here. If he can find some cutters we can be out of here in a couple of minutes. We just need our luck to hold for a bit longer."

"Luck, luck, shit, Simon, the only luck we have is bad." He had no answer for her.

They heard him clumping back up the wooden stairs and the broken door bounced back against the hinges as Fuzz flung himself through. He struggled in, dragging a massive steel mallet with one hand, in the other he hefted a pair of bolt cutters with long wooden handles. "Yes! Those, those." As he shouted out in excitement, Simon nodded his head over and over towards the cutters. "Perfect, Fuzz, you're a marvel."

It didn't take them long to snap the metal rods that the chain was linked through and then Simon held out his arms as the chain itself were severed. "Gloria, do Gloria!" The remnants of chain hanging from his wrists clanged and jangled as Simon pulled at the rope around his ankles. By the time he was free of it, Fuzz had released Gloria's hands and she was holding the rope taught for him to slice through to free her feet.

Puffing and groaning they pushed upright, Fuzz heaving on Gloria's hands to help her. She staggered forward and wrapped her arms around him, "Fuzz, thank you." He shook his head and turned away but his face was split in a grin and his eyes sparkled with the joy of success. Gloria set off towards the door. "Hurry up, come on. Simon, what are you doing?"

"I'm having one of these." He had reached into the trolley and lifted one of the cardboard boxes.

"What the hell for? Let's just get out of here."

"I want to know what this is all about. After all this, I want to know."

"Leave it, leave it, Simon. Let the police handle it."

"What if they get rid of them, eh? What if they come back and see we've gone? They're not going to leave this stuff here. Fuzz, grab one of the boxes from the other trolley." He did and they left, clattering down the stairs and into the kitchen, just in time to see the green Peugeot turn into the farmyard.

Chapter 59

The slam of car doors and the sound of angry voices carried easily to where they were sheltering. Gloria, Simon and Fuzz huddled behind the bulk of a wood store, while the dogs yapped and jumped at the two men facing off in front of the house. "I didn't sign up for this!" As he yelled, the driver they had followed from the veterinary surgery, in what now seemed another lifetime, jabbed his finger at Patrick Coleman who in turn faced him square on, his hands clenched at his side, head held high.

"Oh yes you did, Robert. The first payment that you clutched with your grubby little mitts signed you up well and truly, so don't kid yourself."

"No, not this. Okay a bit of fiddling with the books, a bit of carting and carrying but not this. I'm not ending up like Colin Bliss. No way am I taking the fall for you and your lunatic wife." Gloria glanced at Simon, her eyes wide, her mouth round with shock.

"Colin Bliss, don't compare yourself to that knobhead. He was far more use to me than you could ever be. You, you aren't worth this." He snapped his fingers close in to the other man's face. "His transport connections alone were worth more than years of your paltry deliveries. You are just one of many, you're less than nothing to me. He brought more to the table than you ever could and look what happened to him. Look where trying to be clever got him." The man called Robert turned and took a step towards his car, his head was shaking back and forth, his face twisted with fury.

"Yes, well okay but, you're about to lose that as well, aren't you? From what I hear she's not going to last much longer, then where will you be?" He flung his arm in a wide arc. "You're welcome to this, Coleman, this crappy place and your mad wife but I'm out of it. I'm gone, don't contact me again."

"Oh no, no. You're going to come and help me with that mess upstairs and when that's sorted, you're going to help me find Lily."

"No, no way. It's not happening. This is your mire, you clean it up. As for Lily, it'll be a day too soon if I ever see that mad bitch again." As he turned away Gloria gasped and grabbed out at Simon's arm. Patrick Coleman had reached to a pile of logs stacked beside the front door and stepping forward he raised it high. In the nick of time Robert turned and jumped aside. "You bloody madman. You're insane, just like your cow of a wife. What the hell do you think you're doing?"

"You're not leaving here. You're going to help me and when you've done that, we are having a serious conversation about your future."

"Oh, right. Yeah, that's right." Though his face had paled with fear, Robert stood his ground, his hands raised in defence in front of his chest.

"And while we're doing that perhaps you'd like to discuss your future, or actually your past. I know! Colin Bliss told me before he was thrown in jail, he told me. He knew how evil you really are and he told me about that poor young girl and how you didn't raise a hand when he landed in the shit. I reckon I know who really ran her down, and I know other things."

He paused, seemed to gather himself and after a moment he raised one hand now in a supplicating gesture, the palm towards Patrick.

"Look, look. There's no need for this. We both have stuff to keep quiet about. You let me go and agree never to get in touch again and I'll keep schtum about the girl and the accident and what I think really happened. I don't suppose it was on purpose after all. I mean..." he stopped and took a step backwards at the look on the other's face. "Shit." The one-word expletive said all they needed to know.

"Right. So, now you know and you know what that makes you? That makes you an accessory. Ooooops. So, shut up and come and help me get rid of those pillocks upstairs. They need to have a nasty accident in that car."

"No, I'm not doing that. That's murder. No way. Bloody hell, you're as mad as your wife. No, I'm not doing that."

The dogs had quieted and skulked in the corner, their heads lowered, their eyes flicking from one yelling furious figure to the next but when the Land Rover screeched through the gateposts they ran bouncing and barking towards it. As Lily climbed down, the rifle in her hand aimed towards the two men, they jumped a couple of times at her legs and then fell in behind to escort her across the dirt and rubble of the yard to where her husband and Robert had turned to watch her approach.

Robert tried to move behind Patrick Coleman but the woman's yell stopped him in his tracks. "No, keep still. You, keep still." Her eyes flicked back and forth and it was strange and unnerving to hear the pleading in her voice when she addressed her husband. "Patrick. What do you want me to do? Tell me what to do with him?" He cocked a head to one side and turned to Robert, his face impassive. From where they were, they could see him start to grin.

"Now then. What shall we do? All that threatening, all that bravado, where is it now? Shall I just let her please herself? Should I let her get rid of you and then go and finish the others upstairs on my own?"

"Patrick, Patrick, please. Don't let this go any further. I'm sorry. I know she's…"

"She's what? What is she?"

"Well, she's a bit excitable isn't she, a bit unpredictable. Don't let this get out of hand. Look, look, I'm sorry and yes of course I'll help you with that other stuff." He gestured over his shoulder towards the house. "Of course I will. You know, I could up my deliveries as well. And I can take some of the stock off your hands if you like. I can always find a market for some of it."

Patrick Coleman laughed and shook his head. "Put the gun down Lily love. It's alright. He's going to give us a hand, did you hear?" The woman looked undecided, but eventually taking the lead from her husband she lowered the rifle. "Come on now. We've got unfinished business inside and we've a delivery due tonight. My people are turning the product around pretty quick these days."

He grabbed Robert by the upper arm and then reaching out a hand to his wife, Patrick Coleman ushered the little group up the steps and into the house.

Chapter 60

As the three figures disappeared behind the scarred, old door, Simon, Gloria and Fuzz hobbled and staggered as quickly as they could along the back wall of the property and then, pushing and dragging each other they were over the top and heading across the moors. Simon was limping badly. As she ran, Gloria wrapped an arm around her waist, clutching at her side. Fuzz glanced behind over and over and when it became clear that she was really struggling he dropped back, looped her arm across his shoulders and took her weight, slowing his pace to accommodate her staggering progress. She grunted with pain and Simon fell back now and with his free hand around her waist he tried to help.

"Which way?" She croaked out the question and as Simon turned to answer he was shocked at the grey pallor of her face and the pinched and pained expression around her lips.

"Stop. Stop, Fuzz. Hold on." They lowered her gently to the damp grass and Simon knelt beside her.

"Where do you hurt?"

"My side, it's just my side. It's okay."

"No, no come on. You're not okay at all." He glanced around. "Fuzz, take Gloria over behind the wall. I'll go and get the car."

"You can't, how can you, Simon? You can hardly walk and anyway you can't drive, not with that ankle."

"I'll manage. You can't go on in this state."

"It's alright, Simon, I'll go. You and Mrs Bartlett stay here. Have you got the keys?"

"Can you drive, Fuzz?" The look that he threw at them negated any further questions and Simon simply shook his head. "I reckon they're still in the car. They were. If they're not, then we're screwed."

"Okay, let's get her into some shelter, then I'll be as quick as I can."

She groaned with every movement and by the time they reached the wall, Gloria was leaning heavily on the boy. They had dropped the boxes in the field and before he ran off, Fuzz went and grabbed them up, throwing them to the ground beside Simon as he scurried past.

Gloria leaned her head back against the wall and closed her eyes. "Are you alright?" Simon whispered the question because he could tell from her ashen colour and shallow breathing that she was far from alright.

"I think I need the doctor. It'll be okay though, don't worry." He was riven with guilt, her stoicism in this desperate situation, which was mostly his making, unmanned him.

"I'm sorry, Gloria. I'm so sorry."

"Oh shut up. I'll be alright. Once we get away from this sodding place, I'll be okay. Anyway, now you've got them, what's in those bloody boxes? I don't know why you had to bring them."

"I just needed to know what it's all been about and I needed some evidence to show the police."

"Well you'd better hope that's what they are and not boxes of bloody paper towels." She tried to laugh but instead gave an agonised gasp and shook her head.

Simon tore at the tape holding the flaps on the box nearest to him and pushed his hand inside. "Well? She had opened her eyes now and was watching as he turned the small cardboard package back and forth in his hand. They're just pills. Nothing special at all, just pills." He handed them to her.

"Antibiotics. I wonder if they're for the sheep then? They're just ordinary."

"Shit." Simon kicked out at some loose stones sending them flying across the ground. "It was just coincidence then. They aren't anything to do with it and we've hauled them with us for nothing."

"Well, even worse than nothing really."

"How do you mean?"

"Well, not only are they ordinary pills, they're useless as well."

"Why, why are they useless?"

"They're out of date, aren't they? Silly bitch has kept them up in that room so long that they're no longer any good. Might even be dangerous to use them, although I don't really know enough about it. I do know that you're not supposed to keep them and they can't give you them or sell them to you at the chemist. Look." She held the box towards him and pointed at the use-by-date printed across the bottom.

"Huh. I wonder if they're all like that." He lifted them to peer at packet after packet and nodded as he turned them to examine the tiny date stamp. Because it was nearby and because he needed to do something he tore open the second box. "Different sort." He muttered. "Ah, now these are okay. These are well in date." He passed them to Gloria's outstretched hand.

"Yeah. She just been careless then, hasn't she? I'm surprised she needs so many, mind. Not that I know anything about sheep farming but it seems a bit odd, doesn't it? There must be thousands in that room. Oh..."

"What?"

What's today's date?"

"I don't know, about the sixteenth I reckon. I've lost track a bit. Why?"

"But it's March, isn't it?"

"Yeah, course it is."

"So, how can these pills be manufactured in July?" Simon shook his head.

"No, you've lost me. I don't know what you mean."

"Well, beside the 'Use by' date there's a 'Manufacturing date', have a look."

"Oh yeah, yeah I see. 'July'."

"Well, it's not possible, is it? They can't be made in July when it's only March now. It's this year. Hang on let me look at the other ones. Yeah, yeah see there. They're all in the future."

"But I don't see. I mean, how can it be?"

"I don't know..." She opened the box and took out the blister pack inside. "If they are out of date then they have to be thrown away, don't they?"

He shrugged.

"Well, what if you took them, repackaged them, put a new date on them and resold them?"

"You could get the money for new drugs and you wouldn't have the expense of making them. Bloody hell."

"So, is that it then? Is that what all this has been about? Just money, all about greed."

"I guess that could well be what Melanie was blackmailing him about. If Fiona worked it out and told her. I wonder what that driver, what was he called – Robert? Yeah, I wonder what he meant when he talked about Patrick losing his contact… oh, of course… the transport. Maureen Clegg, she worked in the haulage business, didn't she? You'd need to be able to move them around first to repack them and then to distribute them and she would have the right contacts. Oh, what will that do to Charlie?"

Any further discussion was halted as the door from the farmhouse flew open and Patrick, Lily and Robert charged out and clambered into the two cars. The dogs in the yard ran yelping to their kennels when stones flew from beneath the screeching tyres and the cars sped down the drive towards the paved road, and presumably the place where Gloria's car had been left.

"Oh come on, Fuzz, come on." As she muttered under her breath, a slightly recovered Gloria stretched upwards to peer over the wall. "He's here, he's coming. Help me up, Simon, grab those boxes as well if you can. I don't think I can carry anything. Come on." They stood as Gloria's car, a grinning Fuzz at the wheel, bounced to a halt at the end of a narrow, rutted sheep track. In moments they were inside and hurtling towards Ramstone.

Simon had taken the front passenger seat and from where she was sprawled in the rear, Gloria croaked out her request. "Don't go to the hotel, Fuzz, just go straight to the hospital. I don't feel very well at all."

Chapter 61

The waiting room in Accident and Emergency was busy as always but when the staff saw the difficulty that Gloria was in, she was whisked away to a cubicle. Simon registered her details and was persuaded to wait to see a doctor about his ankle, which was now hugely swollen and discoloured.

They hadn't had a chance to discuss how they were going to explain their injuries and how they had happened but it didn't seem to matter as he watched a pale and shivering Gloria helped into the examination area. She could tell them whatever she wanted and for his part he would simply say he had been lost too far away from his car and had to walk back. They could think what they liked. As the events played repeatedly in his mind, he found it hard to believe that they were now safe, being cared for and it was over. Yes, she could tell them anything and if she blamed him then he had it coming after all.

"Fuzz, you're a hero. I don't know how we can ever thank you." The boy blushed and stared down at his feet as Simon held out his hand. He took it and for a moment seemed overwhelmed but quickly recovered his teenaged cool.

"Yeah well, somebody had to sort you out I suppose. What do you want to do about Mrs Bartlett's car? I can ask my mate to drive you back to her place in it later if you like. Only he's got a licence, I suppose I shouldn't drive it again really."

"That'd be great, Fuzz. I don't think I'll be able to do it and we can't leave it here. Once they let us see her, I'll check with Gloria."

"She's going to be okay, isn't she? Only she looked pretty bad."

"Yeah, yeah of course she is." Simon nodded his head but in truth it was as much for his own reassurance as for that of the youngster beside him. The wait was endless and each time a medic walked towards them they straightened a little on the hard plastic chairs, only to be disappointed as another worried, bored or irritated member of the unfortunate public was attended to.

Eventually, they were allowed to creep into the little space beyond the curtain where a sedated Gloria looked at them from behind the plastic face mask. Her eyes were heavy with the effect of drugs but she seemed comfortable and the doctor had reassured them that she was in no danger in spite of the broken ribs and damage to her spleen.

Simon leaned close and took hold of her hand. "You're going to be fine love." She nodded drowsily. "You have to stay here tonight but I'll come and see you tomorrow. We're arranging for your car to be taken home. There's nothing to worry about. You're safe now." She smiled at him, closed her eyes and drifted into medically induced oblivion. He heard his name being called and hopped back to take his turn to be poked and prodded and x-rayed and ultimately given an appointment for his ankle to be encased in plaster, once the swelling had lessened. They bandaged and splinted it and told him to not even think of removing the support as he had done with the plastic boot, causing even more damage. They made it plain that they didn't think he could be trusted.

Once he was back in the quiet of Mill Lodge, a glass of whisky in his hand and Fuzz safely sent home to his gran, Simon picked up his mobile phone and dialled one of the few numbers in his address book.

"Prentiss."

"Hello. Detective Prentiss, this is Simon Fulton. I wonder if I could have a word, you did say that if I needed advice to give you a call."

"Is it about your case? Only there isn't anything new at the moment. We are still working on bits of it, Simon, but nothing for you to worry about. It's all over for you, you know that, don't you?"

"No, it's not that. I've done what you said pretty much and put that behind me. No, it's something else. I wonder if you could come to Mill Lodge. I've got my leg strapped up and Gloria's in hospital right now but there's something I think you should know about."

"Is it urgent? Only, you could just call the local nick."

"Maybe not urgent exactly, though to be honest I think it's true to say that I, or rather we, could be in some danger." He heard the sigh at the other end of the line and the response was unenthusiastic but resigned.

"Okay, I'll tell you what. Why don't I call in later? I can go home that way."

"Thanks, thanks so much."

"Yeah. Okay."

Gloria had been right, he should have called Prentiss much sooner but hindsight only ever showed you your mistakes, and it was all too late now.

He pulled the little stack of index cards towards him and began to sort them. He made notes on a few of those already used and started some new ones. The clock ticked quietly in the cosy room, the fire hissed gently in the background and he didn't register the bark of the dog at the hotel across the road or the quiet click as the rear door was levered open. He didn't hear the soft footsteps through the darkened kitchen, or the pad of feet on the hall carpet and it wasn't until the room was plunged into sudden darkness that he understood that what he thought had been a slight exaggeration talking to the detective, had been no exaggeration at all.

Chapter 62

He felt the prick of a knife blade against the soft skin of his neck just below his ear; he was frozen.

"Don't bother moving. Don't bother shouting. In fact, don't bother doing anything other than just as I tell you."

He recognised the voice as that of Patrick Coleman but there was someone else there. He was aware of a second person breathing, the sounds of someone shuffling behind the settee, footsteps around the darkened room. As his eyes adjusted to the gloom, he recognised the figure of Lily.

"Right, we are going to get up and walk down to the kitchen, we are going out into the drive and then we are going to get into the back of the van. Are you clear?" As Simon nodded, a trickle of fresh blood, warm and nauseating ran down his neck and he felt it spread and cool as it hit the collar of his shirt.

"Do it now, just do it now. It's best to do it quick. Like with the sheep, quick is easiest." It was Lily, she was leaning close in, he could smell her – dogs and sheep and earthiness.

"Not here love. We can't risk DNA, prints. Somewhere else, away from here. We need to be able to come back anyway. For the woman. We can't do that if the place is swarming with police. No, just wait, go out and tell Steve we're coming. Open the van."

Simon's mind was racing, if he told them he'd called the police they might run, but equally they might decide they had nothing left to lose and use the knife on him right there.

He sensed Lily move away and recognised the change in illumination as light through the glass of the front door leaked into the lounge. There was the shuffle of her feet in the hall, then clicking as she moved across the kitchen tiles. He stood up and, using the crutch that had been leaning against the settee, he took a couple of painful steps forward. Coleman came close up behind him and with the knife now against the back of his neck, Simon was prodded forward across the room. The kitchen door was open, he could feel the stir of cold air and smell the damp musk from the garden. They moved on. Coleman had hold of the back of his sweater, dragging a handful into his fist, causing the shirt underneath to tighten around Simon's throat, the fabric straining under his arms, against his chest.

He knew that once they had him outside, he wouldn't be able to run, if he started to yell it would be the work of a moment to jab with the knife, into his neck, his face, his back. By the time anyone came, if anyone came, it could well be too late. The best chance for fighting back had to be now, while they were still inside and there were doors to slam, where he knew the surroundings, where in the dark he could find his way.

He effected a stumble, let out a grunt and adjusted his hold on the handle of the elbow crutch, sliding it round and underneath so that he held it now like some strange, elongated hammer.

Coleman's grip was broken and he snatched out as Simon tumbled towards the floor. Grasping the crutch with both hands he jabbed upwards, over and over, and he swung it side to side, clattering against the wall, the banister rail, the floor but also against Coleman's hands, face, head, anything and everything, trying to hit as often and hard as he could at Patrick as he was unbalanced and flailing, trying to re-establish his hold.

Simon shuffled away, staggered to his feet and, ignoring the objection in his injured leg, he careered along the corridor, into the disabled access room where he had left the door open after his shower. He slammed it closed behind him and flicked the lock, realising too late, that lock of all of them had an override feature. He moved to the other side of the wooden chest of drawers which was against the wall and leaned his weight on it, heaving and pushing it across the laminate boards until it was wedged behind the door. He scrambled across the bed and pushed that so that it sat kitty-cornered across the room, so that it too was part of his barricade. He heard Coleman cursing out in the corridor, calling for his wife and 'bloody Steve'.

He heard the clatter of their shoes and then mayhem in the hall. Then they charged against the door shoving and pushing and hammering, ignoring the lock but just intent on smashing through. He could go into the bathroom, but that lock also was accessible from the outside. He ran to the window. The catch had been painted over at some stage and wouldn't shift, he took off his shoe and flailed at it but it was soon obvious it wasn't going to move. The door was open a crack by this time, he could see the movement of the people in the hall. Once the furniture began to slide on the smooth floor it would all be over, they would be inside and he would be trapped. He had no option but to break the window and risk being cut to pieces as the old glass shattered. He smashed at it, once, twice. They were working together out in the hall and the dresser began to shift.

He looked desperately around the room for something heavier, something sharp, something other than a stupid, soft trainer that might stand a chance at breaking the glass in the window. Gloria wasn't one for extraneous objects in her guest rooms, especially not in this one, no ornaments or knick-knacks, a painting on the wall in a heavy wooden frame was the only decoration. The bed had slid and rumpled up the square of carpet that was in the centre of the room. The dresser caught against it, it creased and rucked and held them back for just a little longer. He grabbed the painting and dragged at it, but it was screwed tight to the wall. He would have to jump, he was just going to have to jump through the glass and if he was sliced to ribbons on the shards and splinters, surely at least he would have been trying to help himself. He took several steps backwards until his legs touched the end of the bed frame. He nodded to himself just once, took a deep breath. It would be okay. It had to be okay because this was the only chance.

Chapter 63

It was a moment of exquisite timing that saw the headlights sweep down Mill Street and swing into the kerbside, as Ian Prentiss drew up outside of Mill Lodge. Simon ran to the window thumping, yelling and waving out to him so that even as he opened the car door the policeman looked up in surprise. He took in the sense of panic, the Clegg's haulage van drawn onto the drive with all doors hanging open and the frantic face at the front window and immediately called for assistance from the local force.

The Colemans and the *'fat lad with a daft beard'* who was driving them around heard the shouts and realised they were in trouble. They ran for the rear of the premises, pushing at each other to escape the threat of the police. They charged through the garden and scrambled over the low stone wall and out into the rough land beyond. Coleman and his wife turned instinctively in the direction of the farm but Steven, the driver, took the easier route to the road. He jumped the water-filled ditch, straightened his clothes and, attempting to display an air of nonchalance, walked along the grass verge. By this time, Prentiss, who had run down the side drive just in time to see the trio dispersing into the night, was back in his car relaying descriptions and directions and, with his obvious bulk and the Clegg's Haulage sweatshirt, it wasn't long before Steven was bundled into the back of a patrol car and driven off to the local police station to await questioning.

Prentiss didn't bother with a pointless and unnecessary pursuit across the hills but instead went into Mill Lodge where Simon was struggling to pull the furniture from the doorway and hobble to the lounge. They could hear the scream of sirens in the distance and shortly afterwards the thunder of the police helicopter overhead.

"They'll get them now. Once that has you in its sights you don't get away." Ian Prentiss helped Simon to the couch where he sat with his head in his hands, waiting for the pounding in his chest and the throbbing in his leg to subside.

"Well, this is going to be interesting?" He glanced up to see the officer pouring two large measures of whisky into heavy-bottomed glasses. He handed one to Simon and lowered himself into the chair that was usually Gloria's and sipped at the golden liquid as he waited for Simon to collect himself and begin the explanation.

* * *

"So, have you got the boxes here?"

Simon shook his head.

"No, neither of us could carry them. In the end we left them out in that field. We just wanted to get away, to get Gloria some help, you know. There were dozens of them though, in the room at the farm."

"I'll get someone up there as soon as I can and we'll just have to hope they haven't got rid. Then there's all this about the hit and run, unless we can convince Bliss that it's in his interests to give us the real story, that's going to be a hard one to sort. Can you come down and make a statement about what you know and we'll have to make a start. There's going to be a great deal of work from the sound of things and it's going to take a while. I could send someone here?"

"No, I'll come, will the morning be okay? Only I feel absolutely shattered now."

"Yes, I'll send a car for you. We'll have to talk to this boy of course, Phillip?"

"Yeah, but make sure you let him know he's not in any trouble. He's a good kid and he got us out of there. I'd hate to see him upset. And, Fiona Carpenter, you won't forget her, will you? Please can you see if there's anything there. I don't have any proof at all that they were involved but it's a bloody coincidence." Prentiss put his empty glass on the table and then laid a hand on Simon's shoulder. "Are you going to be okay on your own? I could arrange for someone to be with you?"

"No, I'm fine really, I'm good. To be honest I'm just glad it's all come to a head and I'm bloody glad you turned up when you did. Thanks. One thing though – well two really. Can you let me talk to Gloria before your people do? I can just phone her possibly or get over there in the morning."

Prentiss pursed his lips. "I can't really agree to that. It's better if we get your statements separately you know. Tell you what, I'll go personally and make sure she isn't upset. I'll let her know you're alright and we'll take care of her. Okay?"

"Okay. And Clegg. Can I let Charlie know?"

"No, I'm sorry. Again, I have to ask you to keep away from him for the time being. I understand your feelings, I do, but for now at least why don't you leave all this to us? I'll ask a car to pass a couple of times in the night but my guess is that, by the time I get back to the station, Mr and Mrs Coleman will be there waiting for me. You don't generally escape once the 'copter has you and out there on the moor they'll be sitting ducks."

* * *

He didn't think he would sleep but after another couple of whiskies and hours sitting in the dark replaying events in his mind and thinking through the various tangled threads, Simon realised that, though it hadn't been the outcome that he would have hoped for and there was still a lot of it to be clarified, there was nothing more he could do. He double-checked the locks on the doors and windows and went through to lie on Gloria's bed fully clothed.

* * *

He was surprised when the morning light woke him. He'd slept well but felt battered and sore and slightly hungover. He had a long, hot shower and was just finishing his second cup of coffee when a police car pulled into the drive. He wanted to see Gloria, he wanted to speak to Fuzz and although he wasn't looking forward to it, he really needed to have a meeting with Charles Clegg, but none of that could happen until he'd taken care of business. He picked up the bundle of index cards and his laptop. He didn't know if they would let him refer to them but right now they made him feel as though he knew what he was doing, as though he had accomplished something.

Chapter 64

They kept Gloria in the hospital for several days. They needed to make sure that the injuries caused by the fall were healing but they wanted to protect her as well from the flurry of reporters outside Mill Lodge and the buzz around Ramstone. Simon tried to keep most of it from her without lying and by the time he went to collect her in a taxi there was no crowd around the gates.

He helped her into the living room and to her amusement insisted on covering her knees with a blanket. "I'm not cold."

"No, but you need cuddling. You've been through it, you really have. I was so worried about you."

"Well, I'm alright now and you can fill me in on what's happened. The police didn't tell me much and I'm not daft, I know you were hiding things. Come on, I want to know all about it. What's this about, them coming here, the day I went in hospital? Please tell me, otherwise I'll just be left to imagine and you know that's worse."

He sat on the settee, his leg on the footstool and gave her his account. It was as near to factual as he could make it without distressing her too much but in the event she accepted what he said. She could see that he was recovering and in any case had gleaned a lot from newspapers that he didn't know she'd bought and gossip from visitors to the other patients.

Some of it hadn't been reported and that was what she needed to know about, the truth of it without spin and conjecture and so she questioned him.

"How did he make his money? Who bought the drugs anyway, there can't be that many surely?"

"You'd be surprised. The rules are pretty strict. They are supposed to be returned within a certain timescale, the government stockpile some for emergencies, some are sent to developing countries where the rules aren't as closely followed. Apart from out-of-date, or almost expired, there are returned ones, when the packs have been opened and they can't be used if they're not finished, all sorts of stuff like that. As for who buys them, well, don't forget these were being sold as perfectly good drugs so it was on-line suppliers, private hospitals, little chemist shops, vets of course, all those sorts of places. They didn't know they were doing anything wrong, they just thought they were getting them cheaper, a good deal. That wasn't the case with the people who were giving him the stuff though, pharmaceutical reps we know about, basically anyone who had access to drug stocks. Apparently even some health trusts where he had contact with the pharmacists who were pocketing a bit of cash. Lots of people who might be in trouble of course, could lose their jobs as the investigation goes on. Nobody would question that the stuff had gone, it was written-off inventories, worthless for all intents and purposes. Although the police seem to think there might have been some out and out theft as well, here and there. He also had an online business of his own. Coleman's Chemicals, there was a website with pictures of his R&D team, his factory, but it was all just Google images and clever work with the computer. The real places were in Eastern Europe, Spain, even India, anywhere he could find cheap labour and cheap packaging and, of course, it was easy to get his 'tame' drivers to transport the stuff for him, as part of bigger shipments mainly. Then there were a couple of little industrial units down on the South Coast where he shipped the stuff from. All over the place; actually, that was where a huge amount of the money came from, just little orders, but lots of them, in Europe and America where people have to pay for their medicine. We've all had adverts on the internet, well they do work apparently. Sad thing is that according to what I've been able to find out, most of the drugs are okay anyway. The sell-by dates are more to do with marketing and the big pharmaceutical companies making even more money. There's no need for the dates to be so short. Well, I suppose the good thing is that nobody will have been hurt by taking them. None of it would have been as serious, if it had just been the drugs, bad you know, but not what it became. Now it looks like it's murder. Colin's giving them everything they need. Well, he's got nothing left to lose, has he? He was keeping quiet about not being the one who ran over Melanie because of his involvement with the drug thing and his fear of Coleman. Now that's all out in the open and Coleman is no longer a threat. Maureen's not going to get better and they don't think she'll ever be well enough to stand trial. He got her into it and they reckon that now she's so poorly, he's eaten up with guilt. At the end of the day though it's like you said, all just greed until sex and jealousy and blackmail became a part of it and it got totally out of hand."

"And what about Lily?"

"I don't know. They reckon it's doubtful that she can stand trial. She was already disturbed, had been for years. It was why he moved here with her, trying to give her a quieter life. So he's not all bad. But it seems that she's gone completely over the edge now that she can't be with him. They're probably going to commit her."

"Well that's good, she's evil."

"Well, in a way I suppose but she was really just trying to protect him. He was the one who ran down Melanie, because she was going to go to the police. She just moved her."

"She moved her, bloody hell."

"Yes, when she knew Colin Bliss was coming with a delivery. She took her from their own drive and dumped her beside the road. The police never had any cause to look at them, why would they? After all they had Colin on the CCTV, his car was damaged, which was just a coincidence as it happened, but it fit the scenario very nicely."

"But Fiona, what about Fiona?" Simon shook his head.

"No that wasn't Lily. But they've viewed the CCTV footage and Patrick Coleman's car was definitely in the area. They are looking into that and at least the inquest has been postponed, but she wasn't there."

"How do they know? Maybe she helped him."

"No, she was where Fuzz said she was. They have it on film."

"What, Tesco!"

"Yup, well there and the bank and the feed store. Just shopping. The picture is getting clearer by the day. It'll be ages before any court cases I think but now at least we know what happened. I have to go and see him."

"Charlie?"

"Yes, the police have said it's okay now for me to get in touch. They have all they need from him and Beryl, so I'm meeting him this afternoon. I have to say I'm dreading it a bit."

"It's not your fault. None of it's your fault."

"Oh, I know that, of course I do, but I just feel so bad for him. Anyway, come on, let me make you a drink and then you should probably have a bit of a sleep. They said you should take it easy for a while yet."

"Okay, doctor." She grinned up at him and he leaned to give her a kiss.

"You know, Gloria, I would never have forgiven myself if anything had happened to you. I lost Sandie, I lost my mum, I can't lose you. I... Well, you know – I care about you a lot."

"I know and I care about you as well. But..."

"But what?"

"Well, I don't know what you're going to do now. I know you haven't decided. But I have to tell you that if you go on with this idea, this enquiry thing I can't be a part of it. I can't do stuff like this. It's not me, danger and crime and all of that. I had enough when I was a kid, I don't want it."

"No, I know, I know. Like you said eh, you're a B&B landlady with aspirations." He expected her to laugh but she turned away from him to stare into the fire. "Hey, sorry. Don't be mad, I was joking."

"I know, it's not that. It's just that I've had an offer for the hotel, I had a phone call while I was in hospital."

"Oh. Well, okay that's good, isn't it? It's what you wanted."

"Yep. Thing is though, after all this I'm not sure I want to stay around here. I thought I might move away, back to Leeds maybe, or even Manchester, well, Salford or perhaps Cheshire somewhere."

She smiled at him as he knelt before her and took her hands in his. The tears wobbling on the edges of her eyelids trickled down her cheeks and he wrapped his arms around her.

"You don't have to do anything you don't want to, you know that, don't you? But, Gloria..." He couldn't go on, the thought of her not being there for him to turn to, to talk to, was overwhelming, and so he pulled her to him, lowered his head onto her shoulder and tried not to think about it.

Chapter 65

They met in The Oak. Simon arrived early and chose a table in the corner, away from the scrum of drinkers around the bar and sheltered from the flurry of cold rain that blew in with every customer. He was shocked at how much Charles Clegg had aged in the short time since he last saw him. Deep lines around his eyes and the dark circles beneath told of sleepless nights and worry but as he approached the table with his hand held out before him, he managed a smile.

"Good to see you lad. You look well, all things considered."

"I'm fine thank you, and you, how are you doing?"

"Oh, fair to middlin' I suppose. A lot has happened. Perhaps we should talk it through, clear the air and that."

"Okay. Let me get you a drink."

"I'll have a pint of bitter lad and thank you."

They talked quietly, aware of one or two glances in their direction, which they ignored as best they could. Charles Clegg insisted on buying a second round with some crisps and pork scratchings. As the afternoon wore on, they filled in the gaps in knowledge and shared what they understood about the next stage of the police investigation and the future of everyone involved.

"And what about Beryl?" Simon had thought a lot about the stylish woman with the worried eyes that he had met.

"It looks as though they'll be able to mostly keep her out of it. My lawyers'll do their best anyroad. She didn't really do anything wrong, she wouldn't, not my Beryl. All she was trying to do was to save me from hurt. The daft lass, as if I'm some sort of soft kid. She knew they were up to no good, Maureen and Colin, but she didn't know just what, except that they were using the vans for sommat that wasn't kosher and that they'd got in with some bad sorts and it was causing them strife. She was trying to persuade Maureen to put a stop to it, but she had her lips buttoned up tight and anyroad, it was too late. Maureen didn't really have any clue how bad it was. She just organized what transport she could for shipments of boxes. Ringing round, using her contacts. She thought it was perhaps booze, fags that sort of thing. She never imagined it was to do with the medicines. No, I reckon she'll be alright. That was the reason that daft woman was watchin' us all though, that Lily. It gives me chills, thinking about her following me around. Ah well, it's in the past, best leave it there and move on."

"And you, your company?"

"Aye, there's folks right now poking their noses everywhere, of course there is. Only to be expected. They'll not find anything else, none of my other lads were in on it. It was only that snake in the grass Steven Parslowe that was up to no good, leastways that's what I think. That's painful though, I know his dad, he worked for me for years, a right decent bloke. He's pretty broken up about it all but there, what can you do. Oh, and there were others elsewhere. Seems like quite a network, different companies but they're not my concern, I've enough on me plate right now."

"Will you be alright?"

"Aye. We'll weather it. Oh, I don't doubt we'll take a pasting here and there but we'll hang on, we'll come through. We have no choice. I've a deal of folks working for me. There's kiddies that need school trips, girls wanting weddings, it all has to be paid for, I can't let my people down. No, we'll get through it. What about you lad?"

"Me?"

"Aye, what are you going to do now?"

"I don't know. I didn't expect what I did to come out like this. It feels like a failure."

"Nay, lad nay. Colin's going to be let out on bail. He wasn't involved in that young lass's death, like I said all along. Alright, I reckon he's still going to get his comeuppance and quite right too but you did what I asked of you, and he'll have the chance to see Maureen, have time to make their peace. Not only that, you and that friend of yours, that Gloria, you put your bodies on the line to find the truth of it all. You didn't fail lad. Folks like Colin, Steven Parslowe and I hate to say it, even my Maureen, they failed, but not you. You should keep on, do this if you want to, help folks like me. Anyroad. I've written out a cheque for you. I didn't reckon you'd know what to ask, you being new at it and all so I asked my legal people and they reckon this is fair. There's sommat in there toward a new car as well. If I know owt about insurance they'll cut up rusty now about settling."

"Oh no, Mr Clegg you can't." Simon tried to push the envelope back across the table.

"Oh aye, Mr Clegg, is it? I thought I was Charlie. Now lad, you'll learn, if you go into business on your own account, that you don't turn down payment. Not when it's been honestly earned." He put a finger on the envelope and pushed it back, then he gathered up his scarf and gloves. "If ever I can be of service young man, you have my number." And without another word he turned and walked out into the grey drizzle.

The End

If you enjoyed this book, please let others know by leaving a quick review on Amazon. Also, if you spot anything untoward in the paperback, get in touch. We strive for the best quality and appreciate reader feedback.

editor@thebookfolks.com

www.thebookfolks.com

More fiction by Diane Dickson

Also featuring these characters:

TWIST OF TRUTH

Standalone titles:

LEAVING GEORGE
WHO FOLLOWS
LAYERS OF LIES
PICTURES OF YOU
YOU'RE DEAD
THE GRAVE
SINGLE TO EDINBURGH
BONE BABY
HOPELESS

The DI Tanya Miller series:

BROKEN ANGEL
BURNING GREED
BRUTAL PURSUIT
BRAZEN ESCAPE
BLURRED LINES

The DI Jordan Carr series:

BODY ON THE SHORE
BODY BY THE DOCKS
BODY OUT OF PLACE
BODY IN THE SQUAT
BODY IN THE CANAL
BODY ON THE ESTATE
BODY BELOW THE BRIDGE
BODY IN THE WAY

Selected titles

TWIST OF TRUTH

Having been jailed for a murder he didn't commit,
Simon Fulton returns to his quiet hometown with one
thing on his mind: revenge! But when he starts to enact it,
he realises he has the wrong target. And the consequences
of his mistake will be terrifying.

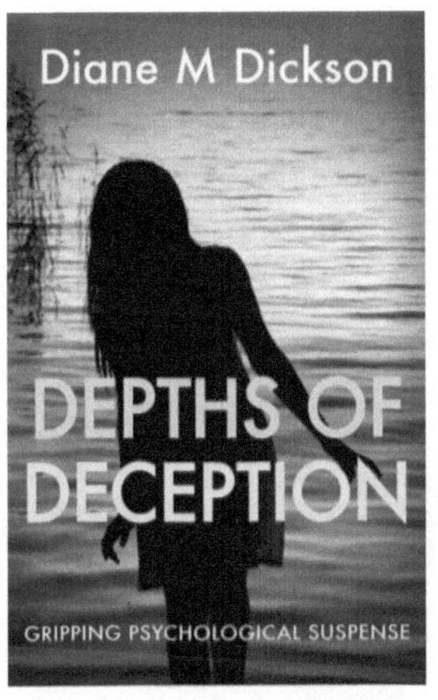

DEPTHS OF DECEPTION

Allured by the promise of a big pay out and praise from
his superiors, real estate agent Jed turns a blind eye to
certain irregularities in a lucrative new deal. The question
is, by the time he realises all is not as it seems, will he be in
too deep to surface?

PICTURES OF YOU

Recently widowed, Mary has been leading a rather dull life. When a young man helps her out, they begin to develop a strong bond. But when he becomes a lodger in her house, events begin to take a disturbing turn.

Other titles of interest

MURDER ON A YORKSHIRE MOOR by Ric Brady

Ex-detective Henry Ward is settling awkwardly into retirement in a quiet corner of Yorkshire when during a walk on the moor he stumbles upon the body of a young man. Suspecting foul play and somewhat relishing the return to a bit of detective work, he resolves to find out who killed him. But will the local force appreciate him sticking his nose in?

THE GIRL IN THE MEADOW by John Dean

When the body of a young woman is discovered under the floorboards of an isolated house during its renovation, questions are raised about DCI Jack Harris' own potential connection to the site. Will he clear his name, or will his reputation be forever besmirched in the rural Pennine community?

Sign up to our mailing list to find out about new releases and special offers!

www.thebookfolks.com

www.ingramcontent.com/pod-product-compliance
Lightning Source LLC
Chambersburg PA
CBHW030928210726

48290CB00007B/2110